CATHOLIC, RELUCTANTLY

Christian M. Frank

CATHOLIC, RELUCTANTLY

John Paul 2 High,
Book One

Imagio
CATHOLIC FICTION
FROM SOPHIA INSTITUTE PRESS®

Excerpts from "A Capella," which first appeared in *Like Taxes: Marching Through Gaul*, copyright 1989 by David Craig and *Scripta Humanistica*, used with permission.

Sophia Institute Press®
Box 5284, Manchester, NH 03108
1-800-888-9344
www.sophiainstitute.com

Library of Congress Cataloging-in-Publication Data

Frank, Christian M.

Catholic (reluctantly) / Christian M. Frank.
    p. cm. — (John Paul 2 high school series ; bk. 1)

Summary: The seven students of a newly-established, "real" Catholic high school try to learn and do what is right as they face the possibility that their building will be condemned, personality conflicts, and problems with the nearby public high school, where two of them are on the wrestling team.

ISBN-13: 978-1-928832-99-7 (pbk. : alk. paper)

[1. Catholic high schools–Fiction. 2. High schools–Fiction. 3. Schools–Fiction. 4. Interpersonal relations–Fiction. 5. Christian life–Fiction. 6. Conduct of life–Fiction. 7. School shootings–Fiction.] I. Title.

PZ7.F84912Cat 2007

[Fic] — dc22

2007026990

www.johnpaul2high.com

To Katie with love

ONE

THE FIRST DAY

ALLIE WEAVER SAT BACK FROM HER MOTHER'S

computer and wiped her eyes. There were still a few sniffles left in her, but they were going away, slowly but surely. She was 15, and she was a sophomore now, and no matter what happened, she wasn't going to cry again.

> **angelgirl785: u there tyler?**
> takedownman: yeah wats up
> **angelgirl785: moms pulling me out of school**
> takedownman: wat!!!!
> takedownman: no way!!!!! Y?
> **angelgirl785: becuz of wat happened today**
> takedownman: the gun scare?
> **angelgirl785: yeah**

She knew it would seem bizarre to Tyler. And paranoid of her mom. But Tyler didn't know what really happened today. She hadn't told anyone except her mom and the police. She ran a hand through her long blond hair as she waited for Tyler to finish swearing. *Gotta stop crying, my mascara will run!* Finally she typed:

> **angelgirl785: thats how I feel**
> takedownman: shes overreacting
> **angelgirl785: maybe**
> takedownman: tell her you want to stay
> takedownman: becuz of me.
> **angelgirl785: yeah right thatll do it**
> **angelgirl785: thats not the worst part**
> **angelgirl785: shes sending me to some**
> **angelgirl785: weird new catholic skool**
> takedownman: wat?

3

angelgirl785: john paul 2 high
angelgirl785: not far from sparrow hills
angelgirl785: thats good i guess

She paused, and shivered. She'd never had a gun pointed at her before. Part of her felt almost as if she had died, as though she *had* been shot . . . the glint of a cold gray eye peering through that hood at her . . . if it had been a gray eye . . . she really wasn't sure . . .

angelgirl785: tyler
angelgirl785: im scared.
angelgirl785: really really scared.

BEEP! George Peterson backpedaled hard and tried to bring his bike to a stop. He heard the sharp, screeching sounds of brakes — and then, with a tooth-rattling shock, something hit his back tire. His bike shot forward, swerved, and headed for the side of the country road.

Jesus, he thought, as he saw the curb approach. *Jesus, help me . . . I gotta do something!*

Then the bike hit the curb, and he was flying over the handlebars. Almost instinctively, he threw out his hands in front of his face. *Hit the ground rolling . . .*

His shoulder hit the grass first with a painful jolt, and then he was somersaulting on the grass. He turned over three or four times before he stopped. The air was knocked out of his lungs, his sunglasses had flown off, and the top of his backpack was digging into the back of his neck.

For a few moments he lay there, stunned; then, with a gasp for air, he got up on all fours. Nothing seemed to be broken . . . He rose to his feet shakily and turned to face the thing that had hit him.

A large black car was pulled to the side of the road. It was old and dusty, with a huge dented hood and a tarnished silver grill.

I just got hit by a car . . . but I'm okay. Relief flooded over him, followed by anger. He glared at the black car. *It's probably some old guy, half-blind; he probably hits people all the time.* He knew how close that had been; he was lucky to be still alive. *Moron.*

The car door opened with a low *creak*, and someone stepped out. It wasn't an old man. The figure that emerged was a tall and bulky teenager, dressed in a large black trench coat, white shirt and tie, with a plump face and bushy brown hair. He looked a year or two older than George, but it was hard to tell.

The boy glanced at George for a moment. There was something strange about his eyes, almost disembodied. Then, suddenly and almost casually, he turned away, walked to the front of the car, and bent down to examine the front bumper.

Feeling irritated, George stepped forward. "Hey! Buddy!" he shouted. "What's the deal?"

"You scratched my bumper," the boy said without looking up.

"I scratched your *bumper?*" Anger flared in George's chest. "Oh, geez, I'm so sorry. Maybe it would have better if you had just run me over, right?" He grabbed his bike and pulled it upright.

"If you do that sort of thing all the time," the boy said, and looked up at him. "I'm surprised you *haven't* been run over." He stood up, straightened his tie, and fixed George with a scornful look.

"Do what?" George snarled.

"Ride in the middle of the road," the boy said.

"What? What are you talking about?"

The boy sighed mightily, and rolled his eyes. "Listen carefully," he said. "If you *ride in the middle of the road* —" he put a sarcastic emphasis on the words, "You're liable to get *run over*. Got that?"

George felt blood rushing to his head. His hands tightened around the handlebars of his bike. "Got *this?*" he shouted, and then lifted his bike off the pavement and threw it as hard as he could against the car. There was a *SCREECH* of metal on metal. "Huh?"

The boy's eyes narrowed. "Now you *definitely* scratched it," he said.

"Did I? Oh, I guess I did," George retorted. "Watch where you're going next time!"

The boy's face suddenly went blank again; he said nothing more but just stared at George with an unreadable expression. It was almost as if he were a robot that had just gotten turned off. George felt a little creeped out. *There's something wrong with this kid . . .*

Then, suddenly, the boy turned away and got back into the car. Still breathing hard, George watched as the old car pulled back onto the road and drove away.

"What a jerk," he muttered, and turned back to his bike, picking it up and rotating the pedals experimentally. It didn't seem to be broken. *That was freaky.* He let out a harsh laugh. *I bet he goes to Sparrow Hills. There's a lot of crazies at that school. Wasn't there something on the news last night about another gun scare up there?*

He picked up his sunglasses, and then cleaned himself off as best he could, running his hands through his curly hair to smooth it down. He had been wearing a windbreaker, so his white school shirt and tie were untouched; but he had two large grass stains on the knees of his school pants.

Thanks a lot, buddy, he thought savagely. *Scratches? He's gonna total that thing. . . I hope he gets into an accident . . .* he stopped moving for a second. *No. That's not right.* He sighed heavily.

"Lord," he muttered. "Okay, guess I could have handled that better . . ."

He sneaked a guilty look back down the road, but the black car was out of sight. *Too late to apologize. Oh well.*

As he got back onto his bike, feeling his bruises, he tried to stop himself from cursing the guy to Hell, or imagining a very nice car accident waiting for him around the bend. Better think about something else, he told himself in a surly voice. "Okay, God, please help me to be a better Christian . . ." *But he almost killed me!* a voice inside him screamed. He gritted his teeth and went on. "Please help me to be a better Christian . . . and please help me to get to school on time."

Until recently, he hadn't been praying like this. George had been Catholic all his life, but he hadn't started really taking it seriously until he'd started wrestling last year at St. Lucy's. It had started with praying before matches, and somehow, once God had gotten his attention, it was hard to ignore Him. Not that this made things any easier; in fact, sometimes it made things harder.

And now he was going to a new school, a school that was supposed to be a "real" Catholic school. So lately he had been trying even harder to be a "real" Catholic, whatever that meant. *As if my life isn't hard enough...*

He checked his watch and almost swore. It was 7:30 already! He had been having trouble getting to school on time, mostly because at John Paul 2 High, opening bell was at 7:50 — earlier than he was used to — because they started the day with a Rosary...

He shook his head, pumped hard on the pedals, and shot back onto the road.

Allie Weaver sat in the back seat of her mom's car, slumped down, her blond hair spread behind her over the leather seat of the car. It was her first day at John Paul 2 High, and she was dressed in the official uniform: black skirt, white shirt. She looked exactly like a waitress.

She saw her mother's eyes glancing at her anxiously from the rear-view mirror. *Here comes the pep talk...*

"So, Allie," her mom began in a hopeful voice. "How are you feeling?"

Allie knew that she should just say "fine" and go back to moping. But suddenly, all her frustration welled up inside, and she burst out, "*Why* do I have to go to this stupid school, Mom?"

"You know why," her mom said shortly. "Because it's safer for you."

"Not much safer. It's right next to Sparrow Hills," Allie muttered, but not too loudly. Her mom and step-dad had talked about sending her to some snobby boarding school instead, and that would have been much worse. Fortunately they couldn't afford it. She glanced longingly out the window at the yellow buses unloading at Sparrow Hills, then ducked down again in case anyone saw her.

A few minutes later, the car came to a stop. "Here we are!" her mother said. "At least, I *think* that this is the address she gave me . . ."

Allie straightened in her seat and looked out the window. What she saw made her more depressed than ever, if that was possible.

It looked like a school building, at least, but a very old and ugly one. The walls were built of dingy red bricks. The rows of windows were stained and dusty, and in some places the glass was cracked and fixed with peeling tape; yellowing blinds shrouded the inside. Allie and her mother had pulled into a parking lot of cracked gray asphalt, and a rusting aluminum porch stood directly in front of them, shading the front doors.

"This is *it*?" Allie whispered, awestruck by how ugly it was. The building was . . . a *dump*. A *sty*.

"This is it," her mom said firmly as she opened the car door. "Come on."

"Haven't you seen inside?" Allie asked, yanking her book-bag out of the car.

"There wasn't time. You know this is sort of last-minute. But I'm sure that Emily Costain's husband has everything under control. He's the principal. You remember Emily?

She and I were in college together, and she has a daughter your age."

Allie was barely listening; she had noticed a sign taped to the doors with the words "John Paul 2 High" on them. She read more of it, and gasped. "Hey, Mom, this sign says — "

"Come *on*, Allie," her mom said, pulling open the door and pushing her through. "I don't have much time. I've got an early meeting."

They walked into a darkened hallway, lined on either side by rows of rusting lockers with a musty, decrepit look about them. Her mom found a light switch and turned it on. One by one, rows of dim, flickering, fluorescent lights went on, bathing the hallway in a sickly light.

"Ah," said her mom in satisfaction. "That's better."

"Hello!" a voice called out. A stout lady with red-gray hair had emerged from an office door. "You must be the Weavers," she said, walking up to them. "I'm Jenny Flynn. Welcome to John Paul 2 High."

With a wonderful feeling of relief, George reached the top of the hill and started coasting down. The road sloped gently for a full mile, curving slightly. He picked up speed, his tires making a soft, steady *buzz* on the asphalt, and as he rounded the curve, he saw the huge complex of new buildings that was Sparrow Hills.

He glanced at the public-school buildings wistfully as they flicked past. *I bet they have a bunch of gyms*, he thought. Gun scares or no, he was envious. Life there had to be so much easier. *Heck, the wrestling team probably has its own gym.* That reminded him painfully that he wasn't on the St. Lucy's wrestling team anymore. He wasn't on *any* wrestling team anymore. His new school didn't have sports. How could it? There were only five kids enrolled, including him.

And wrestling's pretty much the only thing I'm good at, he thought glumly as Sparrow Hills flicked out of sight, to be replaced by woods on either side.

He had made it onto the varsity team. He had made it to States! *States!* It didn't happen often, a freshman making it to the state championships. He had gotten his picture in the paper . . . *Stop it,* he told himself again. *Better think about something else. After all, like Mom said this morning, the Costains need us to be at John Paul 2 High. The school's just getting off the ground; they need the students.*

The story of my life: Mom and I do everything with the Costains. The Costains lead, we follow. Mr. C. is the general and we're the . . . supply team or something. He gave his forehead a quick swipe. *At least you'll stay in shape from all this biking.*

To his right, a pasture replaced the trees, with a few black-and-white cows grazing in it. George backpedaled and slowed down. Finally, he turned up a driveway of crumbling asphalt and coasted into the parking lot of his school.

He had heard that the building was supposed to be knocked down before Mr. Costain had leased it for a rock-bottom price. But every time he saw it, George couldn't help thinking that the building might have been better off as a pile of rocks. It was pretty much the ugliest school he had ever seen.

Pulling up to the doors, he dismounted and checked his watch. Awesome — it was only 7:40. He had ten minutes left before the Rosary started.

"George, could you help me?"

He turned to see Mrs. Simonelli getting out of her car, balancing several grocery bags together with her briefcase. As usual, the science teacher was wearing high heels, clunky jewelry, a faultless suit, and a tense, pained expression on her narrow face. Every blonde hair on her head was perfectly in place, as though held there with super glue.

"Sure, Mrs. Simonelli," George hurried to grab the door for her, partly to be polite and partly because you didn't mess with Mrs. Simonelli. "Hi, Liz."

Mrs. Simonelli's daughter (and polar opposite) Liz was slouching out of the car with a few grocery bags of her own. As usual, she had a sour look on her Italian features as though she would rather be dragged down the street behind a Ferrari than attend school at John Paul 2 High.

"What's the food for?" he asked, by way of making conversation. He recognized a pumpkin pie and a few cans of whipped cream in the plastic bag she was carrying.

"Refreshments for the fundraising meeting after school," Mrs. Simonelli said. "Liz, make sure those get into the refrigerator in the cafeteria."

Liz grumbled something unintelligible in answer. George let the door close behind them and returned to his bike.

He had just locked his bike up and was about to go inside when something — he wasn't sure what — struck him as odd. Slowly he turned around.

Then he saw a car that had never been there before in the parking lot next to the Simonelli car: a big, battered, black car with a huge hood and a tarnished silver grill.

No!

That creep . . . he's coming here?

It was the same car.

Then George remembered hearing rumors last week about a new kid enrolling at the school; Mrs. Flynn and Mrs. Simonelli were really excited: the student body was growing, the school was getting off the ground. He glanced again at the old car with a sinking feeling in his stomach. It all made sense now. *So that's our new classmate,* he thought sourly as he headed for the front door again. *Great. As if John Paul 2 High isn't weird enough already.*

He was so distracted that he failed to notice another new car — a shiny red coupe — looking distinctly out of place in the old parking lot.

TWO

UNDER INSPECTION

These premises

JOHN PAUL 2 HIGH

are under inspection for
structural integrity
in accordance with county
building code MCBC-1200043TR

_____

signature of building inspector

date 7/15/17

GEORGE, HIS HAND STILL ON THE HANDLE, frowned as he read the sign that was taped on the front door of the school.

"Under inspection"? he thought, frowning. *What does that mean?*

"Hi, George!"

He turned to see Celia Costain getting out of the battered Costain station wagon. She waved and eagerly cut across the lawn toward him, her dark curly hair swaying in a ponytail behind her. She was wearing a knitted white sweater over her school uniform and her usual upbeat smile. They were the only two sophomores in the new school.

"Hi — " A sudden movement caught his eye behind Celia. "Watch out!"

He dodged just in time as a stream of water came around the side of the building. But it caught Celia, who had turned to look, full in the face. "Aacccck!" she yelled.

They both heard maniacal laughter disappearing around the other side of the school building.

"Guess Mrs. Flynn got here early," George said dryly. "J.P. has time on his hands."

Celia examined her dripping sweater and pulled it off. She didn't seem too upset — George was constantly amazed at her patience. She probably got it from being the oldest of six Costain kids. "Yeah," she said, "but there's a new student coming. Isn't that great?"

"Huh." George's bad temper returned. "I'm not so sure. Students like this one could probably sink the school."

As if in answer, a man opened the door, pulling on his coat as he came. Black-haired, with a silver goatee and half-glasses, his face was usually as good-humored as Celia's, but right now, Mr. Costain — main teacher and principal of the school — looked distinctly stressed out.

"George!" he said, "Good to see you!" Mr. Costain had a way of speaking, as though you were just the person he wanted to talk to. Usually it made people feel special. But lately it just made George nervous.

"Uh, yeah?" George said. "What's up, Mr. C?" Sometimes he had a sneaking feeling that Mr. Costain considered him an oldest son.

"Emergency again. The town inspector seems to have found another reason to deny our permit. I've got to run down to the town planning office," Mr. Costain said. "Look, Mrs. Simonelli and Mrs. Flynn are busy with the new folks. Can you get the kids in class and start the Rosary? We need to make sure the day starts on time."

"They denied the permit again?" George said. Not that he cared, but he knew Mr. Costain did. The Costain family had been working overtime to get this new school started, but this part of the process had turned into a mini-drama. The first day of school, the Fire Marshall had closed the school down. They'd had the first three days of classes outside until the building was declared safe for entry.

"Yes. God created order, but the Devil invented bureaucracies." Mr. Costain sighed. "If you and Celia could start the Rosary and be the student welcome wagon, that would be fantastic. Between the Rosary and my signature in person on a few more release forms, we might just get school started today." He jogged to his beat-up Volvo station wagon. "Glad you're here, George."

George was sure Mr. Costain knew he'd rather be at St. Lucy's, where he could wrestle. Trying to sound happy, he said, "Thanks," and turned away.

"Oh," Celia said, wringing her wet sweater. Her eyebrows were worried. "I hate this. I hate that even now they can still close us down."

"Don't worry, Seal," George pulled at her ponytail. He'd been calling her that ever since they'd been kids. "Your dad'll take care of it."

"I hope so," she sighed and then smiled again. "I know he's glad you're here, George. He really depends on you."

"Yeah, I know," George muttered as he opened the door for them to go inside, hoping he didn't sound sarcastic. Mr. Costain trusted him to welcome the new student. But then, Mr. Costain didn't know that George had already put a nice deep scratch in the middle of the new student's front fender. *Some welcome wagon.*

"What happened to your pants? Did you crash your bike?"

"Not exactly . . ."

"Hi, Liz!" Celia said. "What's up?"

Liz Simonelli had gotten to her locker. She merely grumbled as she yanked her dirty blond hair into a ponytail. She was 14, a freshman with an athletic build, about the same height as Celia — but she looked a bit shorter because of the way she was slouching. "What's up with that sign?" she said.

"That's from the county," George said. "They're going to shut us down and demolish the building."

19

Liz brightened. "Really?"

George snorted with laughter, and Celia looked reproachfully at both of them. "*No,*" she said.

"Darn," Liz said. "I was in the mood to see something get demolished. That would be a great welcome for the new kid my mom keeps blabbing about — Hey, George, what happened to your pants? You got, like, the worst grass stain in history."

"I'll tell you what happened," George said. "The new kid happened. You know, the psycho?"

Celia looked at him in surprise. "The what? You can't be serious."

"Oh yeah," George said. "I already met the mental case this morning."

"What? How?"

George was about to reply when something heavy slammed into his back and pinned his arms to his sides. A voice whispered in his ear. "You're dead meat, Peterson."

George groaned, "Get off me, Flynn," he said. "Before I break your skinny Irish neck."

The grip tightened. "Skinny? Irish? You got a lot of guts, Peterson. Just because you went to that big bad state championship, you think you can escape my mighty grip — *oof!*"

George had twisted hard and thrown the weight of his right shoulder up and backward. Immediately the other boy fell to the floor.

"Real smooth, J.P.," Liz said.

J.P. was already back on his feet. He was a freshman, younger and a little bit taller than George, but thinner, with a shock of reddish-brown hair that he clearly didn't make an effort to comb. The most arresting thing about him were his eyes, which glinted from his pale freckled face with a slightly crazy gleam.

"I can't believe you pulled that wrestling move on me, Peterson!" he crowed in a strangely triumphant way. "You're lucky! I was gonna take you *DOWN!*" He shouted the last word in a roar that made Celia and Liz jump. "There are few who can withstand one of the mighty Flynns . . ."

"Yeah, yeah, yeah," George said, making as if to smack J.P. on the head.

J.P. sprang away. "Don't touch the hair! *NOT* the hair!"

"Oh, yeah, J.P.," Celia giggled. "You must have worked *really* hard on it."

"You should know better than to take on a state wrestling champion," Liz said, fiddling with the combination lock on one of the lockers.

"Why *do* you have a lock on your locker, anyway?" J.P. shot back. "I mean, don't you *trust* us?"

At that moment, one of the hall lights suddenly flickered and went out. "Not again!" Liz complained. "Why does that always happen?"

"Maybe it's a poltergeist," J.P. said. "This looks like the kind of building that would have one . . ."

"Speaking of which, we should go start the Rosary," Celia said. "Hurry up and come into home room."

George groaned and opened his locker. J.P. sidled over conspiratorially. "Hey, I heard there's a new kid today. Do you know anything about that? I hope it's a girl, at least."

"It's not," George said sourly. "Sorry."

"*Whoah!*"

J.P. had opened his locker and was standing in front of it, something white on his hands. There was more white stuff coming out of the locker that looked like . . .

"*Whipped cream?*" J.P. said, aghast, and pulled a white-smeared can out of the locker.

"What the heck?" George laughed. "Who would — ?"

Just then, Liz ambled back from her locker, her hands full of books, obviously trying to keep a straight face.

J.P. saw her. "*YOU!*" he said, shaking the can in her direction. "It was *SO YOU!*"

"Me?" Liz said, grinning nastily now. "Me what? What happened?"

"YOU put whipped cream in my locker!"

"Oh, did someone cream your locker?" said Liz in a mock-sympathetic voice, smirking. "Maybe it was the poltergeist." She walked away triumphantly.

"Oh ho *HO!*" J.P. yelled after her. "So, you think this has ended, little missy!" He grinned crazily at George. "But it has only just begun!"

With that, he sprinted down the hallway in the opposite direction, still clutching the can of whipped cream.

"What's only just begun?"

Brian Burke, a slim, African-American boy with thick glasses and an impeccably neat uniform, had joined the group. Another freshman, the former homeschooler was polite, earnest, smart, hardworking — a bit of a geek. But he fit well into John Paul 2 High, mostly because there weren't enough kids to form any cliques.

"Nothing. Liz just found something else to do at school besides complain." George said.

"I wish she'd cheer up," Brian said. "A good attitude makes a better atmosphere."

Celia beamed at him. "Way to go, Brian!" George didn't say anything; he was too busy trying to stifle a laugh.

Brian apparently didn't notice, though; he just smiled in some surprise. "Well . . . yes. Anyhow, I was concerned about the sign on the front door. Do you know what's going on?"

"Dad drove into town to find out," Celia said. "He said we should start school without him and he'll be back as soon as he can. He doesn't know why they should need another inspection."

"I don't like it." Brian said, frowning, and asked in a quieter voice, "Do you think that the government's going to try to shut us down? You know, because we're Catholic, and we're actually trying to follow the Church's teaching?"

George and Celia stared at him. "Oh, come on, Brian," George said. "They're just going to inspect the building, and honestly, can you blame them?"

"You don't understand," Brian said seriously, shouldering his book-bag. "You haven't been homeschooled. I know what it's like to get persecuted."

It was hard to handle Brian sometimes. "I think this is a little different," George said, as Brian disappeared into the large classroom that served as their homeroom.

"Liz, did you really have to do that?" said Celia as Liz returned to the hallway, tossing a hackey-sack ball from one hand to the other. "What if J.P. goes off and does something stupid?"

"Well, *that* would be surprising, wouldn't it?" Liz said cuttingly, tossing the ball at Celia, who dropped it. "Besides, I did it to get him back for all the pranks he's pulled on *you* since the first day. You can't just roll over and take it, Costain. You got to fight back."

"He's just being a goof," Celia shook her head with some irritation, picking up the ball and tossing it back. "Honestly, Liz, I don't care."

"Well, I care! *Someone's* got to stand up for women's rights!" Liz said, catching the ball deftly on the side of her black uniform shoe and tossing it to George. She was an excellent shot. "So who's this psycho creep of a new student who's starting?"

"How do you know the new student is a psycho creep?" Celia asked again.

"Believe me," George said, batting the ball back to Liz with his ankle. "A mental case, like I said. A complete psycho. I wish your dad wasn't so desperate for tuition money, Seal, or he wouldn't take weirdoes like that one."

"Weirdoes like who?" a steely female voice answered.

George turned in surprise and nearly hit himself in the face with the ball.

A girl was standing there — a girl with long blond hair, a slim, graceful build, and clear blue eyes. She was . . . beautiful. She could have been on the cover of some teen girl magazine, except that she was dressed in a white blouse and a straight black skirt like the other girls — it looked so much *better* on her — and she was clenching a notebook to her chest. And those blue eyes, full of fury, were looking right at him.

"Uh . . ." George faltered, and Liz snickered.

The gorgeous girl tossed her blond hair. "Not that *I* could do much more to bring this school downhill," she said, and walked past him down the hall.

"Like I said," Liz asked hopefully as the girl vanished into the ladies' room, "Is she really a psycho creep?"

"Um — why don't we go start the Rosary now?" Celia said brightly, pulling him away. "Hey! Dad's back!"

George had slunk into his desk by the time Mr. Costain entered the room, followed by a tall fat boy with bushy hair and dead gray eyes, still wearing the black trench coat over his white shirt and tie.

At Mr. Costain's entrance, the atmosphere had immediately changed to more of a semblance of school. John Paul 2 High might be disorganized, but the main reason it was working was because Mr. Costain was a teaching genius.

"I'd like to announce a momentous event," Mr. Costain said. "As of today, we have a *junior class*. Meet James Kosalinski." With a wave of his hand, he introduced the boy to the rest of the class, as though there were sixty other teens in the room instead of just six. "James, these are our sophomores, George Peterson and my daughter Celia. We have another new student, who should be arriving shortly. Here are two of our freshmen, Brian Burke and Elizabeth Simonelli. And I expect that Mr. John Paul Flynn is around here somewhere."

James Kosalinski's flat, pallid face turned toward them without making eye contact — until he saw George. For a moment, he blinked; then a sour smile came to his face.

He lifted one hand. "Greetings," he said in a low voice, fixing his eyes on George. Then he walked over to one of the many empty desks in the classroom, sat heavily, pulled out a paperback with the title *Hostage to the Devil,* and began to stare into it.

George stared at James, feeling his anger from earlier that morning returning. *Why is this kid here?*

Celia raised her hand. Mr. Costain beckoned. "Yes?"

"Excuse me, Dad — I mean, Mr. Costain," Celia said. "Can I ask what happened at the permit office? I mean, lots of kids were wondering about the sign . . ."

"Yes, the sign," Mr. Costain said with the sigh. "I went down to the county municipal office this morning. They informed me that the building is being inspected for . . ." he cleared his throat, "'structural integrity.' But we're still allowed to use the building, so there's nothing to worry about right now. Let's get started. Rosaries out, morning prayer commencing — George, why don't you lead?"

Mr. Costain usually asked George to lead the prayers. Slightly resentful, George fished his wooden bead rosary out of his backpack and folded his hands. Everyone followed suit.

Glancing over, George saw the new boy remove a ponderous, black, fifteen-decade rosary from his trench coat and cross himself solemnly.

Okay. Weird. George took a deep breath and began, "I believe in God, the Father Almighty . . ." For the umpteenth time, he wished that he was in a classroom with sixty other kids, an anonymous face at the back of the classroom, doodling in his notebook, putting in time until wrestling practice — but he had to be here instead, leading the Rosary and looking like he was trying to be some kind of spiritual leader.

He barreled through the first part of the Creed on auto-pilot, and the class began saying the second half, "I believe in the Holy Spirit . . ."

". . . Ghost," the new boy said at the same time, choosing his words smugly.

The rest of the class faltered momentarily, and George's eyes flashed to the new boy's. Even when his voice was sneering, his eyes were expressionless, but when he looked at George, James Kosalinski's eyes sneered too.

George reddened. James wasn't fooled. He knew George wasn't some kind of saint: he had seen George yelling and throwing his bike against James' car. And now that he knew that George knew he knew, he was enjoying watching George squirm.

George's anger from the morning boiled up again. *Why does* he *have to be here? This is not fair!* Trying to keep his temper, George stared at the floor and tried to remember what he should be saying next. *Ignore him, ignore him . . .*

"For the intentions of our Holy Father, the Pope, we pray, Our Father, who art . . ."

Suddenly a loud shriek echoed down the hall.

Allie had decided that she was going to skip her first homeroom at John Paul 2 High. As she brushed her hair out in front of the bathroom mirror, she wondered if she should just call her mom on her cell phone and announce she was quitting school right now.

"Why?" she could imagine her mom saying.

"They all think I'm a psycho creep," she would say. "They were all talking about me in the halls."

The embarrassment of that moment came back to her, and she clenched the hairbrush and pulled it through her thoroughly brushed blond hair for the hundredth time.

Why am I not good enough for them? she wondered. She had always been popular at school, and the thought that in this school, she might be an outcast hit her with a smack. *They hate me. They don't even know anything about me and already they don't like me!*

The bathroom mirror was cracked, the ugly green paint was peeling off the walls, and the few fluorescent lights were dim. Allie looked at her reflection in the smudged mirror, and suddenly she felt so out of place and lonely that she wanted to cry.

Why should I be surprised? Everything in my life is different now. Why should I care about being popular? I should be glad that I'm alive. And safe.

Safe, she thought ruefully. *Yeah, Mom, this place looks safe. No locks on the doors, no security guards. Bet they have policemen frisking kids right and left at Sparrow Hills. I'd probably be safer up there . . . from . . .*

She shivered. No, she wouldn't be safer back there: a pointless attack like that could happen only in a big place like Sparrow Hills, with kids so bored and deadened that they'd grab a random sophomore girl, put a gun to her head, and then vanish . . . *I hope they find him. They have to find him. Stop him before he . . . Okay, stop thinking. Focus. Got to deal with this new school now . . . Figure out how to make it to the end of the year here . . .* She touched up her lipstick. *Well, at least my hair looks good today . . .*

Suddenly there was a loud *bang* as one of the stalls in the bathroom slammed open. In the mirror she saw a dark figure behind her, and her heart jumped. She screamed and turned to fight, to run . . .

But instead of a gunshot, there was a hiss and something cool and sticky splattered against her face.

Wiping her face frantically with her hands, she realized what the stuff was. Whipped cream. All over her.

Standing in front of her looking horror-stricken, was a tall, thin, freckle-faced boy. The can of whipped cream dropped from his hand and clattered on the floor.

"Oh!" he said. "Thought you were Liz — "

The bathroom door banged, and he was gone.

THREE

THE GREAT WALL OF QUOTES

If you want the truth,
you must look for it.
It's that simple.
If it's there, it will stick a foot out
as you pass; he will hold his side laughing
as you fall...
It will be more than you expected.

But then, of course, you must decide
what you're going to do with him.
He might start to follow you around --

You can just picture him
down on the corner with the boys,
trying to fit in--

No sir,
you won't be able to take him anywhere.

-- David Craig

AS THE SHRIEK ECHOED DOWN THE HALL, the classroom fell into stunned silence. George heard pounding footsteps echoing down the hall, and then J.P. rushed into the classroom, slammed the door, and leaned against it, breathing hard.

"Ah, Mr. Flynn," Mr. Costain said. "Nice of you to join us. Where have you been?"

J.P.'s face reddened underneath his freckles. "Nowhere," he mumbled. "I just went to the bathroom," he added as he sat down.

George caught Mr. Costain's eye, and they both winced. George could tell Mr. Costain didn't want to deal with the situation. George tentatively said, "Our Father. . . ?" and Mr. Costain nodded, got up, and walked toward the door.

The door opened before he got there. A very angry Mrs. Flynn entered, followed by the blond girl, whose hair was now damp and whose uniform was spattered with white foam.

"Sorry about the disturbance, Mr. Costain," Mrs. Flynn said, glaring at J.P., who was huddled in his chair clutching his rosary and apparently praying to become invisible. "It seems that *someone* played a practical joke on our new student."

"Really," Mr. Costain said, his voice much colder. "Well, I'm certainly sorry to hear that — especially since it's her first day here," he added, glancing at J.P. "Everyone, this is Allison Weaver, our new sophomore. Allie, you can go ahead and find a seat."

"I'll bring you a towel to clean up with," Mrs. Flynn murmured and left the room.

The new girl's face was beet-red. She gave J.P. a murderous glance, and then stalked over to an empty desk, sat down, and sullenly stared into space.

"All right," said Mr. Costain. "Let's continue. George?"

After she had cleaned up, Allie stared at the wall, too angry and humiliated even to pretend to pay attention to the unfamiliar words of the prayer. *I have* got *to get out of here:* the words ran through her head again and again.

Somebody nudged her elbow. She looked up as a girl with dark, curly hair pushed some rosary beads into her hands.

"Try to follow along," the girl whispered. "I'm so sorry about what happened!"

Allie just stared at the rosary, an object she had never actually held before or even seen up close. Confusion replaced her anger as she held the string of colored glass beads with little knots and medals on it.

"Glory be to the Father and to the Son and to the Holy Spirit . . ." someone said.

Everyone else said automatically, "As it was in the beginning, is now, and ever shall be, world without end, Amen. O my Jesus, forgive us our sins, save us from the fires of Hell, lead all souls to Heaven, especially those in most need of Thy Mercy."

The prayers droned on, sounding strange and slightly creepy to Allie. She started following along on the little beads, but she didn't actually say the words; she was too busy sneaking looks at the other kids.

It was a diverse group, despite the fact that there were only — she counted rapidly — six of them. Was this the *whole school?* Two girls and four boys. The redhead, a black guy, a fat guy, and the praying guy — the one who had called her a psycho creep. She checked him out again. He was the only guy here who could be called cute — tall, curling light brown hair, hazel eyes, nicely built. She'd never seen a guy like that praying before, and even though she knew he was a jerk and a hypocrite, there was something compelling about the way he prayed. *Weird.*

So this is a Catholic school, and they're praying. . . It was a bizarre experience, sitting there with six other teens just . . . saying words. Over and over again. To no one who was in the room. Okay, to God. It hit her that suddenly she was on a different plane, a different universe; a world where things like prayer were important. Her stomach sank. *How am I ever going to fit in here?*

After what seemed like forever, the brown-haired guy was saying, ". . . Our Lady, seat of Wisdom . . ."

"Pray for us."

"John Paul the Great . . ."

"Pray for us."

Silence. Everyone made the sign of the cross, including Allie. At least she knew how to do *that.*

"Okay!" Mr. Costain said, clapping his hands together and rubbing them with a warm smile on his face. "Let's go, people! Freshmen to math — no, wait, freshmen to science first — sophomores and junior to math class. James,

Allie, that means you're going to Mrs. Flynn's classroom, two doors down on the left — "

"Allie!" the rosary girl said, picking up her books and coming over. "I'm so sorry about what happened!" she said again. "J.P. can be *such* a pain. Are you okay?"

The girl seemed to know her, which was equally weird to Allie. "I guess," she said, cramming her wet sweater into her backpack and trying to pretend she wasn't freaked out. *Who* are *these people?*

The girl turned to prayer guy, who was gathering up his books and clearly trying to ignore them. "George, you didn't mean to say Allie was a psycho creep, did you?"

The boy turned, and Allie saw he was red with embarrassment — which made him look as cute as a confused beagle. "I didn't mean *you*," he muttered. "Sorry."

Despite her defensiveness, Allie was amused. "So who *did* you mean?"

"I meant him," George said in a low voice, and the fat boy walking up the aisle paused and turned around.

The fat boy's face betrayed no expression, but his gray eyes sparked. "Georgie Porgie is not very nice," he said. Then his eyes fell on Allie.

They lingered on her a little too long. Uncomfortable, she flipped back her hair and turned away to pick up her books. *Okay, another weirdo.*

She glanced back at George, who was sneaking away, his face still bright red — at least she wasn't the only one embarrassed.

Allie slung her backpack over her shoulder and walked down the hallway with the girl, whose name, she found out, was Celia Costain. "So," she said, "let me guess. Is Mrs. Flynn J.P.'s mom? Or is he an orphan?"

"Mrs. Flynn's his mom," Celia said. "And Mrs. Simonelli is Liz's mom. Mr. Costain is my dad. There's just three teachers."

"So that means," Allie said slowly, "that about half of the kids here are *related* to the teachers?"

"More or less," Celia said, shrugging. "And anyway, George and me might as well be related, we're so close. I don't know the other kids as well, though. I knew Liz a little bit from St. Bridget's — that's the Catholic grade school — "

"I know," Allie said distantly.

"But I never met Brian or James before they came here. They were both homeschooled, I think."

"What about J.P.?" Allie said.

Celia laughed. "J.P. is the youngest kid in this *huge* family. He's got, like, ten brothers and sisters. So yeah, I knew him from St. Bridget's and from church. And because his dad writes for magazines my parents get, and his mom speaks at conferences my parents go to, and organizes things my parents do . . . The Flynns are, like, Catholic to the max."

So, Allie thought glumly. *A bunch of homeschoolers and Catholic school kids. That's who goes here. I'm* really *gonna fit in.* Her family hadn't even been to Mass since last Christmas. Everyone here was probably halfway on their way to being nuns and priests or something. *Catholic to the max. Great.*

"And you used to go to Sparrow Hills, right?"

"Yeah," Allie said as they sat down in a smaller classroom with about five desks.

"Weird."

Yeah, Allie thought darkly. *Weird for you to have to deal with me.*

"I mean, *we* must seem really weird to *you*," Celia corrected herself.

Allie did a double take. *Did she just read my mind?*

But Celia just smiled and said, "If anything here freaks you out, just let me know. I can explain things, okay? I really want you to feel comfortable here."

"Okay," Allie said, still suspicious. Celia was the principal's daughter. Maybe she said this to everyone. But did she really *mean* it?

Before either of them could say any more, Mrs. Flynn walked into the classroom.

"Everyone here?" Mrs. Flynn said briskly, as she plopped an old battered textbook entitled *Intermediate Algebra* on Allie's desk before going to James's desk and doing the same. "My, we've doubled our class size! Let's get started."

Allie took one more look around. Three other students, besides her. *Yeah, I guess going from two students to four is doubling the class size. At least I know that much math. . .*

Then she doggedly cracked the old book open and fished a brand-new spiral notebook and mechanical pencil out of her backpack. School, after all, was still school.

Completely embarrassed, George tried to focus on algebra, but he couldn't help sneaking glances at the new girl. She *definitely* wasn't the type of girl he had expected to come here. How did she end up here, anyway?

"George?" Mrs. Flynn said, tapping on the board with her pencil. Tall, heavyset, and grandmotherly, she was a capable, sometimes formidable math teacher. "Why don't you take this problem?"

He looked up, startled, and his eyes flashed to the algebra equation on the blackboard. "Uh — just a sec." He tightened his grip on his pencil and started scribbling frantically in his notebook.

This was the hardest math class he had ever been in; mainly because there was no crowd to hide in, but also because Mrs. Flynn had the tendency to fire off complicated problems and expect you to solve them by yourself. He scribbled some more, trying to reduce one side of the equation so that only the x remained.

"Come on, George," Mrs. Flynn said encouragingly. "There's only one variable. You can do it!"

"The answer is 13, Georgie Porgie," drawled James behind him.

"Oh, that was quick, James. Can I see your equation?" Mrs. Flynn asked.

"I did it in my head," the flat voice said. "I don't like writing anything down."

George felt a stab of annoyance and pushed it aside. *Okay, the* x *has got to be divided by two. . . How do you divide an* x *by two?* His brain seemed to freeze, and all he could think of was the pretty new girl's bored expression . . .

Mrs. Flynn leaned over his shoulder and checked his notes. "You have to just multiply both sides of the problem by two," she said patiently. "And then what do you get?"

George gritted his teeth, thinking of how stupid he must look in front of Allie Weaver, and finished the problem.

"Very good," Mrs. Flynn said, watching him. "*X* equals 13. Now, that wasn't too hard, was it?"

George was glad when the bell rang. Next up was history class with Mr. Costain, and it was sure to be less difficult.

He and the others went back to the homeroom. The whole school took all of Mr. Costain's classes together, so now the classroom actually looked full for a change.

Mr. Costain had passed out papers already, and stood in front of the blackboard smiling. George had never had a teacher who enjoyed his work so much.

"All right, people," he announced as soon as everyone had taken their seat. "Because we have two new students today, I thought that we would review some essentials. Time for a quote."

This was a standard Mr. Costain-ism: he'd done it in his classes at St. Lucy's too, starting class with a provoking quotation from a saint, historian, poet, or theologian. The class would discuss the quotation before diving into the meat of the lesson.

Today's was a poem by David Craig. George scanned the handwritten words on the sheet before him as Mr. Costain read them.

If you want the truth,
you must look for it.
It's that simple.
If it's there, it will stick a foot out

as you pass; he will hold his side laughing
as you fall . . .
It will be more than you expected.

But then, of course, you must decide
what you're going to do with him.
He might start to follow you around —

You can just picture him
down on the corner with the boys,
trying to fit in — your friends will hate him
but won't be able to ask him to leave because of his size.
He'll try to sing the bass part, completely destroy the
    harmony.

No sir,
you won't be able to take him anywhere.

No one said anything, except James, who gave a prodi-
gious yawn. "Modern poetry," he said, as though it was
something smelly.

Mr. Costain merely smiled. "Question: Everyone says
they want to find the truth. But do you really want to?"

Silence fell. Then the new girl, Allie Weaver, raised her
hand.

"Well, what is the truth, really?" she said. "I mean, can
we really ever know what it is?"

"Very good question, Miss Weaver," Mr. Costain said.
"Why don't you go on? Elaborate a little. Why do you
think that truth is so hard to find?"

"Well, you know . . ." Allie twirled her hair nervously
with one finger. "There's so much bias and prejudice and
stuff. There's two sides to every story. I mean, the truth isn't

something you really know, it's something you — have to keep seeking. If you want to be a good person. You know, you always have to be open to finding the truth. I don't know if you ever actually find it." She looked around as though to find support, and suddenly, to George's surprise, she glanced in his direction.

He gulped, and suddenly seemed to lose about 50 I.Q. points. "Uh . . ."

Mr. Costain turned to him. "Well, Mr. Peterson? Do you have an opinion?"

"Uh . . ." he found himself saying. "I don't agree. You can find it. It's there."

"And according to the poem of my friend Dr. Craig, it's when you find the truth that your problems actually begin," Mr. Costain said.

George felt himself turn red. "Right." He glanced at Allie, who looked somewhat annoyed. *Smooth, George. Real smooth.*

From the back, James's voice said a touch smugly, "Christianity has not been tried and found wanting. It has been found too difficult and left untried."

"G. K. Chesterton," Mr. Costain said. "Excellent, Mr. Kosalinski."

George wished again that everyone wouldn't keep complimenting James.

Brian raised his hand. "So the poem is saying that the problem isn't finding the truth; the problem is knowing the truth?"

"Yeah, because it's impossible to understand," Liz grunted.

"Catholicism can be very complicated, true," Mr. Costain acknowledged. "But understanding the faith is not the whole problem."

"Living it is harder than understanding it." Celia said.

"Very good," Mr. Costain said. "I'll leave you to ponder that. Celia, why don't you take this copy and tape it on the wall? That can be the start of our 'Great Wall of Quotes' for the year. I've been a little late starting it, but there you go. Now. Let's go back to the Apostolic Age and see what other troubles the early Christians had." He handed his paper and a roll of tape to Celia. "Everyone else, notebooks out."

As George slapped open his notebook, he saw James looking sideways at him. Again, George felt a stab of anger. James seemed to think he was scoring points against George with every right answer he made. George didn't even want to play that game, but at the same time, he was mad that James seemed to think he was winning.

What a rotten day.

FOUR

FOLLOWED

CATHOLICISM. TRUTH. IT WAS HARD TO TALK

about things like this — it was like using muscles she'd never used before.

Allie creased the poem in half and put it in her notebook, but she couldn't shake the image of a nerdy, troublesome Truth following her around. *I've had enough of weird people following me around, thank you very much.*

She was extremely grateful when the bell rang to end the history class, and rushed off to the bathroom before the next class started. Once she was safely inside, she pulled out her cell phone, hoping to catch Tyler during the class break at Sparrow Hills.

He picked up on the first ring. "Hey, babe! What's up?"

Allie breathed a sigh of relief. "Hey, Tyler. Are you free?"

"For a little while. How's the freak school going?"

"Terrible. Hey, listen, could you pick me up after school today? I really want to see you."

"Sure thing. I don't have practice today." She could tell he was pleased she'd called him, and for the next few minutes she actually started feeling okay.

As she was walking back up the hallway a few minutes later, she met Celia.

"Hey, Allie! I just wanted to make sure you knew," Celia said. "Next class is Theology, with my dad."

"Again? Your dad teaches two classes?"

"Three, actually. After lunch, he'll be teaching English. What did you think of history? Wasn't it interesting?"

"I guess," Allie said vaguely.

"Theology should be neat, too. We're going over St. Thomas Aquinas's five proofs for the existence of God!"

Yippee.

George walked into the cafeteria for lunch. Small as the building was, it did have a little cafeteria between the two wings of the school. There was no kitchen staff, of course; every student paper-bagged it, and everyone tended to sit together, at one of the many long folding tables.

But the two new students, James and Allie, each found a separate table and sat down alone. When Celia saw this, she turned to J.P. with a fierce look on her face. "What did you do to her?"

"Nothing!" J.P. said defensively, shifting in his folding chair. "Well, I didn't *mean* to do anything. You see . . . well, there was this little mix-up in the girls' bathroom . . ."

"What were you doing in the girls' bathroom?"

"Nothing! . . . Well, you see, I had no idea who she was, and I just saw someone . . . and . . . well, I got her."

Celia looked at him stonily.

"With whipped cream," he mumbled. "I thought she was Liz."

There was a clatter of metal as Celia stood up. "Come on," she said to J.P. "You're going to apologize. George, make him apologize."

"Oh, all right," George sighed. "Come on, J.P." All three went over to the table where the new girl was sitting alone, flipping through her math book as though trying to ignore them. There was no lunch in front of her.

"Allie?" Celia said. "J.P. wants to say something to — "

"Hey," J.P. interrupted. "What's Allie short for?"

She didn't look up. "Allison," she said in a toneless voice that made it clear that she wasn't interested in conversation.

"Really?" J.P. said. "Oh, well, I just wanted you to know that I *totally* did not mean to hit you with that whipped cream. You see, that girl over there, Liz, is my arch-enemy. This morning she put whipped cream all over my books, and I was just trying to get her back . . . so when I saw a blonde come into the bathroom, well . . . I didn't even know there *was* a new kid in school today! . . . I'm really sorry. You are *way* too good-looking to get creamed like that."

Allie turned a page of *Intermediate Algebra*.

"So . . ." J.P. fumbled for a moment. "Uh . . . well . . . you want to go out with me?"

Allie's expression didn't change, although George thought he saw her lips curl upward, slightly.

Celia immediately started dragging J.P. away, calling back to Allie. "I'm really sorry! He's the worst student in the whole school! He only got in because of his mom!"

"I did not!" J.P. protested while being dragged. "I got in on my good looks! Ow! Don't pinch!"

George was left standing in front of the new girl. Not knowing what else to do, he sat down across from her.

He was still holding his lunch bag, and awkwardly started taking out his lunch. The girl's eyes flickered upward at the sight of the food, but otherwise she made no sign that she had even noticed he was there.

George unwrapped his ham sandwich and pushed half of it toward her. "Here. Did you forget your lunch?"

She looked at it, but shook her head. "No, thanks. I'm not eating lunch today."

"Really? Aren't you hungry?"

She turned another page of the textbook. "Nah."

George shook his head in amazement. *What is it with girls and not eating?* He left the sandwich half on the table, between them, just in case she changed her mind; then he opened his bottle of orange juice and took a swig. "My name's George," he said. "In case you didn't catch it."

She didn't even look up. "Yeah, I caught it." She raised one hand, her eyes still glued to the book. "I'm Allie."

Nice to meet you too, George thought. "So," he said doggedly, "how did you end up here?"

She looked up and stared at him, as though debating whether he was worth talking to. "It's a long story," she said finally.

"I'm really sorry that this place is so disorganized," George said, changing the subject.

She shrugged. "It's not *your* fault."

George tried again. "Why are you reading that textbook, anyway?"

"Because I'm bored. Look," she sighed. "I'm sorry I'm not . . . more friendly. I'm just . . . just . . ."

"You're just getting used to the place," George finished for her. "So am I."

"Really?"

George smiled. "Yeah, really. I used to go to St. Lucy's until this year, and this is way different."

"Yeah, but at least St. Lucy's was, you know, a *Catholic* school," she said. "I went to Sparrow Hills until last week."

"You miss it?"

"Well . . ." she considered it for a moment. "Right now . . . yeah, I kinda do. Sort of."

"Oh," George said, not knowing whether to feel defensive about John Paul 2 High, or honored to be in her confidence. "It's not so bad."

"So far I'm not too impressed," she said.

"Why'd you come here?" George tried again.

Allie shrugged. "It was my mom's idea." Her voice sounded edgy, and George saw she looked a little pale.

They sat in silence for a while. Then, absentmindedly, Allie picked up the half of George's sandwich that still lay in front of her, and took a bite.

"Fo," she said with her mouth half-full. "Wafoo mif-famos . . ." she swallowed. "Sorry," she said. "I guess I am hungry, after all."

"That's okay," George said, acutely aware that there was a stupid grin on his face. "What was that?"

"What do you miss the most about St. Lucy's?"

"Wrestling, I guess." George said, trying to stop grinning and sound more casual. "I was on the squad at St. Lucy's and I miss it a lot."

"You were a wrestler?" She sounded interested.

"Well, uh, yeah," George said, running a hand through his hair. "Actually, I like to think that I still am."

"That's really funny!" Allie said. "I'm dating a guy on the Sparrow Hills wrestling team."

George felt a slight deflating in his chest. "Really?" he said, keeping his voice nonchalant. "Then you must know all about wrestling already. Cool."

51

"Not much, actually," Allie said. "I can't stand it."

"Oh." George said, suddenly finding himself at a loss for words. He compensated by taking an extra-large bite of his sandwich.

English class was next. George cringed as he walked down the hallway with Celia and Brian. They were reading *Romeo and Juliet. Love* poetry. Just what he needed right now.

He chanced a glance backward. Allie Weaver was walking alone ten feet behind them. She looked more tense than a girl that gorgeous should be, facing a weenie school like John Paul 2 High. *Something's bothering her.*

Celia noticed him looking back. "So," she whispered. "How's Allie doing? After I dragged J.P. away, I tried to make friends with James and didn't get a chance to stop by your table again. It was nice that you sat with her."

"No big deal. We really didn't talk much."

"She used to go to Sparrow Hills, right?" Brian said. "I wonder what she's doing here."

"I dunno."

Brian glanced back at Allie. "Well, I think it's pretty neat to have a public school kid here. I don't like it when everybody's got the same background; it's not very interesting."

George didn't reply. He was a little surprised at Brian's words; it just wasn't what he had expected from a homeschooler.

"Afternoon!" Mr. Costain greeted them from the front of the class. "I hope everyone had a lovely lunch. Now, we'll be going back to the Bard's masterpiece of young, tragic love. We were on Act I, Scene IV last Friday . . ."

Allie yawned again. *How many more classes are there?* She had read *Romeo and Juliet* in freshman English class, and hadn't liked it then, either.

She happened to be sitting next to that freshman girl . . . what was her name again? Liz. "Hey!" she whispered.

Liz glanced up. "What?" she hissed.

"What's the next class?" Allie whispered

"You got Science with my mom! Mrs. Simonelli!" Liz muttered back, pretending to write some notes.

Oh, Allie thought. *Another teacher's kid.* "Is it interesting at all?"

The other girl gave her a pitying look. "Are you kidding? My mom's the worst!"

She sure was right, Allie thought glumly. Mrs. Simonelli's classroom was on the other side of the school, near the girls' bathroom, in a long, narrow classroom that seemed to suit long, narrow Mrs. Simonelli herself. She was thin with stiff, blond, poufy hair, an immaculately pressed suit, and a high-pitched, singsong voice.

"Are we all here?" she said. "It's so good to have a few more children in my classroom. James, Allison, here are your textbooks . . ."

Children? Allie thought as she took a dog-eared *Elementary Biology* from the teacher.

"Let's start with Chapter 4," Mrs. Simonelli began. "Cell Division and Mitosis . . ." She began to lecture and write on the board, and Allie's mind started to wander. She had never liked science class at the best of times, and this one was particularly boring. She propped her chin on her hand and pretended to listen.

But the other classes . . . Some of them hadn't been so boring. Especially that history class. What was up with that? Reading poetry in history? She pictured the Truth Nerd following her around — it was too weird, that poem . . .

Flashes of memories hit her like bullets: being grabbed from behind by a dark, hooded figure; the short, guttural *heh-heh-heh* laugh; the flash from the muzzle . . .

Her elbow slipped, hitting the textbook which hit the floor with a *bang*. She nearly screamed. Everyone — Celia, George, James, and Mrs. Simonelli — turned to look at her. "Sorry," she muttered.

Fifteen excruciating minutes later, the school bell rang. No one got their things together quicker than Allie Weaver. She shoved her textbook and notebook into her book-bag, and said to George and Celia. "It was nice meeting you guys. Guess I'll see you tomorrow."

"Where are you going?" George said.

"Home," Allie said, a wonderful feeling of relief coming over her. But it dwindled when she saw their faces. "What, isn't this the last class?"

"Yeah," George said. "But . . ."

"She doesn't know," Celia said. "After classes, we pray a Divine Mercy Chaplet. It only takes about ten minutes."

"A divine mercy chapel?" Allie said, surprised. "I didn't know you guys had a chapel. Where is it?"

"No, no," Celia said, and Allie noticed with annoyance that she was suppressing a smile. "A *chaplet*. It's a sort of prayer. We say it on the rosary."

"Oh," Allie said, thinking about all those beads. They had to pray again?

As they walked back to the homeroom, George pressed a rosary into her hand. It was made of wooden beads strung together on brown twine. "Here," he said. "You can use mine this time."

George glanced over at Allie as everyone took seats for the chaplet. Her face had the expression of a girl who was too cool to pray: a faintly bored, skeptical look. *She's probably having a religion overload,* he thought. *I bet she's starting to hate Christianity or something because we're so strict. . .*

Still, he had to admit she was cute, even if she did have a boyfriend. He wondered if he knew the guy she was dating. He had been at meets with Sparrow Hills High before. *Stop it,* he said to himself. *I'm praying now.*

When the chaplet ended, she handed over the beads with a slight smile. "Thanks."

"No problem." Out of the corner of his eye, he saw James lumber out the door, and felt a sense of relief.

"Well, I gotta go," Allie said. "Do you want to meet my boyfriend? He's probably waiting outside right now; I told him to pick me up at 2:30."

George felt that deflated sensation again, but he quickly suppressed it. "Sure," he shrugged.

By the time they reached the parking lot, James's car was gone, but a new yellow car was parked in its place. Allie yelled and ran happily over to the dark-haired guy with muscular arms standing beside it.

"Tyler!" Allie wrapped her arms around the guy and glanced over her shoulder as he nuzzled her. "Hey, George! Come over here!"

"Hey there," Tyler said, giving George a toothy smile and keeping an arm around Allie's shoulders. He looked a year or two older than George. "Haven't I seen you before?"

"George Peterson," George said, "Wrestled for St. Lucy's last year."

Tyler nodded. "I saw you at States." His eyes fell on the rundown building behind them. "So what kind of a squad do you have at this school?"

"The kind that doesn't exist," George said, a bit irritated by Tyler's broad grin. "Why?"

"You want to try out for our team?"

George was startled. "But I'm not from your school," he said suspiciously.

Tyler shrugged. "Doesn't matter. We've even had *home-schoolers* try out before. I'm squad captain, and the coach told me he needs more guys to fill out the roster this year. Why don't you come up tomorrow after school for tryouts?"

"Okay. Thanks." George recognized Tyler Getz now, but hadn't remembered him being this nice.

Tyler grinned widely. "Don't sweat it. I know you'll be better than the freshmen losers we usually get. Ready, babe?"

"Yeah," Allie was already in the car and putting on her seat belt. "See ya, George."

"See ya," George said, but his mind was elsewhere as their car pulled away. Wrestling for Sparrow Hills . . . wrestling again, period! He felt his face warm up. *Yes, God, I could handle going to John Paul 2 High, if I could wrestle again —* and wrestling on a public school squad! He knew the public school could afford better equipment, better coaches; he would be in a bigger pool of wrestlers, but that was okay, he could handle the competition — assuming he made the tryouts. He'd have to get back in shape. He'd have to talk to his mom about rides . . .

"Who was that?" Brian Burke had come out of the school.

"Allie's boyfriend. He's captain of the Sparrow Hills squad — I mean, Sparrow Hills wrestling team," George answered absently.

"Really?" Brian said with interest. "I was thinking of going out for wrestling."

Snapping out of his plans, George stared at the slight boy, a bit dumbfounded. "You were?"

"Homeschoolers can play on public school teams, and my dad was all for me trying out for a team this year . . . but it's sort of intimidating. I wouldn't know anyone," Brian said.

George didn't want to answer. He thought of going to tryouts with a thin, nerdy kid in glasses tagging along.

That would really be — not so hot . . . He shook his head, impatient with himself . . . *Come on, George, grow up. This isn't junior high anymore. Bringing along a kid who's slightly "uncool" is not going to kill me . . .* He swallowed. "Well, I'm going to try out for the team tomorrow. At least, I hope I can. I have to talk to my mom." But he knew his mom would say yes. She'd be happy that he had something to do.

"Really? Maybe I'll come with you then. That would be great!" Brian sounded so appreciative that George felt better. His conscience settled, he grabbed his bike.

"Great! See you then."

FIVE

TRYING OUT

ALLIE FELT GUILTY ABOUT GOING TO SPARROW HILLS

without telling her mom. *It's after school, it'll be safe enough*, she thought. *Weird guys, please stay home.* Still, she wished that she had gotten Tyler to pick her up instead of going with the John Paul 2 High kids. George and Brian were trying out for the wrestling team, and Celia was going along to cheer for them. They had gotten a ride up to school with Mrs. Burke, Brian's mom, who drove a shiny white van big as a bread truck, and who seemed to have more kids than a daycare center.

Allie winced as she squeezed between two car seats — a drooling baby in one, and a toddler who wanted to grab everything in sight, including Allie's hair and sunglasses, in the other.

"Sorry about Augustine," said a preteen girl with tightly curled brown hair and light brown skin. "He's such a pain."

"Uh," Allie said, not wanting to agree too quickly with the girl. This was totally not a cool way to show up in front of her old friends. She half-thought of asking Mrs. Burke to drop her off at the corner.

Mrs. Burke, a blond lady in sunglasses and a calico jumper, said, "Melissa! Faustina dropped her pacifier. Find it for her. George, where am I going?"

"Up this road, I think," George said, glancing back at Allie from the shotgun seat.

"Yeah, it's up on the right," Allie said, speaking over two more kids in the seat in front of her who were arguing over an *I Spy* book. *Get me out of here!*

Mrs. Burke adjusted her sunglasses, not seeming to realize how much they clashed with her flowered jumper.

"Do you know anything about this wrestling team, George? What sort of character do the boys on this team have? Are they good kids?"

Allie felt sorry for George, who looked only a little less uncomfortable than she was. "I met the team captain, and he seemed all right. It'll probably be a pretty big team. My squad at St. Lucy's had only about fifteen wrestlers, but some of the public-school squads have thirty or forty kids. It'll probably be a big mix."

"I'm sure that if you and Brian stick together, you can stand up to any bad influences those kids might have, right?"

"Uh, sure, Mrs. Burke."

Allie pursed her lips. *What? Are public-school kids contaminated or something?*

"I'm just used to knowing everyone Brian socializes with. I'll be glad when John Paul 2 High is big enough to have its own sports teams."

George turned slightly red, and Allie knew what he was thinking. *Yeah, right, like John Paul 2 High will ever get that big.*

"Mrs. Burke?" She waved a hand. "Why don't you turn this way? The gym doors are closer." *And my friends won't see me getting out of your homeschool bus either.*

Once on the sidewalk, she tried to put as much distance between herself and the car as possible without seeming rude, and wished she had brought a normal change of clothes.

"The gym's right over there," she said over her shoulder to George, Brian, and Celia as the Burke van pulled away. Then she saw her best friend Nikki standing in the parking lot, talking to some boys. "See you guys," Allie said, and took off running.

George had been more than a little nervous about making his public-school wrestling debut in front of Allie Weaver, but realized he had probably been worried over nothing.

"I guess she must really miss her friends," Celia said after Allie had abandoned them without a backward glance. "Maybe she'll catch up with us later."

"Maybe," George said skeptically, and turned away. *Yeah right. She hates wrestling. She told me so yesterday.*

As they walked down the sidewalk, Brian said to George, "What's in the gym bag?"

"My gear," George said, pushing Allie Weaver out of his mind. He decided to do a really good job in prepping Brian for the tryouts. "My singlet — that's the uniform that wrestlers wear — and headgear and knee pads. You're going to need some of this stuff too, you know. But don't worry," he said as Brian's face fell. "They should lend you some gear for the tryouts. Did you bring a change of clothes like I said? Shorts and a T-shirt?"

"Yeah," Brian said in a lower voice. "But I don't know *anything* about wrestling . . . I'll still try out, but . . . I wish I was more prepared."

Celia heard. "Don't worry, Brian," she said. "Seriously. George wouldn't even *let* you come along if he didn't think you could cut it. Right, George?"

"Right," George said, glad Celia was there.

"You know," Celia continued earnestly. "George was the best wrestler on St. Lucy's last year, and he was just a freshman. I heard the coach talking to my dad about him. He said he was a natural, the best freshman he had ever coached."

George rolled his eyes. "Don't listen to her, Brian. She's totally making it up."

"I am *not!*" Celia said indignantly. "Anyway, if he says that you can wrestle, Brian, you can trust him. Honest."

Brian didn't say anything, but he looked a little less nervous. He just walked thoughtfully next to George, glancing up to him every now and then.

George had noticed the police cars in the school parking lot, and there was a policeman at the gym door who asked them their business and searched their bags before letting them inside.

"What's going on?" Celia asked a tall, gray-haired, state trooper with a bored look on his face.

"There was a gun incident here last week," he said. "Everyone going into the building has to be searched."

Allie Weaver's nervous expression flitted through George's mind again, and he wondered. But the next moment he smelled the gym smells of rubber mats and polyurethane. Coming home — to a newer and bigger home — George stepped up his pace.

They found a seat on the massive bleachers around a truly magnificent wrestling gym. George took it all in — the spots for the competition-quality mats, the bleachers, the huge closet at one end to store equipment — and knew he had come to a school that was serious about its wrestling.

A whistle blew, and he quickly snapped back into focus. A tall, burly man in a black and red shirt was saying something. That must be Mr. Lamar, the coach. The boys grouped around him must be the current squad members. The students were looking over the crowd of new kids with somewhat superior expressions. *This is a tough bunch of guys*, George thought. That was okay by him — the St. Lucy squad hadn't been a bunch of wimps either — but George wasn't sure if these guys were the sort that Mrs. Burke would want her son hanging with.

The squad members all looked as if they were in pretty good condition, and he recognized Tyler Getz, senior member and team captain. Last night, George had checked Tyler's stats on the Sparrow Hills website. Getz had put in an excellent performance in last year's state championships. And they'd be in the same weight class: 160 pounds.

After the coach was finished, George, Brian, and the rest of the new kids filed into the locker rooms. The first thing that George noticed was how neat and brand-new everything looked. Fresh-painted red lockers, gleaming wooden benches, clean tile floors, and a scale whose chrome was so shiny that it made his eyes hurt to look at it. It was a public school, so of course they had lots of money. For a moment, he remembered the grubby little locker room at St. Lucy's with a slight twinge of homesickness — but then he thought of how nice it would be to actually use this locker room, and he became more determined than ever to make the squad.

"Come on," George said to Brian, and led him over to a corner of the room.

"Okay," he said, pulling off his shirt. "Listen up. You have to get weighed to find out what class you're in."

"What?" Brian looked up with a panicked look, one foot still in his black school pants. "We have to take a class?"

"Not a class like in school," George said impatiently. "A weight class. All wrestlers have to get weighed before they wrestle. You only wrestle someone in your own weight class. So it's fair. You wouldn't want to wrestle some 400-pound guy, would you?"

"Oh." Looking somewhat relieved, Brian pulled on the pair of ratty sweat shorts, and George groaned inwardly. *No wonder he was so nervous.*

"After you get weighed, wait until they call your name, and then you'll wrestle," he said, pulling his St. Lucy's singlet out of his gym bag. "Just do the best you can."

"But . . . what are the rules?" Brian pulled on a yellow T-shirt that had a picture of Our Lady of Guadalupe on the front. George shuddered, thinking of the likely reaction of the Sparrow Hills wrestlers.

"Well," he said, "you can win a match on points, or by pinning the other guy's shoulders to the ground. You get points if you take down the other guy — if you knock him off his feet. There are a lot of other ways to get points, too — it gets kind of complicated."

Brian was nodding firmly with a frown, clearly trying to remember it all. George looked at Brian, in his sweat shorts and yellow T-shirt, for a long moment. He was awfully thin and frail compared with all those gorillas on the team. He couldn't be much more than a hundred pounds, though, and that was an advantage . . .

"You know what, Brian?" he finally said. "Don't worry about all the details, not yet anyway. The most important thing is *not* to get pinned. Just fight as hard as you can to keep your shoulders off the mat. See if you can stay in the whole match." He looked at Brian again. "How much do you weigh, anyway?"

Brian shrugged. "102 pounds, I think."

Well, at least he'll get into a really small class, George thought.

Come on! Everyone will want to see you!" Nikki linked arms with Allie, and they walked to the school entrance.

"Hi, Madison! Hi, Ginger!" Allie said, feeling a rush of homesickness as she saw her friends gathered on the concrete bench by the door that was "their" hangout place after school.

"Hey, Allie," Madison said, drawing on her ultra-light menthol cigarette. "How's it going? You haven't been around."

Allie was secretly relieved that Madison was still talking to her like a friend. "What have I missed?"

For a few minutes they talked about the latest school news — Madison had broken up with her summer boyfriend, Ginger had gotten caught using her cell phone to cheat on a quiz . . . nothing much.

"Tyler said you go to school in the old grade school down the road," Ginger said. "That place is a dump!"

"Yeah," Madison said, taking another drag. Allie grimaced at Nikki, who giggled. Both of them hated the smell of cigarettes, but it was the price to pay for hanging out with Madison and Ginger, who were juniors and pretty high on the popularity scale. It was so *nice* to be with normal people who wore normal clothes and talked about normal things.

"My dad knows about that school," Madison told Ginger. "He works at the town planning office. He said they leased the building to a bunch of crazy Catholics who were kicked out of St. Lucy's Catholic High. A bunch of whack jobs, he said."

"Really?" Nikki said. "That's weird."

"Yeah, my dad doesn't think it'll last very long." Madison laughed again, but Allie thought there was something unpleasant about the sound. "I don't know why anyone would start a *new* Catholic school. I mean, come on, didn't they ever hear of evolution? Scientific progress? Women's rights? Hello!"

"Hey, *I'm* Catholic," Allie said. Madison and Ginger looked at her, and she hesitated. "I mean," she said quickly and lightly, "If *I'm* Catholic, it can't be all that bad, right?"

"Really?" Ginger said. "Do you go to church?"

"Oh, no," Allie said. "My mom stopped taking me after she got divorced."

"So, what's it like? Are they brainwashing you?" Madison said. "Teaching you to become nuns?"

"Yeah, right," Allie laughed, and the others joined in. She felt a little guilty. *Why?* For a moment, she thought of the Truth following her around, trying to fit into her life. It wasn't a nice feeling.

"Do you know her?" Madison pointed behind Allie with one vermilion nail. Allie glanced back and saw Celia outside the gym doors, peering in their direction.

"Yeah, some guys from the school are trying out for the wrestling team and some of the girls came up," Allie felt awkward ignoring Celia, who was obviously looking for her. "I promised Tyler I'd meet him. Nikki, IM me tonight, okay?"

"Sure will," Nikki said, grinning. "Good to see you Allie! Miss you!"

Irritated with Celia for showing up, Allie walked toward her. "Hey, Celia," she called. "Have they started the tryouts yet?"

"Yes," Celia said. "I saved a seat for you in case you wanted to watch."

"Thanks," Allie said, seeing the football players coming in from the field and wishing that Tyler were a football player instead. The team jogged around them on their way into the school, all of them fresh from practice and sweaty in their grass-stained practice uniforms. The quarterback, Brad, a major hottie, was with them, and to Allie's pleasure, he smiled and waved at her.

"Hi!" Allie said gaily, and Brad did a double take, glancing over his shoulder as he passed. Allie hoped it was because she looked especially cool, and not because she was dressed in a dorky uniform. *Man, I wish I were back here.*

Celia had waved, too. Allie was starting think that Celia considered it her personal mission to be friendly to the entire universe. "Um, has George tried out yet?"

"I don't know — boy, this place is huge!" Celia said, looking in awe at the granite-paved halls that were so big that freshmen regularly got lost in the corridors.

"Yeah, it's definitely bigger than your school," Allie said, half-smiling.

"Our school," Celia corrected her, and Allie felt her insides sink.

"Yeah, *our* school," she said, miffed.

Coach Lamar was sitting on a card table in front of the mats, checking off the names of would-be wrestlers. George and Brian got into the line of hopefuls, George in St. Lucy's wrestling uniform, and Brian in his T-shirt and shorts.

When George came to the head of the line, Coach Lamar roared "Hey!" with a startled look on his face. Then he broke into a broad grin. "You're George Peterson! From St. Lucy's!"

George reddened, but he couldn't help grinning in return. "Yep, that's me," he said.

"What are *you* doing here?" Coach Lamar said. "No, wait. Don't tell me. I don't want to know. But I'm certainly glad to see you here. I watched some of your matches last year." He chuckled. "Not bad, for a freshman. Not bad at all. What's your weight this year, Peterson?"

"One-fifty-nine," George said triumphantly. That had been a pleasant surprise when he had gotten weighed in a few minutes ago. He he'd always been light for the 160-class — a disadvantage — but thanks to some last minute dieting, he had managed to get bumped down to a lower class and wouldn't have to face Tyler in the tryouts.

Coach Lamar looked duly impressed. "Down to the 152, eh? Pretty good, Peterson. We'll let you try out against Flynt. Go over to Mat 2."

He looked over George's shoulder, where Brian was standing, looking nervous and very out of place. "What's your name, son?" Coach Lamar said kindly.

George said quickly. "This is Brian Burke, Coach. I go to school with him. It's his first time wrestling."

"Really? Good for you, Burke. Very brave. What's your weight?"

Brian looked at the floor. "101 pounds, sir," he said, sounding embarrassed.

But Coach Lamar only nodded, "That's a good weight, Burke. A very good weight. Go to Mat 2 with George, and we'll find someone to match you up against."

The two of them walked off to Mat 2, where a fierce match between two 189-pound kids was just winding down. George sat, and Brian slumped next to him, a troubled expression on his face.

"Brian, don't look so depressed," George said in a low voice. "You're going to be fine, seriously."

"I weigh only 101 pounds," Brian muttered. "I thought I would weigh more, but. . ."

"For the last time," George said with good-natured exasperation. "It's *good* not to weigh a lot when you're wrestling."

Brian looked down at his sneakers and said nothing.

George sighed and then got up as the match on Mat 2 came to an end. On the other side of the mat, there was a big, mean-looking kid with spiky black hair in a Sparrow Hills uniform. He glared at George as Mat 2 was cleared for action.

That must be Flynt, George thought, and smiled grimly. *Good. I don't like him already.*

Allie sat down heavily in her place in the bleachers next to Celia, in a thoroughly bad mood. She had decided that after the tryouts, she was going to get Tyler to drive her to the mall.

"Hey, George is up!" Celia said. "He's really good at this." George, in his blue-and-black singlet, was shaking hands with Neil Flynt, one of Tyler's bigger, dumber friends. They positioned themselves in a circle on one of the mats. Suddenly, George looked up and saw her looking at him. He grinned back.

Allie felt her heart skip a beat. She had to admit George was cute.

Then the referee's whistle blew. Flynt dove forward, trying to trip George up; but George was too quick for him. He grasped Flynt by both forearms. There was a flurry of movement, almost too quick for Allie to see, and suddenly Flynt was sprawled on the mat, and George was on top of him. Just as quickly, the referee was lying down, trying to see if George had forced Flynt's shoulders to the mat. For a moment there was no sound but the grunts of the two wrestlers. Then the ref smacked the mat with an open palm, and blew the whistle. Pin!

Allie was impressed, despite herself. She didn't know a lot about wrestling, but even she knew that it was unusual to get a pin so quickly. *He* is *good*, she thought. *I wonder if Tyler saw that?* She glanced around, and saw Tyler had indeed been watching from the sideline. He had a frown on his face, and Allie saw that he was impressed, too.

George got up, chest heaving, and offered his hand to Flynt — but the other wrestler got up with a scowl, ignored him, and stalked away. Allie felt a flush of annoyance. *That is so typical,* she thought.

Brian was up next. He was standing in the center of the mat with a totally clueless look on his face. The coach, meanwhile, was looking around; apparently there was no one light enough to wrestle him.

Finally, one of the smaller Sparrow Hills wrestlers came forward; but he didn't look as small as Brian. Allie watched as they shook hands. Then the whistle blew . . . and the match was over about three seconds later. Allie winced as the larger, more experienced wrestler unbalanced Brian, threw him on the mat, and pinned him. It was over even more quickly than George's match.

For the next ten minutes, Allie watched as Brian got beaten again — and again, and again. Every wrestler he faced was bigger than he, and he never had a chance in any of the matches. Even though she hadn't really noticed Brian until this afternoon, Allie was starting to feel sorry for him.

The matches went on for a half an hour. George wrestled two more times, and won each match. After getting clobbered five more times, Brian was finally given a break when Coach Lamar announced that the tryouts were over.

The last few matches broke up, and the crowd of kids milled around, waiting for the results to come in. The coach and the wrestlers had already gone into the locker rooms. Allie sighed, looked at her watch, and wondered how much longer the mall would be open.

"Hey, George! Hey, Brian!" Celia said as the two boys sat down on the bleachers. "Good job!"

"What do you think? You think you made the squad?" George asked Brian.

Brian looked as though he thought George was making fun of him. "Did *I* make the squad?" he said in a bitter voice. "Are you kidding? Did you see how I did?"

"Oh, don't worry about that. Everyone gets creamed their first time out. The important thing is that you . . . that you show some potential."

"I don't think I showed anybody anything," Brian muttered. "Unless it was how to get your butt kicked."

"*Everyone* gets their butt kicked sometimes, Brian."

"Well, all I can say is that if I get in, *everybody's* going to get in," Brian said, more despondent. "I mean, I lost every single time."

"Yeah, but don't forget, everyone was heavier than you," George replied.

"I think you did fine," Celia said. "You could tell you were really trying hard. That's got to count for something."

As Celia encouraged Brian, George looked over at Allie. "How are you doing?"

He looked very happy. "Okay," she said hesitantly. "How 'bout you?"

"Good," he said with a grin. "I feel . . . normal. It's really cool."

Suddenly, Allie realized that she knew exactly what he meant. This was where he belonged — here, in the wrestling gym. This was where she belonged — here, in public school. *Neither of us really fits in at John Paul 2.*

"Yeah," she said. "It *is* really cool."

George hadn't felt so good since — well, since the last time he had wrestled. He hadn't expected Brian to do as well, although now he wished he had thought to teach him a couple of moves. He knew he'd done well himself, but maybe the squad already had enough wrestlers in his weight class. But, it had been great to be in the zone again. He loved being out there on the mat.

Coach Lamar blew his whistle. He had come out of the locker room, followed by the members of the wrestling squad, now back in their street clothes.

"I'd like to thank everyone for coming out today," Mr. Lamar said. "As you know, we have a limited number of spaces on the squad . . . but I do have some names here to read." He looked down at his clipboard and cleared his throat.

"Burke, Brian . . ."

Brian looked stunned. George clapped him on the back, hard. "All right!"

"Geraghty, Jim . . . Hanus, Patrick . . . Mahoney, Frank . . . Olmstead, Dennis . . . Peterson, George . . ."

"Yeah, George!" Celia yelled, grabbing George's shoulders from behind and shaking him.

"Quit it!" George said, grinning.

"Pester, Sean . . . Tarrant, Daniel . . . Vickson, Marshall . . ." Coach Lamar finished reading and looked up. "That's it. Everyone whose name was called: practices are Mondays, Wednesdays, and Fridays, and we begin next Monday after school. If you'll just come forward now, we've got some information for you . . ."

But George was too busy explaining things to Brian to

pay much attention. "I bet you got in because of your weight. They probably don't have anyone as light as you."

"Really?" Brian said, looking less thrilled.

"Well, yeah," George said. "But that doesn't mean you can't be a good wrestler. The weight thing just helps, that's all. I'll practice with you, don't worry."

He was thoroughly excited, but before his mind could race away, he remembered to say a prayer: *thanks, God.* He knew he owed God one. After all, this is where it had all begun — he'd prayed his way through every wrestling competition, and won. He was just glad God had found a way to let him wrestle again.

How did I do?" Tyler crowed, strutting up to Allie as George, Celia, and Brian went outside to wait for their rides. "Not bad, eh?"

"Oh . . ." Allie suddenly realized that she hadn't even been watching Tyler. "Oh, you did awesome," she said smoothly, and hoped it was true. Not that Tyler would notice; he obviously *thought* he had done awesome.

"Yeah," Tyler agreed. "Well, I didn't have much for competition. Looks like I'll have to carry the squad again this year, as usual."

Allie thought of George's spectacular performance, but decided not to mention it.

"You know what's really going to be fun, though?" Tyler said, with a wicked gleam in his eye. "The first day of practice."

Something about his tone of voice made Allie look up suspiciously.

"Why?" she asked. "What happens the first day of practice?"

Tyler laughed. "You don't want to know. Let's just say that we give 'em a *warm* welcome."

An unpleasant memory cropped up in Allie's mind: getting off the bus and seeing some guy — he looked like a freshman — tied to the school flagpole. Apparently he had been on the football team, and everyone figured that the seniors had something to do with it. But it was also apparent that no one would be punished for it. It looked like that sort of thing happened in wrestling, too.

Then an even worse thought came to mind: the thought of something like that happening to George, or Brian. She glanced at Tyler, and thought, *would he do something like that? I wouldn't put it past him . . .*

"Why am I even dating you?" she grumbled.

"Because I'm so cute," said Tyler, grabbing her hand. "Come on, babe. I'll take you to the mall. Buy you something."

Allie grimaced. She hated Tyler calling her "babe."

SIX

INTO THE WOODS

THE REST OF THE WEEK PASSED MORE QUICKLY

for Allie. She still longed to be back at Sparrow Hills, but she had to admit that Mr. Costain's classes were interesting.

Still, she was drowning in the unfamiliar information about Church history, saints, theology, the *Catechism of the Catholic Church*, and the people with weird names Mr. Costain loved quoting: Von Balthasar, Von Hildebrand, T. S. Eliot, C. S. Lewis, G. K. Chesterton, and too many others. *None of this is going to be helpful on a college application*, she thought. It was just too different from anything else she'd ever studied.

What made it more confusing was that Creepy Boy, as she thought of James, argued with Mr. Costain whenever he quoted these people, saying they were modernists, heretics, or something else that was supposed to be bad. Allie couldn't see what the problem was, and most of the time she wished James would just shut up. But Mr. Costain, like Celia, was always patient with him. She could tell this drove George nuts too.

Friday, during a particularly interesting history lesson on the early heresies, where Mr. Costain explained that *The Da Vinci Code* was just a reworking of something called "Gnosticism" that had been proven to be false ages ago, Mrs. Flynn came into the classroom.

"Sorry to interrupt," she said, her forehead creased with worry. "The inspector's on the phone again."

Mr. Costain excused himself for a few minutes, but didn't return. Finally Mrs. Flynn returned to say that history class was dismissed for the day.

"*Yes!*" yelled J.P. His mother looked at him severely.

"But math class for freshmen will be starting early," she said crisply. "J.P., Brian, Liz — in my classroom, now."

The older students remained in the classroom. James was reading another thick black book, this one with red flames on the cover. George stared out the window, while Celia talked about a book she was reading, something about theology for the bodies. Allie's mind wandered.

"Do you think we could run down to SpeedEMart?" she said when Celia paused for breath. Allie was not in the mood for the leftovers her mom had packed for lunch, and was really missing the salad bar at the Sparrow Hills cafeteria.

Celia looked doubtful. "I don't know . . ."

But George was interested. "Why not? It's right through the woods. We just need to get permission. Celia, go ask Mrs. Flynn. Don't bother asking Mrs. Simonelli — she'll just make us mop floors or something to pass the time."

Allie had already picked up that Celia would do anything that George asked her to do. "All right," Celia said and left the room. George grinned at Allie — she could see he was feeling happy today; probably still riding high over making the wrestling team.

Celia returned in a short time, saying they could go, but they had to be back ten minutes before the next period started.

"James, do you want to come?" Celia asked, and to Allie's surprise and disappointment, Creepy Boy eased himself out of his chair to follow them.

It was a brisk fall day, with the leaves falling carelessly from the trees. Allie went ahead as the four of them walked out the front doors and around to the back of the school. George noticed that she seemed to know where she was going. She led them through the woods to a well-worn dirt path that none of them had noticed before.

"This goes to the SpeedEMart," she said. "If you go the other way, you can get to Sparrow Hills. It's shorter than going by the road, and we used to run down here after school — or during school — to get snacks."

George found himself walking next to Allie, because Celia was walking with James, trying to make conversation. Celia was doing all the talking.

"Weird rock," George said to Allie as they came to a large, odd-shaped boulder, sort of triangular-shaped, sitting beside the path. It was as big as a shed. He noticed a dry stream bed nearby that ran deeper into the woods.

"That's Chimney Rock," Allie said.

"Why's it called that?" George asked.

"Uh, because it looks like a chimney," Allie said, smiling with her usual knowing look.

George couldn't see what the joke was. "Right."

"Hey, when does your next wrestling practice start?"

"Next week," George said, surprised she was asking about a sport she couldn't stand.

She had a serious look on her face. "Be careful," she said enigmatically.

"Of what?"

She shrugged, coloring. "Maybe *you* don't need to be careful, but if I were you, I'd watch out for Brian."

"Why?"

"Just keep an eye on him, okay?"

"Sure," he said, staring at her. He was surprised that someone like Allie cared about a geek like Brian. It was a different side to her than he had seen.

The trail ended, and they came out of the woods into the parking lot of the SpeedEMart. Celia checked her watch. "We better hurry up," she said. "We have only thirty minutes."

Inside, they split up to buy things. Allie and Celia headed for the deli at the back. James went straight for the magazine rack and picked up a newspaper. George dug in his pockets and counted his money. He had only a few quarters. *Maybe I could get a candy bar*, he thought glumly. *Nah*.

He meandered around the store, checking out the shelves halfheartedly, and trying to ignore the clerk, who was watching him suspiciously as if he expected him to shoplift something. *Relax, buddy*, he thought.

His eyes fell on some of the magazines by the checkout counter — the usual trashy magazines. There were girls in bikinis on all the covers, and his eyes kept being pulled in that direction. George tried to look somewhere else, half-afraid that Allie or Celia would notice him.

In a few minutes, the girls came back, Allie with a salad and Celia with a bagel. They all paid for their purchases and walked out.

Allie and Celia were talking together as they walked back through the woods. George walked behind, trying to ignore James. When they came to Chimney Rock, he turned toward the dry streambed. He felt an urge to get a more of a feel for the lay of the land around here.

"Guys! Wait up," he said. "Hey, Seal! Check out that dried creek. Doesn't it look like the one at your uncle's place in the Poconos?"

She stopped. "Yeah, it does," she said with interest. "Where we played Capture the Flag last Thanksgiving?"

"Yeah — let's go check it out." He added, before she could look at her watch, "You said we had thirty minutes before we have to be back."

Intrigued, she gave in, and, stuffing the remains of her bagel in her pocket, jumped down behind him.

George led the way down the streambed, which soon deepened into a narrow gully. In the thickening woods, he leapt from rock to rock with ease, smelling the mossy air. But he kept having to wait for the others: Allie and Celia couldn't go as fast in their school shoes, and James was lurching and stumbling behind them with a disagreeable look on his face. He clearly wasn't enjoying the exercise.

The streambed curved sharply. The gully walls loomed up on either side like miniature cliffs, and, where the stream rounded, there was a hollow in the cliff wall, like a small cave. Sunlight spilled through the leaves onto the ground. There was no breeze: a quiet, still, oasis of green.

"Wow," Celia breathed, halting in admiration.

"I've never seen this before!" Allie skipped forward.

They all stood there for a few moments in silence, taking it in.

"What a great place," Celia said softly. "It would be a cool place to . . . build a shrine to Mary. Or something. Wouldn't it?"

"A what?" Allie said looking skeptical.

"A place where we could come and pray," Celia explained. "A private place. It's a shame it's not closer to the school. George, can't you just see it? That space right there in the hollow of the rock — it looks like it's asking for a statue of Mary to be put there."

George could see what she meant: the natural cave in the crevice of the creek bank seemed like a picture frame, standing empty. "Yeah, that would be cool. Seriously, that's a great idea."

Allie had that weirded-out frustrated look on her face again. "Can't you guys look at *anything* without thinking about Mary, or Jesus, or something?"

George was embarrassed, and looked at Celia to see how she would respond. But Celia didn't say anything right away. Then her eyes glazed over. "No, Allie," she said in a misty voice. "We . . . can't . . . help it."

George started to snicker, and put on the same monotone. "Yes, Allie, we're . . . *Catholic*." He started to walk toward Allie, stretching out his hands. "You must . . . join us . . ."

The look on Allie Weaver's face was precious. Her eyes widened until she couldn't keep the too-cool-for-you look anymore. Gaping at both of them as they closed in on her, she seemed to realize they were joking.

"Back! Back!" she yelled, holding up her fingers to make a cross as though she were warding off a vampire.

A sinister look crossed Celia's face and she giggled and kept advancing. "No, that won't work, Allie . . . we're *Catholic*, remember? We *love* crucifixes . . ."

Both girls collapsed in giggles and even George had to

laugh, relieved that Celia had figured out a way to defuse the situation. He glanced back at James. He wasn't laughing. He was leaning against a tree, a jealous, hungry look on his face.

At last the girls recovered and started talking about the grotto, Celia imagining how they could arrange benches or fallen logs, and wondering where they could get a statue. Tuning out, George picked up a couple of acorns and practiced slinging them through the fork of a tree. James remained where he was, brooding.

"I guess it all depends on who owns this part of the woods," Celia was saying to Allie. "If it belongs to the land our school is on, then maybe we could do it."

Allie looked thoughtful. "Maybe it belongs to the haunted mansion."

"What?" Celia said.

"Oh, you never heard of that? Look over there." Allie pointed through the woods.

George looked where she was pointing. Through the tree trunks and underbrush they barely make out an iron fence, and far beyond it, the high roof of a house.

Allie said, "I've never been there, but I heard kids go over there sometimes. Like, at Halloween, to do séances and stuff like that."

"Séances? Weird." George said.

"And dangerous," Celia shivered.

Allie shrugged. "Nobody knows what they do, but I've heard some pretty creepy stories."

They all strained their eyes, trying to catch a better glimpse of the house in the distance.

"BWAHAHAHAHAHAHAHHH!"

They jumped, and the girls screamed.

James chortled with laughter, and pointed at the three of them. "Ahahaha! I got you! I got ALL of you!" He advanced on them, wiggling his big, long fingers. "Oooh, scared of things in the woods, are we?"

Celia laughed nervously and backed away. "You really got us there, James."

"And I have *you*," James snickered. "Right where I *want* you — BOO!" he lunged at Allie, who leapt back.

"All right James, you got us," George said. "Give it a rest, okay?"

Allie had turned white.

James was laughing harder than any normal person would laugh. He kept wiggling his fingers and laughing, and George's scalp began to prickle. Unconsciously, he put himself between James and the two girls.

"Cut it out," George said brusquely. "No one else is laughing."

"That's because no one else knows what I know," James sniggered. "And what I know is . . . *Bang!*" He pointed his finger at Allie as though it were a gun.

"SHUT UP!" Allie screamed suddenly. "Just shut up!" She lashed out at James. "You stupid gross fat CREEP! You total LOSER! Get AWAY from me!" Then she turned and ran, stumbling, back down the streambed in the direction of the school.

"Allie!" Celia ran after her, distressed.

George barred James's way on purpose. "You stay away from her."

James had a stupefied look on his face. He blinked, his mouth open, as Allie vanished around the bend. He didn't seem to comprehend why Allie had laughed at Celia and George but had screamed and run away from him.

For a bare second, George had a glimpse of a guy who was fumbling in a strange world, watching everyone else's behavior and trying to make sense of it; a fat, lonely guy who had no clue what was normal but was trying to do his best to figure it out...

And then the cold familiar mask settled back onto James's features, and the vulnerability vanished. James sneered. "What makes you think she's yours?"

George was so disoriented by the change that he couldn't understand what James was saying. "What?"

"I mean you," James sneered, his face still red. "You watch her too."

George turned away. "Shut up," he said brusquely. "We better get back."

He started down the streambed, painfully aware that he had his back to James. After a moment, he heard James walking slowly behind him.

Celia sidled up to Allie during biology class while they were dissecting crickets. "Hey, you okay?"

Allie had been pretending that she was a very studious person who didn't even notice that there were other people in the classroom. So when Celia came up to her, she barely looked up.

"I'm okay," she said, a fake expression of concentration on her face.

"You sure?" Out of the corner of her eye, Allie could see Celia's worried expression.

For a moment, Allie wavered. *Can I trust her? Can I trust anyone here?*

No. I don't want to deal with it. No. "Yeah, I'm fine. I just got freaked out." Allie frowned and pulled antennae off her specimen. "I don't like the woods."

"James was a little overboard," Celia said.

"I don't understand," Allie said, placing the antennae on the napkin in front of her, " — what his deal is." And before Celia could begin explaining, she added, "And I really don't want to know."

After school, she got into Tyler's car and nestled up against him.

"Hey, babe," Tyler said, surprised and pleased.

Appreciating his strong arms and bulky muscles, she said, "Hey. Can we go to the mall?"

SEVEN

FEAST OF
ST. FRANCIS

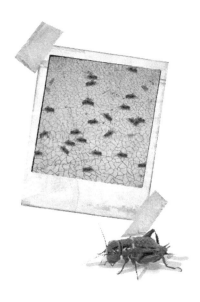

GEORGE PEDALED INTO THE PARKING LOT ON Monday morning. He was early again; the only cars in the lot were Mr. Costain's Volvo and Mrs. Flynn's blue minivan. That meant that Celia and J.P. would be there. Celia would be in the office, helping her dad. J.P. would probably be doing something that would get him into trouble. He had been acting especially crazy since his mom had taken away his laptop: he'd been playing *Praxor's Game* on it with the sound turned off during school.

As he walked down the hallway, George saw J.P. appear from around a corner.

"Hey J.P.," he called out.

J.P. looked up and gave him a goofy smile. "Hey, George!" he said. "You know what today is?"

"No," George said. "What?"

"October 4th!" J.P. said. "The feast of St. Francis!"

"And what are you doing to celebrate it?" George said.

J.P. gave him an affronted look. "Can't a guy walk around the school without being accused of causing trouble?"

"Okay, okay," George said, shrugging. "You better not have damaged anything, though."

J.P. put a friendly arm around George's shoulders. "George, old buddy," he said warmly. "You know I would never do anything like that."

"I do?" George asked skeptically.

When Allie got to school, the first person she saw was Liz, who was rummaging through her locker frantically.

She looked up and yelled, "Hey, Allie! Have you seen my science book?"

"No," Allie shot back. "Good morning to you too."

Liz only grunted in reply and turned back to her locker. "I can't find it anywhere," she muttered. "Knowing my luck, my mom will throw a pop quiz at us this morning. She'd have gotten the idea from Mr. Costain. How do you think you did on his quiz Friday?"

The memory of that didn't improve Allie's mood. "Don't remind me," she said. "I was totally lost. What the heck is a papal bull, anyway?"

"I don't know," Liz said. "I almost put down that it was for the papal bullfighter."

Allie felt her insides sink. "Oh no," she said.

Liz looked at her, a broad grin on her face. "You didn't think . . . it was a real bull, did you?"

"How was I supposed to know?" Allie snapped. "I'm going to flunk out of this school, I just know it!"

"No way," Liz said. "Costain can't afford to lose any students, don't worry."

At that moment, Celia burst out of the homeroom. "Liz! Liz!" she yelled, running over to them. She was holding a textbook in her hand.

"You found it?" Liz turned around. "Oh, thank God, Celia! Where was it?"

"No," said Celia, skidding to a halt, "I didn't find your book. Brian said you could borrow his. He said — " She giggled. "He said that he already read it all."

"Oh." Liz pondered that for a moment. "Okay. Wow. That's weird . . . Thanks, Celia."

"No problem," said Celia happily. "Glad I could help."

Something about Celia's voice, always so cheerful, rubbed Allie the wrong way. She brushed past both of them and started down the hall, muttering, "I have to go to the bathroom."

"Wait up!" Liz said. "I have to go too! Come on, Celia. It's a trend." She slammed her locker door, and, much to her annoyance, they both followed Allie.

"So, Allie," Celia said as they walked down the bleak hallway and around the corner to the other wing of the school, "How did you do on the quiz Friday?"

"Celia," Liz said, quickly. "Don't ask."

"Oh, well," Celia sounded sympathetic, "don't worry too much about it. It's only one quiz."

Allie knew better than to reply.

They reached the bathroom doors, and Allie had just put her hand on the door handle when she hesitated. "Do you hear something?"

They all hushed and listened. There was a strange, high-pitched sound coming from the bathroom.

"What is that?" Celia asked.

"Let's find out," said Liz. Pushing past Allie, she threw the door open. All three crowded into the bathroom.

Allie shrieked. Celia and Liz laughed. All over the floor, in the sinks and in the stalls, were crickets. Scores of little brown crickets, every one of them chirping happily.

"Great! Just great!" Allie said after recovering her breath. She hated bugs of all descriptions, and dissecting crickets in biology hadn't improved her opinion of them. "How am I supposed to go to the bathroom now?"

"I can't believe this!" said Liz. "Where did he get these?"

Celia couldn't stop laughing. "This is so funny!"

Allie's self-restraint snapped, "What's so funny?"

"They're just so cute!" Celia gasped.

A cricket jumped onto Allie's shoe. She screamed in alarm, and shook her foot frantically. "Aah! Get it off, get it off!"

This set the other girls giggling hysterically as Allie danced around, shaking her leg and squashing crickets by the score.

"Stop, stop!" Celia said finally. "I'll get it off." She knelt down and examined her shoe. "He's gone! Be careful not to step on any more of them. It's the feast of St. Francis. We should be nice to animals today."

Allie's irritation suddenly ballooned into anger. "I don't care what feast it is, Celia," she said savagely. "All I care about is that there are vermin in this trash heap of a school! You know it's a trash heap! You just don't want to admit it 'cause your dad's the principal!"

There was dead silence at her words. Celia's face suddenly crumpled as she stared at Allie. Slowly she stood up and walked out of the bathroom.

Liz turned to Allie, her face hard. "Why did you have to say that to her? She's a better person than you are." And she, too, left the bathroom.

Allie stood there for a moment. Then, mechanically, she opened the bathroom door, and re-entered the hallway.

She felt the first waves of guilt come over her as she walked back up the hall. *Probably that Truth person following me around*, she thought. *Man! I wish he would leave!*

Mrs. Flynn was manning the homeroom desk when George came in. "Mr. Costain's going to be a little late," she said. "He had to visit the county municipal office again this morning."

A few moments later, the door banged open, and Liz and Allie came in. "Mrs. Flynn?" Liz said. "There are crickets in the bathroom!"

"Crickets?" Mrs. Flynn said in surprise.

"Hundreds of them!" Liz said. "They look like the ones you buy at the pet store."

Mrs. Flynn's face darkened, and she glared at J.P. "Really?" she growled.

J.P. looked up. "What was that?" he said distractedly. "Crickets?" His eyes widened. "Oh my gosh! It happened again?"

"What happened again?" Mrs. Flynn said.

"The *poltergeist!*" J.P. said in an awestruck voice. "He must have put them there! He must know it's St. Francis' Feast Day today! We should have an exorcism!"

"Oh, give me a break!" Allie spoke up for the first time, sounding very grumpy. "Why not just call an exterminator? You people are always so *Catholic* about everything!"

"George," Mrs. Flynn said, "Could you take a look at the girls' bathroom?"

Crisis in the school, so there's suddenly a job for George to do. George got to his feet, wishing he wasn't the student who appeared more competent than everyone else. *Can't someone else manage things for a change?*

But he went down the hall and turned the corner. Even before he got to the bathroom, he could see a few small brown specks on the hallway floor; specks that emitted soft chirps and occasionally hopped. *Great. Crickets in the bathroom. This looks like a job for . . . me, apparently.*

He looked into the bathroom. There certainly were more crickets than he could hope to catch on his own. *Maybe if I get a push broom, I can sweep them out the door.* He headed up the hallway to the janitor's closet.

As he approached it, he heard another sound coming from behind the battered wooden door: soft sobs and snuffles.

He opened the door carefully. Celia was huddled on the dirty floor of the closet, her eyes red. "Oh!" she said, and hastily got up. "George! I'm sorry, I . . ."

"What's wrong?" George asked. "What happened?" It took a lot to get Celia down.

"Oh, nothing," Celia said, embarrassed.

"Come on, Seal, what happened?"

Celia took a deep quavering breath. "It's . . . everything, all together . . ." She paused, collecting her thoughts. "Dad just got back from the county office. He said that the building failed inspection again."

"Yeah, but that wasn't unexpected, was it?"

Celia wiped her eyes. He could tell she was trying to put on a brave front. "I don't know. Dad can't figure out what to do. It doesn't make any sense. My dad and Mr. Simonelli looked over the whole building before we leased it. It wasn't perfect, but there was nothing that couldn't be fixed up. And now, there's all this stuff going wrong, and the people from the county are being so picky, it's almost like they *want* us to fail . . . and then, when we found the crickets, Allie said the school is a trash heap, and it just hit me that she's right, and I can't help it at all,

I just can't. There's nothing I can do about it." She took a deep breath.

"Okay, okay," he said, not knowing what else he could say. "Don't worry about it so much, Celia. Your dad and the other parents . . . they'll get this stuff fixed. And even if they don't . . . we can always have school in your dad's basement or something."

Celia had to laugh at that. "What were you doing down here, anyway?"

"Getting a broom to sweep the crickets outside," George said.

Celia giggled. "That's a good idea," she said. "Don't squish them if you can help it; it would make an even bigger mess. And St. Francis would never squish a cricket."

"Right," he said, grabbing a broom. "Maybe you better get back to class. I think first period has started."

After she had gone, George went straight to Mrs. Simonelli's classroom, knocked, and then opened the door.

Mrs. Simonelli was in the middle of a science lecture, with Brian, Liz, and J.P. sitting in the front row. She looked annoyed at the interruption. "What is it?"

"I'm sorry, Mrs. Simonelli," George said. "But I need J.P. for a few minutes. It's an emergency."

"What's going on?" J.P. said to George as soon as they were out in the hallway.

"Look, moron, you're going to help me get those crickets out of the bathroom, right now, before anyone else finds out."

"What?" J.P. protested. "Why me? I don't know anything about it! I keep telling you guys, it's the polter — "

"Shut up," George said, lowering his voice. "You know

the county might condemn this building! What if the inspectors see those crickets? They'll say the school's infested with vermin, and that's the last thing we need."

"Vermin?" J.P. said indignantly. "Those are high-quality crickets! They cost five bucks a box!"

"You come with me," George said, "And keep quiet." He handed him the broom. "We'll start with these ones in the hallway. You push them out, and I'll hold the door."

Together they managed to get most of the crickets out of the hallway with the broom, catching the stragglers by hand. It was a long time before they got the last one out, and they hadn't even tackled the actual bathroom yet.

"Okay," George said, wiping his brow. "Let's keep going."

"But there's still the whole bathroom!" J.P. whined. "Come on, we'll never get them all out!"

"Yes, we will," George retorted. "And if you don't like it, you can blame it on the *poltergeist*." He pulled the girls' bathroom door open.

"Hold it right there!"

Mrs. Simonelli was striding down the hallway toward them, her eyes narrowed in anger.

"What do you think you're doing? I'm surprised at you, George! I can understand J.P.'s behavior, but you . . . I don't know what to say. The period's almost over, and neither of you came back, and I sent Brian to the office to find you. Mr. Costain had no idea where you were. What is going on?" Mrs. Simonelli's voice got louder as she got closer, her perfectly combed blond hair even stiffer than usual. "What are you doing in the girls' bathroom? And what's that sound?"

At that moment, a cricket jumped past the door that George was still holding open. Chirping happily, it landed on Mrs. Simonelli's black, high-heeled shoe.

Mrs. Simonelli let out a piercing shriek that echoed down the hall.

It took Mr. Costain several minutes to restore order. "This is a very interesting way to celebrate the feast. We'll work together to get them all out."

"I'm not touching them!" Allie said. "I'm scared of bugs, Mr. Costain!"

"Excuse me, I signed up to be a student, not a janitor!" James said with haughty indignation. "If you can't keep an infestation of insects from your plumbing . . ."

"All right, all right," Mr. Costain said. "Who wants to volunteer to help George? Anyone who doesn't can come to my theology class and read over the latest papal encyclical."

George was strongly tempted to laugh as he watched the looks on everyone's faces while they pondered the choice. In the end, everyone except for Allie and James volunteered to help clear the crickets out of the bathroom. George was glad that he didn't have to deal with Allie — Celia looked a little better, but not completely her cheerful self.

"Okay," George said, after the others had gone and he found everyone looking at him expectantly for orders. "Brian and I will use brooms to get them out the door, and Celia and Liz, you catch any stray ones with your hands. J.P., hold the door open."

"And don't squish any of them!" said Celia. "St. Francis wouldn't like it!"

"Yeah!" said J.P. "They were expensive."

It was the most fun any of them had ever had at school. George and Brian ended up doing most of the real work, pushing the bulk of the crickets out of the bathroom and down the hallway to the nearest door. Celia proved to be a woefully bad cricket-catcher; she was too concerned with not killing them. Liz had no such qualms.

"Liz!" Celia shrieked at one point, after Liz dispatched a particularly jumpy cricket with a well-aimed stomp. "How could you?"

Liz lifted her shoe and examined the brown smear on the floor. "He deserved to die," she said. "Too hyperactive."

"J.P. better stay away from you then," said George, and they all cracked up.

"I got to hand it to you, J.P.," Liz said, throwing two more outside by their legs. "That was a pretty cool stunt. It got us out of class, at least."

J.P. sighed deeply. "I keep telling you people," he said with an air of injured dignity. "It wasn't me. It was the *poltergeist.*"

George yawned. "Give it a rest, will ya?"

Brian frowned. "You shouldn't joke about things like that. There *are* real poltergeists."

When the last cricket was finally out of the door, they walked back up the hallway. George was distracted until he overheard snatches of whispered conversation.

"The next one has got to be *really* big."

"But no one can find out it was us."

He glanced over his shoulder and saw Liz and J.P. deep in discussion. He groaned. *If they make this much trouble separately, what will they do together?*

Not my problem, not my problem. He remembered Celia sobbing, trying to save the school. He certainly couldn't save the school, and he was irritated everyone seemed to want him to.

Can't wait till wrestling practice, he thought again.

EIGHT

FRESH MEET

AFTER SCHOOL, WHILE HE AND BRIAN TRUDGED through the woods to Sparrow Hills on the forest path, Allie's warning kept ringing through George's head. He had heard some real horror stories about hazing, everything from getting tied up and whipped, to being thrown naked out of school. He wondered what would happen to them, and whether he should warn Brian.

Maybe she was exaggerating, he thought. *Maybe nothing will happen.* But he couldn't help being anxious for Brian. *Why do people do stupid things like that, anyway? I just want to wrestle.*

They emerged from the woods, Sparrow Hills looming up in front of them. Crossing the soccer fields and rounding the football stadium, they finally walked into the gymnasium where tryouts had been held. There were already several wrestlers in uniform there. Some of them were wrestling each other; some were doing push-ups, sit-ups, and other exercises; and some were just hanging around. Mr. Lamar welcomed them, passed out school singlets and headgear for the rookies, and told them to get changed quickly for drill.

In the locker room, surrounded by friends, Tyler Getz was just putting on his headgear when George and Brian walked in. He looked at them, flashed a brilliant smile, and put out his hand. "Hey there! New kids on the block!"

George and Brian shook hands with him, and Tyler introduced them to the other squad members. All of them seemed to be veterans. "This is Flynt and Brock. I think you and Flynt have met before, Peterson."

George shook hands with all of them. He felt a little awkward about Flynt, who had looked so ticked off when George had beaten him in the tryouts. But now, all of the veterans seemed to be pretty friendly. In fact, it was kind of strange how they all had big toothy smiles plastered on their faces. George didn't like it. But Brian seemed relieved, and loosened up a bit as he shook hands with all of them. "Nice to meet you. It's a pleasure."

"So," Tyler said. "You two go to that school down the road. Isn't it some sort of Mormon school or something?"

"No," George said, trying to sound casual. "It's just a Catholic school."

Tyler shrugged. "Oh yeah. Mormon, Catholic, I don't see any difference."

"Actually, there is a rather big difference," Brian said. "The Mormon church was founded by Brigham Young and Joseph Smith in the nineteenth century. The Catholic Church was founded by Jesus Christ in the first century."

There was an awkward silence, then Tyler laughed. "If you say so, buddy. Well, you two kiddies better get dressed."

George and Brian put down their gym bags and started pulling out their gear. George was into his singlet in about thirty seconds and was stowing his stuff in his assigned locker when Tyler leaned forward again and said, "So, George, how does Allie like your school?"

"I don't know," George said slowly. "All right, I guess."

"You guys seem to be getting along pretty well," Tyler said. His voice and face were still friendly, but George sensed that behind the smile Tyler was studying him closely, gauging his reactions. "Do me a favor, will you? Tell her I said hi. We're sort of going out."

"Sure," George said, fiddling with the open combination lock on his door. Tyler pulled something out of his own locker, a magazine. "Hey Peterson, look at this!"

George looked up. It was a *Playboy* centerfold. For a split second, in his surprise, he gazed at the naked blonde model, then quickly looked away. "Aw, not now," he found himself saying, as he reached down to lace up his wrestling shoes.

"Too bad," Tyler said, thumbing through the magazine. "She kind of reminds me of my girlfriend. What do you think?"

George looked up again, dumbfounded. Tyler was looking right back at him to see his reaction.

I can't believe this is happening. "Yeah, you wish," George finally said, turning away. His face felt hot.

I should say something else. I really should, his conscience nagged him as he got into his singlet. *You totally let him get away with that.*

But anything I say is going to make the situation worse. Yeah, it's not worth it. Just let it go.

Besides, you're not so holy yourself. Remember those magazines in the SpeedEMart? You sure didn't look away too quickly then.

Getz is just being a jerk, that's all. Just go on and show that you can take it, that you can be a good team member. Don't rock the boat.

Rationalizing himself out of action, George walked out of the locker room and hurried into the gym.

He felt better after a half-hour of grueling exercise — push-ups, jumping jacks, suicides, the works. During the break, George leaned over, put his hands on his knees, and breathed deeply. His singlet was hot and sweaty, and his arms and legs had that strong, strangely pleasant ache. It was good to be working out again.

After five minutes Mr. Lamar blew another blast on his whistle, "Okay, everyone! Veterans on this side of the gym, new guys on that side! Everyone sit down and pay attention!" The wrestlers separated as ordered, and two of the veterans dragged out a wrestling mat to the center of the gym.

As Mr. Lamar strode down the center of the gym, his glance fell on George, who was sitting next to Brian on the rookies' side. "Peterson!" he said. "You're no rookie! Go over there!" He pointed to the veterans' side.

George walked over to the other side, feeling a little awkward.

"All right," said Mr. Lamar. "Today we're going to learn the half-nelson. Getz! Brock! Get up here."

Tyler came up, followed by Brock. "Okay, rookies," Mr. Lamar said. "Listen up. Getz and Brock are going to demonstrate this move, and then you're all going to learn how to do it, and do it well. This is what you do."

Standing behind Brock, Tyler put his arm underneath his armpit and grasped the back of his neck. "Does everyone see what he's doing?" Mr. Lamar said. "This is one of your basic moves. You can use it to take control of your opponent's upper body. Okay, Tyler, take him down."

Tyler pushed down hard on Brock's head, and Brock collapsed. There was silence in the gym as the rookies took this in.

"Pair up!" said Mr. Lamar. "Rookies with veterans. Try to stay in your own weight class. Veterans, *teach* your sparring partner, don't beat him! Let's go!"

The wrestlers split up into pairs as ordered, and went to drag more mats out of the storage closet in the back of the gym. George went straight for Brian, but Mr. Lamar said, "Peterson! I want you to get to know other people on the team. Go over there with Mahoney."

Reluctantly, George jogged over to Mahoney, a blond, freckle-faced boy with thin arms and pale skin who was dragging a mat out of the closet. He looked apprehensively at George.

"Well, come on," George said in what he hoped was a friendly voice, and started to get on his hands and knees. "See if you can do the move on me."

As Mahoney fumbled forward and tried to put an extremely weak half-nelson on him, George encouraged and corrected him. "No, harder! Grip my head nice and tight. Go ahead."

Suddenly Mahoney seemed to get the idea, and forced George's head downward to the mat. As his vision whirled, he caught a glimpse of Brian. He was with Tyler's buddy Flynt. Flynt had *him* in the half-nelson.

"Hey!" George grunted in his indignation.

Mahoney released him immediately. "Did I do it right? Did I hurt you?" he asked anxiously.

George rubbed his neck reflexively as he got up, his eyes

fixed on Brian, who was squirming in Flynt's grip with a panicked look in his eyes.

"You did fine," he told Mahoney. "That was great. Excuse me, just a sec."

"Hey, Flynt!" George strode over to where Brian and the older, heavier wrestler were. "What's up?"

Flynt looked up and saw George. As he did, his face darkened.

George faced him. "You're supposed to be teaching him, not beating him; besides, you outweigh him by like, sixty pounds, man."

Flynt released Brian with a grudging air, and got up off the mat. He muttered something under his breath.

"What was that?" George said in a lower voice, coming closer. "I didn't hear you."

Flynt looked up and met George's gaze. "I said, mind your own business, Peterson."

George smiled. "Okay. But if you got a problem with me, take it out on *me*. I don't mind." He turned away, without looking back.

They had been sparring for a half-hour, and Mahoney was starting to develop a pretty decent half-nelson, when Mr. Lamar blew the whistle again. "Practice over! Hit the showers!"

In the locker room, George was getting out of his singlet when Tyler jogged up. "Not bad, Peterson," he said, in the same friendly voice he had used before.

"Thanks," George said, noncommittally.

"I don't know about your friend, though," Tyler continued, opening up his locker as he spoke. "Kind of a shrimp, if you ask me."

George flushed. "He's all right. Just give him time."

Tyler chuckled. Then, in a rustle of paper, the *Playboy* came into view again. "Sure you don't want to look, Peterson?" he asked loudly.

"Nah," George said, and tried to laugh too, although what came of him sounded more like a shaky titter. "Not right now."

At that moment, Brian jogged up, looking sweaty and worn out.

"Hey, Burke!" Tyler said, his grin getting nastier.

Brian looked up.

"Recognize her?" Tyler said, and flashed a page of the *Playboy* at him.

Brian flushed bright red. He turned away, shielding his eyes with one hand. It looked very strange in the locker room, and some of the wrestlers nearby laughed.

"What's the matter?" said one. "Haven't you ever seen a naked chick before?"

Brian made no reply. He didn't undress, but just pulled his clothes out of his locker, stuffed them into his gym bag and walked quickly out of the room. More laughter followed him out.

George ran after him. He found Brian outside, pulling a coat over his wrestling singlet. It was freezing outside.

"Are you all right?" George didn't know what else to say.

Brian was still flushed, but angry, not embarrassed.

"They shouldn't have that kind of crap here," he said. "I didn't come here to put up with garbage like that."

"I know, I know," George said. "It stinks. But it's a public school. I mean, what did you expect?"

"I didn't expect to get it shoved in my face," Brian retorted. "They shouldn't have that in the locker room. I'm going to tell Mr. Lamar."

"I wouldn't do that. The rest of the team will hate you," George warned. "This isn't home school, Brian. You can't tell the other guys what to do."

But Brian's jaw was set stubbornly. "I'm not. I'm just telling the coach what they're doing. He can decide," he said. "Besides," he added in an accusatory tone. "I didn't see *you* saying anything!"

George opened his mouth and then stopped. "I was kind of taken by surprise," he said lamely.

They both fell silent. In the quiet, they heard the sound of a car entering the parking lot. George saw Mr. Lamar coming out of the gymnasium. The car pulled up next to him, and a burly black man got out.

"There's my dad," Brian said. Mr. Lamar and the man were talking.

"I guess the coach wants to meet the parents," George said. "Hey! Brian! Wait!"

Brian had already started walking toward them. "What?"

"Are you really going to tell on those guys?" George said.

Brian looked at him steadily, and George found himself blushing. "I mean . . ." he said hesitantly. "I don't think it's a good idea. Trust me on this."

"But it's the right thing to do." Brian said. Then he turned and walked away.

Frustrated, George turned around and walked back inside, not knowing what else to do.

He showered quickly, and found some comfort that at least he could do it alone; everyone else was already getting dressed. His conscience told him he had really screwed up, and George found himself wishing he hadn't invited Brian to tryouts in the first place. *Great. John Paul 2 High kids are on the team just one day and already they're making trouble.* He saw his wish to just be another anonymous wrestler vanishing before his eyes.

As he got dressed, his thoughts went back to how he had laughed and shrugged it off when Tyler had shown him the *Playboy. You shouldn't have laughed,* a voice inside him said. *You should have said something. Brian* did *do the right thing.*

He put on his jacket, slung on his backpack, and turned to leave.

There were Tyler, Brock, and Flynt. "Hey, Peterson," Tyler said. "You did good today."

George backed away, alarm bells going off in his head, "Thanks, guys . . ."

Tyler nodded. Brock and Flynt lunged forward. Before George could react, Brock had his right arm, and Flynt his left.

They dragged him back into the shower room, keeping a firm grip on his arms. He kicked and squirmed, but it was no good.

Inside, all of the faucets were on, and there were clouds

of water vapor billowing out. But in the center of it, George saw a big heavy plastic bucket there, full of what looked like soupy brown mud with a rotten smell. He kicked and squirmed, but it was no good.

"Okay, in he goes!" Flynt said. "One . . . two . . . three!"

George just had time to squeeze his eyes shut and mouth closed before they plunged him into the stuff head first. George fought to get free. Just as he thought he would suffocate, they yanked him out, and George's vision spun as they tossed him into the shower, jacket, book bag, and all.

The water soaked into his hair and clothes, and he struggled to his feet. Tyler was standing in the doorway of the shower room, looking down on him with a big grin on his face.

George was suddenly filled with a surge of hot anger. He struggled to his feet, and rushed at Tyler.

"Chill out, dude," Tyler said, and shoved him back. George stumbled, slipped, and fell onto something soft.

"Ow! Watch it!" a voice said behind him.

George looked around, and for the first time realized that he wasn't alone in the shower room; the place was filled with dirty, wet, crestfallen kids. There was Mahoney, and several others that George recognized with brown stuff smeared on their faces. It looked like all the rookies on the team were there.

Tyler turned to Flynt, "Did we get everyone?"

"Burke left already," Flynt said.

"We'll get him later," Tyler said with a shrug.

A flash of alarm went through George's brain at those words. "Tyler!" he shouted.

116

Tyler looked down. "Yeah?"

"You better not touch him," George said. "I mean, won't it look bad, hazing a black kid?"

Tyler looked thoughtful for a moment. "I guess so. Maybe we'll let him slide. He's just a shrimp, after all."

"Okay, listen up, twerps!" Tyler stepped into the shower room, and the rest of the veterans followed him, turning off the showerheads and pulling the soaked rookies to their feet.

"Congratulations!" Tyler said, sounding positively jolly. "You've now been initiated into the Sparrow Hills wrestling team. Just remember *one* thing! If you want to pull your weight around here, you got to put in the time. And don't forget who was here first, got it?"

There was a surly-sounding murmur of assent from the crowd of rookies. Tyler grinned again, and seemed to think it was enough. "See you next time!" he said.

For the next ten minutes, George washed his hair over and over again to get the smell out, wishing he could laugh it off. He felt angry, and humiliated; but a small part of him was glad it was over with. *Whatever*, he thought ruefully. *I'll worry about it later. I just want to go home.*

He got dressed again in his wet clothes and headed for the door. But before he got there, he heard Tyler's voice behind him. "Peterson!"

He was starting to hate that voice. "*What?*" he said.

Tyler strolled up, grinning his toothy grin. "Whoa, calm down, man," he said fraternally. "I couldn't let you slide, you know. Everyone has to get the treatment."

George turned away. "Sure, fine."

"But I wanted to say something to you, special," Tyler said, leaning in closer. His grin suddenly vanished.

"They say that you're pretty good," he said in a low voice. "I don't know; I haven't seen anything to impress me, yet."

George thought about his trip to the state tournament the year before, and the stories about him in the newspaper, and his easy victories in the tryouts last week. He didn't have to prove himself to anyone on this team.

"What's your point?" he said.

Tyler's toothy smile returned. "I just wanted to make sure we're clear on one thing: *I'm* the captain around here. I don't want you getting any funny ideas. Now that you know who's boss, stay in line, and you'll do just fine."

George had absolutely no desire to interfere. "Just leave Brian alone," he said.

Tyler waved his hand. "Sure, sure," he said. "As long as he stays in line, too. See you next time, buddy. Glad to have you on the team." And with that, he strolled out, leaving George alone in the locker room.

Only George knew that Brian wasn't going to be toeing the line. And something told George that Mr. Lamar wasn't the type of man who was going to wink at porn in locker rooms. He really, really didn't want to be around for the next practice.

George walked out to the parking lot, tired, wet, cold, and humiliated. His mom should be coming soon, and he shuddered to think of the questions she would ask.

Don't ask, mom, he thought. *Please don't ask*. His book bag was digging into his shoulder, heavier than usual. He took it off, put it on the pavement, and zipped it open. There were his textbooks, notebooks, pens, and pencils — all soaked.

Great, he thought. *Just great.*

veritatissplendor: George! Hey George!
gpwrestler27: yeah
veritatissplendor: Good news about the permit!
veritatissplendor: Dad thinks that its fixed!
veritatissplendor: I had to tell someone :)
gpwrestler27: thats great seal
veritatissplendor: How are you doing?
gpwrestler27: ok
veritatissplendor: Have you talked to allie?
veritatissplendor: She's been avoiding everyone.
veritatissplendor: I think she's still mad
veritatissplendor: about the crickets.
veritatissplendor: Has she talked to you?
gpwrestler27: no
veritatissplendor: Do you think she reported us
veritatissplendor: to the health department?
veritatissplendor: Liz says it must have been her,
veritatissplendor: she was so upset
veritatissplendor: about the crickets.
veritatissplendor: and she;s still not talking
veritatissplendor: to any of us.
veritatissplendor: What do you think?
gpwrestler27: dunno
gpwrestler27: dosnt seem like her
veritatissplendor: You're right. I mean
veritatissplendor: I know she doesn't
veritatissplendor: like the school but

veritatissplendor: it doesn't seem her style.
veritatissplendor: I'll just put it out of my mind.
veritatissplendor: Anyhoo.
veritatissplendor: How's wrestling?
veritatissplendor: How is brian doing?
    gpwrestler27: ok
veritatissplendor: I guess you only had
veritatissplendor: a few practices so far . . .
    gpwrestler27: 1
    gpwrestler27: next 1 is tomorrow
veritatissplendor: Your mom has been asking
veritatissplendor: my mom if I knew why you
veritatissplendor: were all wet when she picked
veritatissplendor: you up at school last week
veritatissplendor: What's she talking about?
    gpwrestler27: nothing
    gpwrestler27: just guys fooling around
veritatissplendor: Gotta go. I'm holding Samuel
veritatissplendor: and he just blurped everywhere :O
veritatissplendor: plus Miranda is yelling that it's her
veritatissplendor: turn to get on the computer.
veritatissplendor: <:[
veritatissplendor: In short, life is happening again.
veritatissplendor: See you tomorrow, ok?
    gpwrestler27: k

George punched the computer monitor button off, feeling sick again. He hadn't told Celia or his mom what had really happened at wrestling. And he couldn't look Allie in the eye without remembering the *Playboy* centerfold. *Thanks a lot, Tyler.* He wished he could wipe that part of his memory clean like a blackboard. Why was she dating that jerk? Every time he turned around, it seemed that she was calling Tyler on her cell phone between classes. *How do girls like her end up with guys like Tyler?* He wondered if Allie knew the sort of things Tyler did behind her back. *Not my problem: forget about it.*

Unfortunately, being at John Paul 2 High didn't give him a clear conscience. Mr. Costain kept talking about how Pope John Paul II told youth to preach the Gospel by their words and actions. *Great*, thought George, staring at his homework folder where the crumpled paper with the "Truth" poem on it was sticking out.

So much for taking the Truth with me . . .

He shoved the poem back into the folder and tried to get back to his algebra homework.

NINE

GUNS

ALLIE WAS STARTING TO FEEL LONELY AT school. She hadn't felt comfortable around the girls since she had snapped at Celia during the cricket episode, and everyone else seemed to ignore her, including George, which was strange. That pained her. *Why isn't George talking to me, or even looking at me?* she wondered as she sat in theology class Wednesday morning.

The answer hit her: Celia's face crumpling into tears as she walked out of the cricket-filled bathroom. *I made Celia cry*, Allie realized. *And George must know about it.*

She felt her stomach sinking. Like everyone else at the school, she knew George and Celia were really close. Allie had never been able to figure out if they were dating or not. No one ever said anything on the subject, but maybe it was something so obvious that no one had bothered to mention it to Allie.

"Yesterday in history, we were talking about the Arian heresy," Mr. Costain said. "We're going to see what the *Catechism* has to say about the matter . . ."

Allie thumbed through her catechism. Once she found the right page, she held it open with one hand, and sneaked a look at George, who was sitting at a desk across the aisle from her. She wished he would at least look at her. Was he dating Celia? *Well, obviously Celia has a crush on George, but does George love her? So hard to tell — George is hard to read sometimes.*

"You'd better take notes," Mr. Costain said, "because these points are very important."

Allie looked at her desk and realized that she hadn't even taken out her notebook. As she dug into her backpack and pulled it out, a magazine fell out of her bag at George's feet. He picked it up, glancing at the cover.

"Sorry," Allie whispered, holding out her hand. He gave her a funny look as he handed the magazine back to her.

Allie knew exactly what he was wondering, as she stuffed the magazine back into her book bag impatiently. *Ho boy. That was swift.*

At least he had looked her in the face. But that didn't make her any happier.

When Mrs. Flynn rang the bell for lunch, Allie decided she needed some alone time. She dropped her book bag in her locker, grabbed her purse, and sneaked down the side corridor with a door at the end that led outside.

George was there, waiting for her.

"Hey," he said. "What are you up to?"

"Just thought I'd go outside for some air," she lied.

George looked at her keenly. *Cute eyes*, she thought again.

"Okay," she relented. "I was going to sneak out to SpeedEMart."

"Why not just ask?" George said.

"Oh — I don't know," Allie said.

"What if I ask if we can both go?"

"You think they'd let us?" Allie asked dubiously.

"Trust me," George grinned. "I have an 'in' with Mr. Costain."

"Don't tell Celia," Allie muttered. George's look darkened so she added, "She'd want us to invite James."

George laughed. "Nuff said. I'll be right back."

A few minutes later, George and Allie were walking together through the woods.

"So why do you have an 'in' with the Costains?" Allie asked.

A ghost of a smile flitted across his face. "So why are you looking through *Firearm Review*?" he countered. "Seems a bit out of character. Has someone really ticked you off lately? I know you don't like it here, but isn't that overreacting?"

Allie's stomach clenched uncomfortably, but she covered up her reaction with a fake laugh, "Ha ha ha, no. It has nothing to do with John Paul 2 High."

"Okay," he said, and gave her another funny look. "I actually know a bit about guns, if you need some help."

"You do?" She looked at him sharply, but no — there was no way that George resembled the kid in the black hood . . .

George shrugged. "I mean, I can shoot a rifle. I go hunting with Mr. Costain and his sons every fall."

"Is that your 'in'?" Allie said.

"Sort of," George said. "I spend a lot of time with them." He hesitated. "I don't have a dad, and I guess my mom wants me around a normal family."

"Your parents divorced?"

"No." He looked around at the trees. "I don't think my mom ever got married."

"Oh." Allie suddenly realized that in the Catholic circles George moved in, this had to be a bad thing. She tried to make him feel better. "I guess you and I are the only ones at this school without normal families." She kicked at a rock sticking out of a pile of leaves. "It stinks, the divorce. I miss my dad. I never see him since he moved to Maryland."

"Yeah," he admitted, and glanced at her with his hazel eyes. "So — what do you need to know about guns?" *Cute — and persistent.* "Does this have something to do with the gun scare at Sparrow Hills?" *Smart, too.*

She tried to cover up, but knew her expression must have given it all away. And she realized she was tired of hiding it from everyone.

Okay, I'm going to trust him. They had reached Chimney Rock. Allie stopped and leaned against it. The rock was scarred with graffiti that Sparrow Hills students had chipped into its surface, but its broad surface and natural seat made it comforting somehow.

She took a deep breath. "I'll tell you so long as you don't tell anyone else. I was the student at Sparrow Hills who got shot at."

George stared at her. "That was you? The gun scare at Sparrow Hills — you're kidding!"

"Wish I was."

"What happened?"

It had happened so quickly.

Spirit Day at Sparrow Hills: one of those silly things that they had at the beginning of the school year, where people dressed up as movie characters. There had been a bunch of kids dressed up as characters from a recent movie, Praxor's Game. She had seen it with Tyler. The main character was this guy who dressed up in a trench coat and sunglasses and shot a bunch of people with a shotgun; it wasn't exactly her kind of movie. But there were a lot of *Praxor's Game* fans at Sparrow Hills: kids dressed up in trench coats and sunglasses and carrying water guns.

She had been walking to the bathroom when he — whoever he was — had gotten her. Only first, it was just a water gun.

She was just rounding a corner, when a heavy stream of water struck her in the face. She stepped backward and banged her head against the wall, sputtering and trying to shield her eyes. Allie couldn't see a thing; she just stood there in numb amazement until she was soaked to the skin.

Across the hall stood one of the kids in costume, pointing a large, powerful-looking water gun in her direction. He was wearing a trench coat and a hooded sweatshirt with the hood pulled on tight. She couldn't see his face — only the glint of sunglasses within the hood.

For a moment she was struck by his odd appearance. Then rage welled up inside her. She rushed at him and grabbed at the water gun. He let it go and bolted away. She followed in hot pursuit.

Her assailant quickly outdistanced her; she could see his big shoulders pumping as he sped down the hallway. He was tall and broad, but she couldn't tell who he was.

He went down a side hallway that she knew was a dead end. Yelling in triumph, she rounded the corner and sprinted toward him.

He had stopped with his back to the wall, and was rummaging around in one of the pockets of his trench coat. She skidded to a halt and aimed the water gun at him.

Then suddenly he rushed her, grabbed her around the neck and pinned her to the wall. He was pointing something at her — something silver and shiny — and saying something

129

with a low guttural chuckle. She caught a glimpse of gray eyes under his shades.

Heh heh heh heh heh.

Disbelievingly, she looked at the thing in his hands as she tried to struggle. That can't be . . . a real . . .

Then there was a loud, cracking sound. The thing in the boy's hand flashed.

She seemed to be spinning in space for a moment as the world reeled crazily. Unable to breathe, she staggered, and fell to the hard, cold floor.

It was a blank," Allie explained. "He must have fired it at the ceiling. That's what the police said. They couldn't find a bullet. But *he* wanted me to think I was going to die. I know it." She sighed. "The police can't figure out who the guy was. So I thought maybe if I found out what kind of gun he had, that might be a clue or something."

"I'm sure the police can find that out," George said cautiously.

"Yeah, but not fast enough to suit me!" Allie said. Ruefully she looked down at the crushed leaves on the ground. "They better find him fast, because I'm sure he's going to try something else."

"How do you know?"

"Well — because of what he said."

"What did he say?"

Allie took a breath and shivered. " 'You're the first.' "

She looked at George sideways. He was looking out into the woods, as though he was listening to something out there. She listened too, but she didn't hear anything.

It was odd that she had told him. George had been so distant these past few days, but now he seemed as if he cared about what had happened to her.

"Scary," George said at last. "So that's why you came here?"

"Yeah. My mom figured I was pretty much a walking target if I stayed there," Allie said. "But don't tell anyone, okay? Not even Celia."

"Why don't *you* tell Celia? I thought you guys were friends."

Allie shifted. "We haven't been talking since the thing with the crickets." Then she had an idea, "Would you tell Celia I didn't really mean what I said about the school? I feel really bad I hurt her."

"Celia's really easy to talk to. You should just talk to her."

"Maybe," Allie hedged. Finally she blurted, "Are you guys dating?"

"Me and Celia?" George laughed. "Nah, we're just good friends."

Allie suddenly felt much better. "How's wrestling practice going? Tyler says you guys are getting on really well."

"It's okay," George said, glancing at his watch. The detached look had fallen over his face as fast as a curtain dropping. "We'd better get back."

TEN

SQUEALER

SO THAT'S WHY SHE'S HERE, GEORGE THOUGHT AS he walked through the same woods on his way to wrestling practice later. *That's why she's so skittish.* Leaves were falling everywhere. He heard them crunching behind him and turned to see Brian coming.

George had avoided talking to Brian since Monday night, but it didn't look like he could avoid it any longer. "Hey there."

"Hi." They walked on for a bit.

Brian finally broke the silence. "I hope that we don't have to see any of that stuff today in the locker room."

George paused before replying. "I don't think we will," he said. "Not since you told Mr. Lamar about it."

"You're probably right," Brian said. "Thank God."

George thought that sounded a little too pious. "Yeah," he replied. "But maybe we shouldn't let it out that you're the one who . . ." he almost said *squealed*, but caught himself, ". . . who told the coach about it."

"I won't go out of my way to broadcast that information," said Brian. "But I'm not ashamed of what I did."

George sighed. "Seriously, you shouldn't tell them anything. There's no reason to." *Just keep your mouth shut. Please.*

They got to the gym before practice began. Nothing seemed unusual about the atmosphere among the team members that day; rookies and veterans were mixing and chatting amiably with each other, as if nothing had happened last practice. Tyler, Flynt, and Brock waved cheerfully at George, but looked at Brian significantly.

George flinched. He hadn't even told Brian about the hazing; at first it had been too embarrassing, and later he just wanted to forget it had happened. Now he wished he had: Brian should know what he might be in for.

"Brian," he muttered, pulling at the smaller kid's arm. "I have to tell you something . . ."

But before he could speak, a shrill blast on a whistle announced the entrance of Mr. Lamar. "Form up!" he yelled as he walked into the gym. "Everyone in center court!"

As he walked up with the others, George noticed that Mr. Lamar's face wore a grim expression. That wasn't good. George had begun to hope that nothing would happen over the *Playboy* thing; but now it didn't look like it would be dismissed.

"It's come to my attention," Mr. Lamar said, "that some members of this team have pornographic materials in their lockers. I can't control what kind of stuff you look at in your homes, but — " He glared in Tyler's general direction. "It's against school rules to have obscene materials on school property. It's also against my own convictions. I'm going to be searching lockers regularly from now on; if I find anything I don't like, it's going to be confiscated, and the person owning it will be punished. You got that?"

There was sullen silence from the ranks of the wrestlers. A few voices muttering. "What's the big deal?" "It's a free country!"

Mr. Lamar's eyes narrowed. "I expect you to respond with 'yes' or 'no.' And if you want to stay on this team, you better answer 'yes.' You got that?"

"*Yes*," everyone chorused back.

"Okay, ladies," Mr. Lamar said. "But I think you all got a lot of testosterone. Maybe too much. Form up for jumping jacks *now!*"

Workout that day was especially tough. They had twice their usual number of jumping jacks, then push-ups, sit-ups, sprints, pull-ups, and *more* sprints, all without a break. Everyone was stumbling with exhaustion by the time it was over.

Mr. Lamar was clearly punishing them all for the pornography. Some vengeful looks were thrown in Tyler's direction, even by veterans. But, to George's discomfort, there were also suspicious looks thrown in *his* direction. And in Brian's. Especially in Brian's. Almost everyone had witnessed how he had reacted to the *Playboy* last practice. Now it didn't seem to matter whether they kept their mouths shut or not; it was obvious that the whole team thought one of the John Paul 2 boys was a squealer.

When all of their muscles were screaming for relief, Mr. Lamar called a halt to the workout. "Five minutes!" he said. "Take a breather, ladies."

George staggered over to a corner of the gym and sat down. Brian slumped down next to him. Neither of them spoke. George closed his eyes, leaned his head back against the wall, and tried not to think about what would happen after practice.

"George?" Brian panted. "I'm going to tell everyone that it was me."

George looked at Brian in astonishment. "No way! It'll blow over."

Brian's face was grim and set. "I did what I did because it was right, and I'm not ashamed of it."

George felt a sudden rush of anger. "Fine," he snapped. "But do me a favor, okay? Leave *right* after practice. Don't take a shower. I don't want you out of my sight until you leave, okay?"

To his satisfaction, Brian looked really scared for the first time. "Okay," he said. "What did you want to tell me?"

"It's not important," George growled. "Just do as I say."

When George got back to his locker, Tyler was waiting for him with a big toothy smile on his face. "Hey there, Catholic school kid," he said. "Calm down, dude, I'm not going to jump you again. I just want to know."

"Know what?" George asked, trying to be casual.

"Did you tell?"

"No."

Tyler's grin grew broader. "All right." He stepped aside, allowing George to get to his locker.

George stepped over and fumbled with his combination lock. He'd told Tyler the truth: George *hadn't* told. How could Tyler make him feel ashamed for admitting he hadn't squealed?

He unzipped his bag and pulled out his black school pants, while Tyler leaned against the lockers and watched. "Nice uniform you got there," he said.

George didn't reply.

"You know," Tyler continued in a louder voice, still grinning. "Some of the other guys thought that you might have squealed. But I knew that you would never do something like that. I told them, 'a guy like Peterson doesn't make it all the way to the States by backstabbing his teammates. No way.' I just had to make sure."

There was some laughter in the locker room at this. George undressed in silence. If Tyler was trying to give him a compliment, it wasn't making him feel any better.

Just then Brian jogged into the locker room. He saw Tyler and swallowed; but he went to his locker anyhow.

Oh please, God, make Brian shut up, George prayed. *Please.*

"Hey there, Catholic homeschooler," said Tyler amiably. "See, I remembered that you're Catholics, not Mormons. Aren't you happy?"

Brian looked taken aback, but said, "Well, I'm glad you figured that out. You see, Catholics and Mormons really don't have a lot in common, so it's good that you can tell the difference."

Silence fell on the locker room. George gulped, praying there were no Mormons present. Brian was being totally sincere, of course; but Tyler's smile vanished instantly.

"I'm glad that I could make *you* happy, buddy," Tyler said in a softer voice.

"No problem," Brian said, opening up his locker and pulling out his clothes.

"I better go now," Tyler said. "I gotta go see my girl-friend after school," he yawned dramatically. "She misses me; I haven't seen her much since she started going to that school of yours." He picked up his gym bag, slung it over his shoulder, and started to walk away.

Just as George was about to breathe again, Tyler stopped,

and turned around. "Oh, yeah." He walked back to George and Brian, who were still half-dressed.

"Burke," he said. "You tell Coach about my magazine?"

"Yep," Brian said. "I sure did."

A look of surprise flashed across Tyler's face. Obviously, he hadn't been expecting to get an answer so quickly.

For the first time, Tyler looked really angry. His eyebrows contracted, and his voice lowered to a dangerous whisper. "Why'd you do that, Burke?" he said. "That wasn't very nice."

George stiffened and inwardly cursed furiously. He was painfully aware of the fact that he was in his underwear. Not the best situation in which to fight people.

Brian didn't look away. "I'm sorry," he said. "I mean, I'm sorry that you got in trouble. But I'm not sorry I told. It's wrong to look at that stuff, and personally I find it really offensive. I — "

"I'm sorry too," Tyler said softly. "You know what happened last practice, Burke?"

Brian looked a little worried. "No."

"Well, if Peterson didn't tell you, I'm not going to ruin the surprise," Tyler said, and glanced at George with a look of contempt on his face. "But you got a free pass out of it, and that pass is now expired. Understand?"

"What do you mean?"

"I *mean*," Tyler said, taking a step closer. "That we weren't going to touch you because you're black. But now it looks like you need to know who's in charge here."

Brian's face turned crimson. "Excuse me," he said indignantly. "What do you mean by 'because you're black'?"

George suddenly felt cold inside. He had forgotten what he had said to Tyler, and now it suddenly came back to him. He hadn't even thought there was anything wrong with saying that, at the time. He was just looking for *something* to say, some way to shield Brian, and that was the first thing that had come to mind.

Tyler saw George's reaction; and suddenly, a malicious smile came to his face. "Well, Burke," he said, in a horribly cheerful voice. "Your little friend here told me last week," he paused, savoring the moment, "that we should go easy on you because you're black. I guess he thought, you know, that you just couldn't take the heat. Anyway, I was afraid that you'd sic the NAACP on me or something, so I *was* going to leave you alone."

Brian turned to George slowly, an incredulous, angry look on his face. George couldn't meet his gaze. He had never expected this to happen. He had been dreading the prospect of getting beat up again, or seeing Brian getting beat up, but this was much, much worse.

Tyler chuckled. He slung his gym bag on his shoulder again and waved to both of them. "I *really* got to go now," he said. "Keep your noses clean, kids. And Burke . . . I'll be seeing you around." He walked away jauntily.

Crap, George thought. *Crap crap crap crap CRAP!*

He couldn't meet Brian's look. He had no idea on how to explain, or even how to begin to explain.

A few minutes later, they were outside, waiting for Mr. Burke to pick them up. It was cold, and a biting wind was blowing in George's face. Brian stood ten feet away, facing the other direction. He hadn't spoken or looked at George since Tyler had left.

George's stomach was churning like a washing machine. *I can't take this anymore.* "Brian?" he said.

Brian didn't even look over. He looked, if possible, even more upset than before. His face was flushed, and his lips were set in a thin line.

"Just listen to me for a sec, okay?" George asked.

Brian deigned to look in his direction. "What do you want to say?"

"I . . . you . . . you see, Brian," he began. "They did this thing to all the new guys last practice . . ."

"You mean they hazed everyone?" Brian said coolly.

"Yeah." George paused and then stared at Brian. "How did you hear about that?"

"I didn't," Brian said. "I figured it out. Your mom asked my mom why you were all wet last week after practice, and my mom asked me. What was it, some kind of stunt?"

George felt the shame come back to him, the memory of how he had felt. "Yeah," he muttered; and for the first time, he felt somewhat justified. *And that's what I was trying to keep you from, Brian.*

"What was it like?" Brian said. "What did they do, exactly?"

"They put our faces in filthy mud," George muttered. "Then they threw everyone in the showers, that's all."

"I see," Brian said. "It was no big deal. So *why*," his voice suddenly turned cold and hard again, ". . . did you think that I couldn't handle it?"

George opened his mouth to reply, and found that he couldn't.

"I mean," said Brian, his voice louder and angrier, "am I *that* pathetic, that I can't handle getting thrown in the shower? Is that it? So you had to tell them to go easy on me, 'cause I'm *black?*"

George examined his sneakers closely.

They were both silent for a long moment.

"I was just trying to help."

Brian turned away again, his face taking on a stony expression. "I don't need *that* kind of help."

Brian didn't speak to George, or even look at him, the whole ride home.

ELEVEN

THAT WEIRD WORD

IT WAS ALMOST 10 P.M. THANK GOD, NIKKI WAS

online. Allie had plenty to say about the recent happenings at John Paul 2; and Nikki was actually interested in hearing about it. Allie was grateful.

> **angelgirl785: so thers little bugs**
> **angelgirl785: ALL OVER the floor**
> **angelgirl785: then 1 lands on my SHOE**
> Jokerbabe: lol
> Jokerbabe: wat did u do?
> **angelgirl785: screamed**
> Jokerbabe: thats wat I thot
> Jokerbabe: u r such a wuss w bugs
> **angelgirl785: I m NOT!!**
> **angelgirl785: their so disgusting**
> **angelgirl785: its not evn funny**

Now that she thought of it, though . . .
Allie found herself giggling. She typed:

> **angelgirl785: the funniest thing was**
> **angelgirl785: mrs simonelli saw the crickets**
> **angelgirl785: she screamed so loud**
> **angelgirl785: like she was being murdered**
> **angelgirl785: AAAAHHHHEEEEEKKK!!!!!!!**
> **angelgirl785: hehehe**
> Jokerbabe: wait a sec
> Jokerbabe: CRICKETS?
> **angelgirl785: yeah**
> Jokerbabe: crickets r cute
> **angelgirl785: thats what celia said**

Jokerbabe: whos celia?
angelgirl785: principals daughter
Jokerbabe: o yeah

Allie felt a twinge of guilt. She wondered if George had talked to Celia yet. She hoped so.

angelgirl785: shes all right shes nice.

Allie sat back in her chair, absently chewing her fingernail. *How could she describe Celia?*

Where would Celia fit at Sparrow Hills? Probably with the really smart kids . . . but not the loser crowd. Celia definitely wasn't a loser . . . but she probably wouldn't be extra popular, either . . . not in the way that Madison and Tyler were popular. She was too nice? Or maybe she just didn't care about that sort of thing. "Hmm," she said out loud, and leaned forward to the keyboard again.

angelgirl785: celia is cool and supernice
Jokerbabe: really maybe we can
Jokerbabe: hang out some time

Allie thought about the things that she and her friends did: hang out at the mall, go shopping, talk about boys. She couldn't imagine Celia doing any of those things. Still, she typed halfheartedly,

angelgirl785: maybe
Jokerbabe: this school is good 4 u
Jokerbabe: i can tell
angelgirl785: ?

A new IM window opened up. The message was from . . . ? Allie peered at the screen.

veritatissplendor: is this allie?

Allie blinked, and looked closer at the strange-looking screen name, trying to sound it out. *Ve-ri-ta-tee-splen-dor? What the heck is that?*

angelgirl785: whos this?
veritatissplendor: this is celia from jp2 high. is this allie?
angelgirl785: yes
veritatissplendor: HI ALLIE!!!!

Allie arched her eyebrows. *What do you know?* She switched back to Nicole's window and typed:

angelgirl785: guess wat?
angelgirl785: celia just IMed me

By the time she had finished typing, Celia had already written some more.

veritatissplendor: sorry to surprise you.
veritatissplendor: my dad had your email address so
veritatissplendor: i thought I'd say hi. whats going on?
angelgirl785: nottin much
veritatissplendor: how did you like the homework for
veritatissplendor: history?

Allie groaned. History homework that night was thirty pages from *Christ the King: Lord of History*, all about ancient heretics. She found it incredibly confusing; but she didn't want to criticize Mr. Costain; she *also* didn't want to look dumb.

> **angelgirl785: it wasnt that bad**
> veritatissplendor: YEAH RIGHT
> veritatissplendor: i lost track between Simon Magus
> veritatissplendor: and Montanus . . .
> veritatissplendor: maybe you could give me some
> veritatissplendor: pointers?

Allie gulped. *Oops.* She considered trying to make up some facts, maybe look something up. But Celia probably knew all about this stuff, and could tell if she was faking it. Then she'd look even *dumber* . . . suddenly, the whole thing just seemed ridiculous.

> **angelgirl785: actually**
> **angelgirl785: i havent started yet**
> veritatissplendor: ah hah!
> veritatissplendor: i WAS kind of surprised
> veritatissplendor: anyway . . .

There was nothing more for a long space of time. Allie quickly switched back to Nicole's window and typed

> **angelgirl785: im talking 2 her right now**
> **angelgirl785: did I tell u**
> **angelgirl785: I thot she and george were dating**
> **angelgirl785: but theyre not?**
> **angelgirl785: so now I like her :)**

Just as Nicole answered,

Jokerbabe: george sounds like a cutie
Jokerbabe: 2 bad ur dating Tyler

another message from Celia popped up:

veritatissplendor: I wanted to apologize for laughing at
veritatissplendor: you last week.

Allie was stunned. *Why is she apologizing to* me?

veritatissplendor: i didnt mean to aggravate you.
veritatissplendor: i know it must be hard,
veritatissplendor: moving to a new school and all
veritatissplendor: and i didnt know you
veritatissplendor: had a phobia about bugs . . .

This is ridiculous, Allie thought. She typed quickly:

angelgirl785: don't be silly
angelgirl785: i was a TOTAL jerk

There was a pause. Allie grinned, imagining Celia with
a baffled look on her face.

veritatissplendor: i could have been a little more nice,
veritatissplendor: though.

No, you couldn't. Allie chuckled. *There was no possible
way you could have been more nice.*

angelgirl785: celia
angelgirl785: i said your school was a trash heap.

angelgirl785: i felt so bad about it all week
angelgirl785: im really really sorry.

Suddenly all her emotions from the week seemed to well up and out of her, and she breathed a deep, heavy sigh. She didn't know how to describe the feeling that followed. It wasn't happiness, exactly, but it she didn't feel sad anymore. She felt *lighter*.

veritatissplendor: i forgive you.

Huh? Allie thought. That was as odd. She'd been hoping for 'that's okay', or 'no big deal'. But 'I forgive you'? That was weird. She pondered the words for a moment. Weird. But not in a bad way.

angelgirl785: thanx
angelgirl785: seriously
angelgirl785: hey wanna meet my friend Nikki?
angelgirl785: from SH
angelgirl785: I mean SPARROW HILLS

There was only the slightest pause, and then:

veritatissplendor: yeah!
veritatissplendor: i would LOVE to

Allie smiled, and pressed the "invite" button, letting Celia and Nikki into a new conversation box. She typed:

angelgirl785: hey nikki
angelgirl785: theres someone I want u 2 meeeet . . .

George couldn't sleep. It had been a strenuous day of school, exercise, and chores, but still he tossed and turned in his bed, his mind churning with unsettled thoughts.

There was the thing with Brian. The thing with Tyler. The thing with . . . *Allie.*

'I'm going to see my girlfriend after school. She misses me.' Tyler walking out arrogantly. The *Playboy* in the locker room. *'Kind of reminds me of my girlfriend.'*

The more George got to know Allie, the more he was bothered that she was dating someone like Tyler. *She can't really know what he's like. When will she find out?*

But there was still a twinge of guilt and fear. Was he, George, that much better than Tyler? Had he stood up for what was right, when it came right down to it?

What could he have said? *Allie is a daughter of God, creep, not a Playboy centerfold. Keep your dirty thoughts to yourself.* Maybe then he wouldn't be in this fix.

Or maybe he still would be. No matter what he did, *someone* seemed to get mad at him these days . . .

It was only after almost an hour of sleeplessness that George gave up. He got up and went to the bathroom. When he came back to his room, on a sudden impulse, he knelt and said a prayer. *Okay, God, I'm sorry I screwed up. Please help me get some sleep. Help me figure out what the right thing to do is, and help me do it and not give in to . . . whatever.*

He took a deep breath. Maybe he just wasn't tired enough. Push-ups might do the trick.

He got on the floor, lying with his face and chest hugging the thin ragged carpet. Then with a heave of his arms he pushed himself up, and then down. Up, and down.

One . . . two . . . three . . . four . . .

The next morning, George got out of his mom's car weary and cranky. Before he got inside, the Burke's van rumbled up and dropped off Brian. As the van zoomed away, the younger boy glanced in his direction, then walked quickly past him into the school.

George restrained a surge of anger and resentment. He was getting used to this. Brian hadn't spoken to him since last practice; this didn't encourage George to try to apologize again; not something that he was inclined to do anyhow.

He walked into school and was opening his locker when Allie Weaver bumped into him, dropping a folder and scattering pages of loose-leaf on the floor. "I'm sorry!" she said.

"Don't worry about it," George muttered, and knelt down to help her pick up her papers. He grabbed at a paper and felt a soft touch on his hand. Allie had grabbed the same paper.

George's heart leaped into his throat. He uttered an embarrassed grunt and stood up quickly.

"Sorry," Allie said, snatching up the remaining papers.

George, struck dumb, suddenly realized that Allie was *blushing*. She'd never looked like this before. Cold, aloof, bored? Yes. Bashful? No.

They stood in awkward silence until George managed to say, "How's it going?"

"Okay!" she said, smiling. "How 'bout you?"

George was again thrown off; this time by that smile. She was dressed to kill, as usual, the white blouse and black skirt looking infinitely more sophisticated on her than on the other girls; but her expression was friendlier than usual. A wild thought flashed through his mind: *She's happy to see me.*

He walked into the classroom in a distinctly better mood. Although it was only 7:30, twenty minutes before the school day officially started, everyone was there, talking animatedly.

"How about a car wash?" Brian suggested.

"Come on!" Liz said. "It's not a fundraiser. It's supposed to be *fun.*"

"What is?" George asked.

Brian turned away, but Celia said, "Dad asked us to think of a way to incarnate our faith in a celebration or an outreach."

"So what can we do?" Liz asked.

"I know!" J.P. said with a meaningful look at Allie, "A . . . Catholic . . . dating game! We can invite all the Catholics from miles around and . . ."

"How about a chess tournament?" Brian interrupted.

"How about a basketball tournament against St. Lucy's?" Liz said. "And if we win, they have to let us use their gym for our own sports," she added hopefully.

"What about an All Saints' Day party?"

Everyone looked in surprise at James, who usually didn't join in conversations except to score points with sarcasm.

"What?" Allie said.

"The feast of All Saints. It's the day after Halloween," Celia explained. "It's a Catholic feast day."

"*Halloween* is a contraction for 'All Hallow's Eve,' " Brian added.

"I thought the day after Halloween was Mischief Night!" Liz exclaimed.

"That's the day before," J.P. said.

"You would know," said George, crumpling up a sheet of incorrect algebra problems and tossing it. He wanted to change the subject. James's smug face still irritated him.

Allie was looking from one person to another, with that bewildered, skeptical look on her face.

"I think it's a good idea," Celia said encouragingly. "We could all dress up as saints!"

George groaned inside.

Liz groaned audibly. "But I wanted to be a pirate for Halloween."

James shook his head. "Curb your disappointment, Miss Simonelli. Halloween is a Satanic holiday."

"What?" Allie asked again.

James nodded. "It's the witches' Sabbath. According to Michael Davies — "

"Give it a rest!" George said. "You're not evil if you dress up and go out trick-or-treating on Halloween."

"But you are being a material participant in evil," said James.

"I think it's best not to go trick-or-treating." Brian said thoughtfully, "My family has a 'Defending the Faith' night on Halloween."

"Come on!" Liz said. "Kill the fun for everyone!"

J.P. pointed a finger at her. "Eeevil, eeevil, eeevil!"

"All right!" Celia exclaimed. "Look, no one's trying to say that you're sinning by going out trick or treating — "

"Except James," Liz pointed out.

"Except me," James affirmed.

" — But there's nothing wrong with the school doing an All Saints' Day party," Celia said.

"Except that it was James's idea," George said.

"Yeah," said J.P., "and James thinks we're eeevil."

"Well — let's still think about it," Celia faltered. "So, Allie, what are you doing for Thanksgiving?"

"Going to see my dad in Maryland," Allie said with a sigh, stretching. "I can't wait."

"Why does your dad live in Maryland?" James asked. James was looking at Allie with a strange expression on his face.

Taken aback, Allie looked back at him distastefully. "Well . . . because my parents are divorced. I live with my Mom and stepdad."

James was still looking at her with his peculiar un-blinking gaze. "Did your parents have their marriage annulled?"

"No," Allie said indignantly. "Not that it's any of your business."

"She's right," Celia broke in, "it isn't."

"So," James said, as if Celia hadn't spoken, "your mom is living with another guy without getting an annulment. That's a mortal sin."

There was a commotion of sound as Allie got out of her seat. "That's not true!" she said hotly. "They're married! My parents are . . . my mom is a *good* Catholic! She sent me *here*, didn't she?"

James' expression didn't change in the slightest. "Actually," he said haughtily, "If she divorced and remarried without an annulment, she's *not* a good Catholic. Celia," he added. "does your dad know about this? Isn't it material cooperation with evil to accept money from a couple that's living in sin?"

Allie's face turned red. An angry tear ran down her cheek as she stood up and stormed out of the room.

"Allie! Wait!" Celia ran after her.

George looked at James with angry disbelief. "Why don't you just keep your mouth shut?" he snarled. "How could you *say* that to her?"

"I was only pointing out the truth. You should know."

"*I* should know?" George said. "What are you talking about?"

"You live with your mom," James turned to him, that knowing smile on his face, the *I-know-you're-a-hypocrite* smile. "Where's your dad? Aren't your parents divorced?"

George sprang out of his chair, planted his hands on James's desk and yelled in his face. "That . . . is . . . *none of your business!*"

There was silence. He could feel his heart pounding in his chest. James hadn't moved or flinched, merely stared back at him, his eyes gray ice. Their faces were less than a foot apart; he could feel James' breath on his face, and knew that James could feel his. *Make one move and I'll hit you.*

TWELVE

DON'T HAVE A COW

WHAT'S GOING ON HERE?" A NEW VOICE

broke the silence, the calm, firm voice of an adult.

Mr. Costain was standing in the doorway. "Mr. Peterson," he said, "please return to your seat. Everyone else, face the front of the class."

George took a deep breath and straightened with effort.

Mr. Costain said, "Mr. Peterson. Tell me why you were out of your seat."

"James insulted Allie," George said. "And me."

"Mr. Kosalinski?"

"That's not what happened. I did *not* insult anyone," James retorted. "All I did was point out the truth. If he can't take it, that's *his* problem. Besides," he added, "according to your silly poem, aren't we supposed to 'take the truth with us'? Isn't the truth SUPPOSED to make us uncomfortable?"

George started to reply, but Mr. Costain shot him a warning look. "Miss Simonelli, in your view, what happened here?"

Liz hesitated. "Well . . ." she said. "James . . . James told Allie that her parents . . . that her mom and step dad were living in mortal sin."

Mr. Costain's glanced at James, but his expression remained calm. "Go on," he said.

"And then Allie got upset and ran out. Celia went after Allie, and George told James to shut up. Then . . . then James asked George if his parents were divorced, too."

Mr. Costain nodded gravely. "I see."

He folded his arms, in deep thought. "All right," he said after a moment. "I want you to listen to me. First of

161

all, Mr. Kosalinski, you need to learn the virtue of com-passion. Put your hand down," he said as James raised his hand indignantly. "Your words *hurt* Miss Weaver. Saying what you said, in the way you said it, was not an act of love. Our primary responsibility as Christians is to love one another, and you failed to do that."

"I'm sorry, sir," James said, but he didn't sound very sorry to George. "I thought that the *truth* was the most important thing."

Mr. Costain didn't bat an eye. "Of course the truth is the most important thing. But were you really looking for it, Mr. Kosalinski?" he said. "Or were you just trying to show everyone that you knew it already?"

For the first time, James looked confused. He frowned furiously at his desk.

Mr. Costain continued. "You also might want to reflect on the fact that if what you said was true about Miss Weaver's parents' marriage, then the best thing we can do for Miss Weaver is to be good examples of Christians. Were you a good example? Think about that.

"And the same thing applies to you, Mr. Peterson," he said, turning to George. "You let your emotions get the better of you."

George looked down and did not reply. His face was still burning red, and he was breathing hard.

"George," Mr. Costain said, and he looked up.

"I want you to go down to the cafeteria and make sure the windows are closed. It's getting colder every day."

George caught Mr. Costain's meaning. He was saying, *Go cool down for a while.*

Once he was out in the hall, George clenched his fists as he walked. He wanted to hit . . . something. Then as he rounded the corner to the cafeteria, George heard a sound that stopped him dead in his tracks.

"*Moooo . . .*"

Oh geez. What have they done now?

He opened the cafeteria door. There, in the center of the room, was a cow. It was large. White, with black spots. A funny smell met his nose. A smell like a barn.

"*Mooo . . .*"

Another crisis in this crazy school. And, as usual, *he* had to take care of it. With a groan, he turned back up the hall to tell Mr. Costain.

Allie slumped against the wall of the girls' bathroom, her face buried in her hands.

She felt a cold hardness in her chest. She hated this school. She had tried to make it work, and just *look* at what had happened.

Divorce, annulments, mortal sin — what did she care? All she wanted to do was go to a normal school . . . *I ought to call my mom right now*, she thought. *I'll tell her what happened, and she'll pull me out today.*

"Allie?"

Allie didn't look up. She heard the door creak open, and the *pock, pock, pock* of Celia's shoes. Allie stiffened, wondering if she'd have to explain herself or defend her parents.

"You don't need to talk," Celia said softly.

The coldness in Allie's chest lessened. She laughed ruefully. "Some kids you got in this school."

Celia laughed too. "You're telling me."

"So," Allie said, "What do you think?"

Celia looked Allie straight in the eye. "I think James was very rude to you."

Allie bowed her head, immensely grateful that she didn't have to defend herself.

"And I understand if you want to leave," Celia said. "Maybe I would too if I were you. But I don't want you to leave."

"I know," Allie found herself saying bitterly. "If I left there would only be six kids in the whole school again,"

"That doesn't matter," Celia said softly. "Really. I don't want you to leave because you're my friend. And because I think it would be good for you to stay."

Allie looked up. Nikki, Celia, her mom . . . everyone seemed to think this school was *good* for her. What was the big deal about this little Catholic school? Why was it so special?

"Celia — " *Here goes*, she thought. *The real test.* "Is James right? Is my mom . . ." She gulped. "Is my mom 'living in sin'?"

Celia took a deep breath, "Well . . . if you're trying to be a good Catholic . . . and you can't work things out . . ."

"Celia," Allie said wearily, "just tell me."

Celia sighed. "Okay. Are you sure your mom didn't get an annulment?"

"I'm sure. Dad doesn't go to church anymore because of that. Mom only goes at Christmas and Easter."

"In that case . . . yeah, there's something wrong there. Something . . . something that should be fixed."

Allie sat silently for a long, long moment, expecting to feel angry. But she only felt sad. Very sad. She didn't know why, and she still didn't understand why this lack of an annulment was such a big deal. But the way Celia had spoken about it had given her a different take on things.

James' voice had been a sharp finger condemning her because of choices her parents had made. But Celia was saying the same thing . . . but it was different. Celia spoke of something broken; she spoke of the whole thing, the whole divorce, as if it were an undeniable fact, something solid and pitiless, that they couldn't get away from. She looked at Celia's face again; Celia was looking away. Her face was turning red, and she had a tense, drawn expression, almost as if she were in pain.

She's more upset than I am, Allie thought in wonder. And then another thought came: *She wishes that it wasn't like this. She wants it to just go away, but she won't pretend it's not there.*

"What am I supposed to do about it?" Allie said. "Why is this *my* fault?"

"It's *not* your fault," Celia said, and for the first time she looked angry. "You should never think that."

"But if James is right," Allie persisted. "And my mom and step dad are 'living in sin,' then . . . then *what* am I doing here, Celia? I'm not *like* the rest of you. I never will be!"

Celia twisted her hands, her forehead furrowed in thought. "Darn it," she said. "I'm not very good at this

165

. . . Hold on. Okay." she said finally. "Do you know, like, in the Bible, who Jesus always got mad at?"

"Let me guess. Divorced kids?"

"Nooooo," Celia said, "the Pharisees."

"Who were they?"

"They were the high priests — super-religious people — who were always showing off and condemning people," Celia said. "They were mad at Jesus because he was always hanging out with tax collectors and prostitutes."

"Oh yeah," Allie said. That sounded familiar.

"And you know what Jesus said to them?" Celia said. "He said, um, that 'I have not called the righteous to repentance, but sinners.'"

"Oh," Allie said. "That doesn't sound too good."

Celia chuckled a little. "I think that Jesus was being sarcastic, you know? Because, Allie . . ." she turned to her. "There *aren't* any righteous people. We're *all* sinners. You are, I am, my dad is, even *Mrs. Simonelli* is. So you *are* just like the rest of us."

"Oh," Allie said. That also sounded familiar, but *not* familiar at the same time. It wasn't a pleasant thought, but it was comforting, in a mysterious way.

"And you know what?" Celia said. "I think that James was acting more like a Pharisee than like Jesus."

Allie laughed, "The Pharisees never combed their hair?"

"Never," Celia said in a perfectly serious tone. "And they were always reading weird books, too."

"Really?"

"*No*, of course not!" Celia said, and they both burst into giggles.

Allie rubbed her eyes and stood up. "Come on," she said. "Let's get out of this bathroom before we get eaten by a giant cricket or something."

Through the door came the sounds of shouts, running feet, and finally a loud "*Moo . . . !*"

Celia looked at Allie. "Did you hear that?"

"Let's go," Allie said, and they rushed out of the bathroom together.

A cow," Mr. Costain said. He put a hand to his mouth. George, who was closest, saw that he was smiling underneath his hand, but he continued in a loud voice, "Mr. Burke, get Mrs. Flynn, please. Tell her it's urgent."

He turned to the students gathered around him. "I don't suppose any of you know how a cow got into the cafeteria?"

"It must have been *the poltergeist!*" said J.P. in a strangled whisper.

"I think we'll investigate that later. In the meantime, George, let's see if we can get it out of here. The rest of you, please return to class."

But the cow proved harder to move than they expected. Although it followed them easily enough out the cafeteria door, it absolutely refused to go down the outside steps. Finally, they led her back to the cafeteria.

"How about you stay here and keep an eye on the cow, George? I'll ask for help at the farm next door. That's probably where it came from."

George sighed and nodded.

Cow-watching turned out to be a mildly pleasant duty. George got some of his books, sat down at one of the tables, and began his homework. Every few minutes the cow looked around despondently and *moo*ed, but otherwise it was pretty quiet.

After a few minutes of this, George found random thoughts floating through his head, interrupting his history homework: *as big as a cow . . . the cow jumped over the moon . . . content as a cow . . . don't have a cow . . .*

"What is this? A Future Farmers of America meeting?"

George looked up, startled. A short, thin angry-looking man with an intimidating air stood in the doorway.

"Who are you?"

"Herman Bickerstaff, building inspector. Why is there livestock in the building? Is this some sort of field day?"

George stared, conscious only of a growing feeling that this couldn't possibly be good for the school. "I . . . uh . . ." he stammered. At that moment, as if in answer to the inspector's question, there was a plopping sound on the floor.

"I'll answer that, George." To George's relief, Mr. Costain strode into the room, accompanied by a burly man in a flannel shirt and worn jeans who could only be from the farm next door.

"Good Lord!" said the farmer, bursting into laughter. "Smells like a cow in here!"

"Mr. Bickerstaff," Mr. Costain said. "This is Doug Grierson. He owns the adjacent dairy farm and this seems to be one of his cows."

"She's mine, all right," said Mr. Grierson. "The kids in your school must be real handfuls. Still can't figure how they got her past the barbed-wire fence, but she don't look hurt, so I guess it'll be all right."

Mr. Bickerstaff was not smiling. "Someone could have been hurt or even killed by that animal."

"I agree," Mr. Costain said. "And I assure you I'll be taking appropriate disciplinary action, Mr. Bickerstaff. I'm sorry it's interfered with your building inspection. George, thank you — you can go back to class now."

George picked up his books and headed slowly for the door, while the men kept talking.

"Thanks so much for coming to get her," Mr. Costain was saying as the farmer led the cow away.

"No problem," Mr. Grierson replied, "I'll be selling the farm soon anyway — I hear land prices around here are going to jump pretty soon. Hey, I see she's left you some cow pies."

Mr. Bickerstaff said nothing, and kept frowning darkly at the cow.

Cut it out!" J.P. yelped. "Let me go!" said Liz, as George grabbed both of them by the shoulders and yanked them into a side corridor after math class. Despite their complaints, neither of them looked too upset.

"I just want to know how you did it," George said. "And don't even *think* about saying 'the poltergeist did it.'" He gave J.P., whose mouth was already open, a warning look. "Come on, tell me the truth."

Liz spoke first. She seemed to be the most embarrassed. "We got a ride over here at 5 this morning," she said, "And J.P. got the cow out."

"You got a ride? With who?"

Liz shrugged, but her face turned red. George decided to let it be.

"How did you get past the barbed wire?"

"There's a spot where the wire's loose," J.P. said. "Liz held it up while I led the cow through. Aw, come on, George. You have to admit it was a pretty cool joke."

George remembered Mr. Bickerstaff's angry expression. If someone from the county office decided to make a stink about this, no pun intended . . . "No, it wasn't," he said. "You might have gotten the school in trouble."

"Who cares?" Liz retorted. "I hope they do shut us down. Then I could go back to a real school with a basketball team." She tossed her ponytail. "And you could go back to a real school with a real wrestling team. So what's up with you playing cop, George? Why do you care so much?"

George didn't know what to say. "Because I have to," he muttered at last. It was that Truth thing again. *Can't take him anywhere.*

THIRTEEN

'SCHOOLED

THE TRUTH WASN'T DONE WITH GEORGE YET. ON THE bus heading for their first wrestling meet of the season, George was talking with the rookies, who were anxious. Mahoney, the redhead he had wrestled the first day of practice was particularly nervous, and George had decided to give him a pep talk. But then he overheard Tyler talking.

"Oh, homeschooler," Tyler crooned to Brian who was reading his science homework, "You are *so* going to get creamed."

"Yeah, we'll be scraping you off the mats," said Brock.

"Ready for a good pounding today?" Flynt added.

Brian looked out the window, red-faced, and George felt his conscience prick. He'd been leaving Brian alone, but Brian was his classmate and just as worried as the other rookies.

"Ignore them," George muttered to Brian, moving his gear into the seat behind him. "You'll do fine."

It was the first thing he'd said to Brian in a long time. "Thanks," Brian said stiffly. "You don't need to look out for me."

Fine. I don't want to anyhow. George stared out the window. *I don't need to stick my neck out. He can go and get himself beaten up if that's what he wants. . .*

And I'll just stand and watch . . .

. . . yeah, right.

He sneaked a glance at Tyler and his goons. They were looking in Brian's direction and whispering to each other. George resolved to be on his guard.

He was worried about Brian. The heavy workouts in practices had put Brian in better condition, but he still looked pretty light. George wondered how Brian would do in his first competitive match.

Guess I could pray for him too, he admitted to himself. His rosary was still in his pocket from school, and last year he had started praying before his matches. The ride to this meet was long, and he might as well pray that they both would do well in the competition, and be able to handle whatever Tyler was planning. *Even if I never get any thanks for it . . .*

The Sparrow Hills team was taking a beating at the meet. Only George and Tyler had defeated their opponents.

When the announcer called the 103-pound class wrestlers, Brian walked out to the circle as determined as George had ever seen him. But no opponent walked out to meet him.

"The winner of the 103-pound class is Brian Burke: a win for Sparrow Hills!" the announcer blared.

Brian's jaw dropped in surprise. Tyler and his friends hooted with laughter. Bewildered, Brian sat down, amid a scattering of polite applause. In his confusion, he seemed to forget he wasn't speaking to George.

"I didn't wrestle anyone. How did I win?"

"There wasn't anyone on the other squad in your weight class, so you won by default," George explained.

Understanding and shame dawned on Brian's face. "That's why they wanted me on the team," he said in a low voice. "Not because I'm good, but because I'm *light*."

What an upset! You won, man!" Tyler chortled to Brian as the team jogged back into the locker room.

Brock and Flynt chimed in, "You are the man, Burke! Way to go!"

"Homeschooler is a hunk!"

George stayed close to Brian as the bigger wrestlers butted up against him on the way into the crowded locker room.

If he hadn't been watching for it, he might have missed it. Brock and Flynt suddenly turned their playful joshing into gorilla holds on Brian's arms and started dragging him into a side corridor.

Not wasting a moment, George yanked Flynt by the back of his uniform, and thrust his foot between Brock's legs, tripping him. At the same time he grabbed Brian and pulled him out of their grasp.

Flynt grabbed for George's legs in a scuffle of movement but George backpedaled and managed to get Brian behind him. Flynt and Brock got to their feet with looks of surprise on their faces. The rest of the team gave the four of them wide berth as they confronted each other.

"Peterson!" said Flynt. "What are you doing?"

George didn't reply. Breathing hard, he looked both Flynt and Brock in the eyes, watching them for any sudden moves.

"Come on, George," Brock said. "Let us do our jobs. You know the rules."

"Let's pretend I don't," George growled. "What are the rules again?"

Flynt rolled his eyes. "Everybody gets the initiation. This little shrimp missed his. He's got to get it sometime. It's only fair. Come *on*, get out of the way."

George didn't move.

"Look," Brock said, apparently trying to reason with him. "There's two of us and one of you. How do you think you're gonna stop us, anyway?"

"Let's find out," George said. "And see if Coach notices."

Flynt and Brock hesitated, and looked at each other. Then grudgingly, the two big wrestlers backed away. "We'll get him, Peterson. You can't stop it," Flynt warned.

It was only after he saw them disappear toward the showers that George turned to Brian.

"Are you okay?" George asked.

"Yeah, yeah," Brian mumbled. He looked at George with a curiously rueful expression.

"Thanks," he said, finally.

"No problem," George grunted.

"Why did you stop them?" Brian said, a touch of the old anger creeping back into his voice. "Why didn't you just let them do whatever it was? I mean, I'm grateful and all, of course, but . . . if it's going to happen, I'd rather just get it over with."

George bit back an angry retort. When he got control of himself, he spoke again in a softer voice. "Brian, you don't understand,"

"*What* don't I understand?" snapped Brian.

"They're going to do something worse to you, because you squealed on them."

Brian closed his mouth.

George swallowed. "You were right about the porn," he admitted. "And I don't think you should get beaten up for that. I mean, you did the right thing. I didn't."

His face was red. When he looked back, Brian was regarding him with a new respect.

"I don't know what to say," Brian said at last. "Except thanks."

"You're welcome," George muttered.

Okay, so maybe once in a big while I do get thanked.

So I'm the mascot with nothing to do but show up," Brian said as they watched another meet at Sparrow Hills.

Despite their rough start, the Sparrow Hills wrestling team had done considerably well as the season went on. Now they were heading for the playoffs with a strong standing. And Brian was right: his contribution had been a series of default wins in his weight class.

George was too busy watching Mahoney to answer. *Come on, kid, do it . . . do it . . . yes!* George yelled as the referee's hand came down. *Pin!* Mahoney was on his way to being one of the better wrestlers on the squad.

"But you always get points and no penalties," George finally said to Brian. "Way to go, Mahoney!"

"Thanks for the pre-match pointers, George!" the red-faced rookie said as he came off the court.

"Any time," George said, ignoring Tyler's glare in his direction. George turned back to Brian, "I lost the team points in my first match — I totally fumbled that double-leg takedown."

"But you still wrestled," Brian muttered. "I want to pull my weight."

"You ARE pulling your weight."

"I don't like being the token featherweight on the team any more than I like being a token black kid on someone's quota."

"Brian, you know I'm sorry I ever said that."

Brian shrugged. "I don't want special privileges. That's not why I tried out for the team."

George was distracted again. Another rookie, Marshall Vickson, was up next. George had been working on take-downs with him during practice and he wanted to see how the rookie did.

"Looks like we got this meet in the bag," Tyler said, coming down the bleachers. "Lucky they got us pros on the squad, right, Peterson?"

"Yep," George said, his eyes on the match.

"I see you've been doing a lot of assistant coaching," Tyler said, easing himself into the seat next to George, "That's great."

"Thanks," George said, not at all fooled, and concentrating on Vickson's struggle to get a grip on his opponent.

"You know, on the Sparrow Hills wrestling squad, it's usually the squad captain who does that," Tyler said, lightly.

"Really? I had no idea." *I thought the only thing the team captain had to do was throw his weight around,* George silently added.

Tyler put his arm around George's shoulders as though they were friends. "Peterson, I know you're not the kind of guy who sets out to make trouble, so I'm just going to tell you this once: try to take anything that's mine, and you're dead meat. And I mean *anything.*" He paused and added significantly, "When you see my babe at school, tell her I said hi."

FOURTEEN

JAMES' IDEA

ALLIE WAS GETTING IRRITATED WITH TYLER. HE WAS calling her at school all the time, asking to see her, and she had so much homework now that she couldn't keep going to the mall with Tyler and his friends after school.

"Honestly!" she exclaimed, snapping her cell phone closed after a lunch-hour call. "Every time I turn around!"

"Then why don't you just turn your phone off?" George asked. They were the only ones left in the classrooms — the others had already gone to the cafeteria.

Allie looked at him. "Is it bothering you?" He had seemed out of sorts around her recently.

"Yeah, it bothers me. You should break up with him."

"Break up with him?" she repeated. "Why?"

George looked out the window. "It's not like you're going to the same school with him," he muttered.

Allie stared, "So, what? You think I should only date guys I go to school with?"

That got him. George flushed red. "I didn't say that."

"Then what were you saying?"

"Nothing."

Allie tossed her phone from hand to hand. "Maybe you want me to break up with Tyler so you can ask me out?" She was enjoying making George blush.

"No! I'm not that dumb."

"Not dumb enough to go out with me?"

"No!"

"Then what's your problem?"

"You just don't seem to like Tyler very much."

Allie opened her mouth and closed it again. Finally she said, "We've been dating for nearly five months. He's taking me to the Halloween dance. I like him okay. Not that it's any of your business!"

George got up. She could see his embarrassment had turned to anger, "Okay, sorry. Forget I said anything."

"Fine! I will!" said Allie, irritated by his quick temper. This conversation was too strange, anyway.

George started out the door and almost ran into Celia.

"Oh!" Celia said. "Sorry! Was I interrupting?"

Allie felt a sinking feeling in her chest as her anger drained away. From the corner of her eye, she saw George going red again.

"Hey, Celia," he said. "What do you want?"

Celia said, hesitantly, "Well, I wanted to ask you . . . both of you really . . . if you could help me out with something?"

"What is it?" Allie said, sitting down at the closest desk. Somehow Celia always made her ashamed of losing her temper.

Celia's face took on a serious, earnest expression that Allie was quickly learning to recognize. George apparently recognized it too, because he heaved a deep sigh and rolled his eyes.

"I didn't even *say* anything yet!" Celia said.

Allie shot him a dirty look. "Go ahead, Celia."

"You know that idea that James had? About the All Saints' Day Party? I really do think it's a good idea. I think we should do it! It could be a lot of fun. Besides, no one really seems to . . . well, you know, *get along* with James, and using his idea would show that we *appreciate* him. Oh come *on*, George!" George had let out a groan at

James' name. "At least think about it! So I need you guys to help me convince the others. What do you think?"

"Well . . ." Allie said uneasily. "I guess we could try it. Even if it was James' idea."

"Won't that just encourage James in the wrong way?" George said acidly. "Honestly, Celia, he thinks that trick-or-treaters go to Hell!"

Celia sighed. "Would it be so terrible to do something that James wanted to do?"

"Personally, I think it's a waste of time. I don't know why you keep trying to include him in everything," George said. "*He* doesn't like any of us."

"Brian thinks the party's a good idea," Celia said. "And if you guys are on board, I'm sure we can convince Liz and J.P."

Allie shrugged. An All Saints' Party was kind of dorky, but not unbearably so; and it was obviously very important to Celia. "All right, let's do it!"

George was trying to keep a straight face. "And Celia can go as the patron saint of lost causes."

"Oh, come on, you guys!" Celia said, but she smiled.

"Wait a sec." Allie had a sudden thought. "When would this thing be, anyway?"

"Halloween night — this Friday, at eight, so Liz can still go trick-or-treating at seven."

"Sparrow Hills always has a big Halloween dance that night," Allie said wavering. "I'm going with Tyler."

"So go with him," George said grumpily.

"Maybe I could go to both . . ."

That was enough for Celia. "Okay then!" she said,

laughing and grabbing her lunch. She threw open the door. There was a thud and a hoarse cry of pain.

"James! I'm so sorry!"

James was standing in the hallway, holding both hands to his face. His face — what they could see of it — was screwed up in pain, and Celia was apologizing. "I'm so sorry! I didn't know you were out there!"

"What were you doing there?" George demanded.

"Coming back for my lunch," James retorted, nursing an angry red bump on his forehead.

"Maybe you better go put some ice on that," Allie said, trying to be helpful.

"James," Celia said impulsively, "We were just talking again about your idea for an All Saints' Day party. We really like it!"

"Yeah!" Allie said, thinking that she sounded phony.

James hardly seemed to be paying attention. "Really?" he muttered, feeling his bump.

"Yeah, let's do it," George said with a fake smile.

James looked at him with undisguised dislike. "And what saint are you going to be?"

Glaring back, George said, "Isn't that supposed to be a surprise?"

"We can keep our costumes a secret until the party and then everyone can guess which saints we are!" Celia said exultantly.

Great, Allie thought. She had no idea how to dress up like a saint, and if the costumes were supposed to be secret, how could she ask Celia for help? Plus, if she was going to both dances, she needed to find a costume that would qualify as a saint, but not look stupid at the Sparrow Hills Halloween dance.

"I certainly hope *you* will surprise us, Miss Weaver," Creepy Boy said, seeming to read her thoughts. "I suggest you look closely at the cloistered orders of nuns for inspiration."

Allie ignored him and turned to Celia. "Right. So what do saints wear?"

"I've got some books you can borrow," Celia said. "And I have all sorts of ideas for games and things . . ."

"No," James interrupted. "The party was my idea. I will do the planning. The rest of you can help, according to my directions."

George, clearly irritated by this, gritted his teeth. *Why did those two hate each other so much?* Allie wondered.

James waved his hand. "Don't worry, Georgie, I'll let you bake some brownies," he said contemptuously. "The rest of you can take care of the other refreshments. I'll plan the *main event.*"

Celia started talking again, and Allie and George, by an unspoken agreement, both ducked out the door and ran down the corridor as fast as they could. Looking at each other, they stifled their laughter until they were inside the cafeteria and had closed the doors. Then both of them burst out laughing, bewildering the other students.

"What is it?" J.P. demanded. "What?"

But George only gasped for breath, and Allie couldn't have explained it if she tried.

You look happy for a change," George's mom said when she arrived to pick him up.

He eased his bike into the back of the car with a practiced maneuver, then slammed the door and got into the front seat next to her. "Hey, Mom, where can I get a priest's cassock?"

His mom paused. "Hmm. I guess our pastor doesn't wear one. What about asking Fr. Borgia? We'll pass his rectory on our way home from the supermarket. He probably has one — but whether or not he'll loan it out is another matter."

Holy Child Parish was a small, run-down parish on the outskirts of town. It was the only local church that had an early Mass on weekdays. George's mom had been going to the 6 a.m. Mass there for as long as he could remember.

They rang the bell at the rectory. There was a long pause before the door opened. "Mrs. Peterson! George!" Fr. Borgia said, a little too loudly. "What a nice surprise! Come in!"

Fr. Borgia was a wiry Italian priest with iron-gray hair and a black patch over one eye — George used to imagine he'd lost his eye in a fight, and had been a little disappointed when he found out it was glaucoma.

Fr. Borgia seemed to be very interested John Paul 2 High. "How's it going over there?" he shouted, bringing a couple cans of soda into the rectory's living room. "I was in favor of it as soon as I heard of what they did to Dan Costain! The nerve of those people down at St. Lucy's! And they claim to be a *Catholic* school!" he snorted.

George shifted nervously in his chair. For some reason, no one ever talked about why John Paul 2 High had been started. But Fr. Borgia seemed to have no reservations.

"Is it true that they fired him because he was teaching *Humanae Vitae?*" Fr. Borgia roared. "Imagine that! Teaching a papal encyclical at a Catholic school! The horror!"

George, taking a gulp of his Coke, snorted in laughter and sprayed soda across the coffee table.

He apologized and started to clean up, but Fr. Borgia waved him off impatiently. "Don't worry about it," he said. "Do you have a chaplain at your school, son?"

"I don't think so," George admitted. "It's been a little disorganized."

"Hm. So, what brings you here?"

George cleared his throat, nervously.

The night before the party, Allie ignored Tyler's repeated calls and flipped through the four volumes of *Butler's Lives of the Saints* that Celia had lent her. "And that's not even all the saints," Celia had said cheerfully. "Pope John Paul 2 canonized lots more! But I don't have a volume on them yet."

This didn't cheer Allie up. Even with another volume she didn't think she'd find a single saint she could dress up as without looking stupid. Saints all seemed to wear flowing gowns or nun outfits, and she didn't have anything, *anything* that resembled that kind of costume.

"All right, Truth Person," she growled to nobody as she slumped on the floor by her mom's bed, staring into the closet. "If you're still following me around, then maybe you can tell me what I can wear to this saint party."

If you want to know the truth, you must look for it. It's that simple.

It wasn't as though she got an answer. It was just that, as she looked at the white summer dress hanging in her mom's closet, she suddenly got a really good idea. Or a passable one, at least.

She jumped up at once to work on her costume. But before she forgot, she whispered, "Thanks."

FIFTEEN

TWO BAD JOKES

AFTER DINNER, GEORGE GOT A RIDE TO THE school with the Costains and helped Celia unload the party things. Mr. Costain had to pick up one of Celia's younger sisters from cheerleading practice and would be back later.

"Do you think these will be all right?" Mr. Costain asked, handing George and Celia a rainbow pile of *Catholic Answer* tracts through the car window. The little pamphlets had titles such as "Are Catholics Born Again?" "Call No Man Father," "Do Catholics Worship Statues?"

"All right for what?" Celia asked.

"For the event tonight," Mr. Costain explained. "James said you needed Catholic tracts."

George looked at Celia quizzically. Celia also looked puzzled, but then she said, "Brian said his family has a 'Defending the Faith Night' on Halloween. Maybe James was thinking of doing the same thing at the party. I guess they'll be okay."

"It's what I had on hand," Mr. Costain said apologetically. "I don't know if I'll be able to be there the whole time — I was called into work tonight." Mr. Costain had been working night shifts as an assistant manager at the supermarket.

"We'll be fine," Celia assured him. "See you later, Dad!"

Yeah, fine. George thought that sitting around reading Catholic tracts to other Catholics was a pretty dumb idea for a party — what was James thinking? *Maybe he's thinking about educating Allie.* James's holier-than-thou attitude would trip him up there. George's lips curled involuntarily.

When you're finished with that," Celia said, "can you grab some stuff from the furnace room?"

"Like what?" George grunted, dragging the tables into position.

"Dad put soda and chips there earlier. The door's open."

"Okay," George said, walking toward the hallway. "I could use a break." *It's a good thing I'm not wearing my cassock yet,* he thought. *I would have messed it up.* The cassock Fr. Borgia had lent him was immaculately tailored and didn't look like it had ever been worn. It fit George well, but he felt kind of weird wearing it, especially when Allie Weaver kept popping into his mind.

I hope Fr. Borgia doesn't have any ideas about me becoming a priest, he thought nervously. *I mean, it's only a costume . . .*

The furnace room was near the center of the school. George had never been inside it before, but the old metal door opened with a creak when he turned the knob.

He walked into the darkened room, and immediately he was hit by a wave of revulsion. It smelled terrible in here; like there was a dead rat or something. *Gross.*

George found the light switch and turned it on. The sodas were right by the door. But the smell seemed to be getting *worse.*

Where is it coming from? The huge, ancient-looking furnace took up almost all the space, vents sprouting from its top and branching toward the ceiling.

The smell had to be coming . . . he sniffed deeply and almost gagged. It seemed to be coming from the furnace itself. He approached it nervously, wondering if it was going to blow up or something. Wisps of smoke seemed to be coming from one of the ventilators at the top furnace. *But it sure doesn't* smell *like smoke!*

Fighting a wave of nausea, George pulled on the ventilator. Loose screws popped. Clearly, someone had been here recently.

He reached in and felt something smooth and plastic. Mystified, he pulled it out. It was a clear plastic bottle with ugly yellow liquid in it. The smoke — and the smell — was rising from holes in the top of the bottle.

It's a stink bomb, he thought incredulously. *Someone put a stink bomb in the furnace!*

J.P. He growled inwardly. This wasn't funny. It was stinking up the room, and if he hadn't found it, it would have stunk up the whole school through the ventilation system the next time the furnace was turned on. *I can't believe he did this. I'm gonna kill him.*

Right now he had to get the stink bomb out of the school. He looked around frantically and grabbed a box of black garbage bags. He threw the plastic bottle into a bag, tied the drawstring tight, then double-bagged it. The smell grew less pungent; but the bag started to swell alarmingly.

Gotta get this thing outside. George ran for the door. *I am . . . really . . . going to kill J.P.!*

Here are your sodas," George said, clunking them down on one of the tables.

"It took you long enough," Celia said. "The others should be here any minute." She sniffed. "Do you smell something?"

"Uh . . ." George said uncomfortably. He had thrown the stink bomb into the woods outside the school. Then he had spent fifteen minutes in the bathroom washing his hands, changing into his costume and throwing away the undershirt he had been wearing, but apparently it wasn't enough.

"Where's James?" he asked. "I thought he was going to plan everything."

Celia shrugged, but looked worried. "I don't know," she admitted. "He was supposed to meet me here."

George looked around. The tables were covered with tablecloths, trays of snacks, and pictures of saints. One table also had books about saints, along with more pictures and photographs.

"I brought a tub so we could do bobbing for apples," Celia said, a little anxiously. "But I was hoping that James would have more things to do."

A door slammed.

"Maybe that's him now," Celia said. "Nice costume, by the way."

"Thanks." George fingered the cassock's tight collar.

"Who are you supposed to be?"

"St. John Bosco."

"Ah *ha!*" Celia said triumphantly. "You're not supposed to tell!"

"Oh, right." George said. He was still distracted by the stink bomb. "What about you? You're not even wearing your costume yet."

"You're right! Can you stay here and greet people while I get changed?" Celia grabbed her patchwork tote bag and dashed out of the gym. George grunted, not looking forward to having to deal with James.

But it wasn't James. A few seconds later, when the cafeteria door creaked open, George looked up to see — an angel. Allie Weaver stood there, wearing a fluttery white dress and feathery white angel wings. Glittery flecks sparkled in her blond hair and around her blue eyes. Despite her uncomfortable, cornered-again-by-crazy-Catholics expression, she was still a knockout. George felt his jaw hanging.

"Wow . . ." he said. "Hey, Allie. Nice costume. You look beautiful."

She laughed nervously. "Thanks. I was looking for something, you know, that would work for this thing and for the Sparrow Hills dance tonight." Her nose crinkled, "What's that smell?"

George felt his face get hot. *I'm going to kill J.P.*, he thought. *I really am.*

Allie was surprised by the costumes that the JP2 kids had made. First there was George, dressed up as some type of priest. Then Brian, wearing a breastplate of juice-can lids and had a wooden shield and plastic sword. Allie thought he must be a knight.

Next Liz walked in, dressed as an old lady. She had powdered her hair and was wearing a shawl, granny glasses, and, weirdly enough, she had put a pillow under her dress to make her look pregnant.

"Who are you supposed to be?" Allie asked, and Liz had given her a 'duh' look.

"Isn't it obvious?" she said. "Just think of my name!"

"Oh . . . yeah, right," Allie said, and hoped her ignorance hadn't shown.

Then J.P. arrived. *His* costume, at least, was obvious. He was wrapped in a white bed sheet, carrying a staff made from a tree branch, and wearing a cardboard pope hat on his head. When he entered the gym he raised one hand in mock blessing. "Tha Lord . . . be with you!" he said in what was apparently supposed to be an imitation of Pope John Paul II's accent.

"Oh, look who's here," George grumbled. He seemed to be in a bad mood. "The life of the party."

"John Paul is *always* the life of the party, my friend," J.P. said expansively. Then he shook his head. "Whoa: my name is John Paul, I'm dressed as Pope John Paul, and I'm *at John Paul 2 High School.* This is like, mind-blowing!"

"J.P.," Liz said, giving him a funny look. "Is it just me, or did you make your pope hat out of *a pizza box?*"

"Do you know how hard it is to find *white* cardboard?" J.P. said. "Cut me some slack!"

"Is James here yet?" Celia came into the gym wearing a beautiful, old-fashioned gown, her hair flowing around her shoulders. The only puzzling thing about her costume was that she had drawn a thin red line around her neck. It was a little jarring.

"Hi, Celia," Allie said, walking up to her. "Nice . . . costume. What's that thing on your neck for?"

"You don't know?" Celia said, smiling. "Well, just think of my name . . ."

196

"Never mind," sighed Allie. She was glad that no one from Sparrow Hills was here to see her hanging out with . . . well, saints.

George kept looking for a chance to pull J.P. aside and yell at him, but the guy kept bouncing around the room, picking sword fights with Brian, poking Liz with his crosier, and pronouncing random blessings and excommunications on everything. Finally, after Celia had made them pose for a group photo, George caught him alone at the drink table, where J.P. was consigning Diet Pepsi to the depths of hell.

"Hey, J.P.," he said, glaring at him. "Nice stunt you pulled today."

"I know!" J.P. said with a goofy smile. "Of course, I had to put it together at the last minute . . ."

I can't believe he thinks it's a joke! George thought.

". . . but once I found the pizza box, the whole thing came together," J.P. said.

"What?" George said. "I was talking about your other stunt. *The stink bomb.*"

J.P. looked mystified, "What are you talking about?"

"Stop it," George said impatiently. "I *know* you put a stink bomb in the furnace. You could have ruined the whole party. It's *not* funny."

"Somebody put a stink bomb in the furnace?" J.P. said. "Wow. That's pretty cool."

"Uh, *no*, actually it's not," George growled.

"It must have been the *poltergeist,*" J.P. said, his eyes widening. "Whoa! I was joking before, but maybe the poltergeist . . . is *real!*"

George gritted his teeth and prayed for patience.

"Man! We should set some traps for him!" J.P. said. "Maybe we should set them up tonight! We gotta catch this ghost!"

"Traps?" George said and wished he hadn't. He didn't know what J.P. was talking about, and he really didn't want to know.

"Yeah!" J.P. said enthusiastically. "Hold on a sec . . ." He pulled something out of his pocket. "Look!"

He held up a small metal cylinder, with a plastic horn protruding from the top.

"A miniature air horn!" J.P. said conspiratorially. "It'll make the loudest sound you ever heard! Perfect for alarms! We could rig it so when the poltergeist comes in . . ."

"Sure," George said snatching the air horn. "Or blow it in someone's ear when they weren't looking?"

"Hey! I need that!" J.P. said. "Give it back!"

George walked away, ignoring J.P.'s protests

Celia was pouring herself a soda, "What was that all about?"

"J.P. had this," George held up the mini air horn.

Celia took it and sighed. "I'll give it to Dad," she said, slipping it into her purse.

"Don't push that button on the top, or it will make a real loud noise. There's something else," George said, gritting his teeth. "J.P. put a — "

"Dad!" Celia exclaimed. "What are you doing here?"

Mr. Costain had just walked into the gym. "Hello!" he said, smiling broadly. "Well, I have to say I'm very impressed. Very good costumes, one and all." He picked up the Catholic tracts from one of the display tables. "Here's some for you, Liz. And you, J.P., why don't you take the ones on John Paul II? And George, you might as well take the ones on celibacy and the priesthood . . . I think I have — yes, here's one on angels for you, Miss Weaver. Celia, you can take these ones on salvation and indulgences . . . I think that's all of them."

Everyone stared at the tracts. "Catholic trivia, right?" J.P. said hopefully, looking with some confusion at his copy of "Was Peter in Rome"?

But even more confusingly, Mr. Costain didn't explain the rules of the game. He just said, "Ready to go? Sorry to rush you, but I've got to get to work." And with that, he walked out of the gym.

One by one, they followed him out. George caught up with Celia and whispered. "Go where? What's going on?"

"I don't know," she answered, shrugging. "Maybe he's got a surprise for us or something. I wonder where James is? I hope he shows up for this . . ."

They followed Mr. Costain down the darkened hallway and out the front doors, where the Costain's van stood with the engine rumbling. "Come on, pile in!" he said.

One by one, they piled into the van. Allie had some trouble getting in because of her wings, and George helped her slip them off.

"Thanks," she said, and sat next to him in the van. "Hey," she said in a lower voice, "do you know where we're going?"

"No idea."

I wonder where James is?" Celia said again while her dad took a call on his cell phone.

"Do you have to keep asking?" Allie asked in some exasperation. "It's not as though he's the life of the party."

"But it is *his* party," Celia said, a little nervously. "I hope he didn't get into an accident on the way over."

"Okay, Brian, I give up," Liz said, changing the subject. "Who are you?"

"St. Martin of Tours," Brian said. "You know, the Roman soldier who gave his cloak to the beggar. That's why I'm wearing only half a cape."

"Oh. Yeah," said Liz. "How about you, Allie? There are angel saints like St. Michael, but I don't remember any *girl* angel saints."

"Maybe she's Saint *Michelle*," said J.P. "Or Saint *Gabrielle*."

"Who are they?" Allie said grumpily.

"St. Michelle is St. Michael's wife," J.P. said authoritatively. "And St. Gabrielle is St. Gabriel's wife."

The van erupted into laughter, except for Allie and Brian. "Angels don't have wives," Brian said, frowning. "They're spirits."

"Oh yeah? Then where did all those cherubs come from?" J.P. said.

"We're here!" Mr. Costain said suddenly.

To Allie's surprise, the van had stopped at Sparrow Hills. "Everybody out!" Mr. Costain said when no one moved.

Celia opened the door and everyone slid out.

Maybe this is something Catholics always do for All Saints' Day, Allie thought. *I wish someone had told me!* She wasn't exactly prepared to be seen in public with her classmates dressed as they were.

Mr. Costain rolled down his window. "You guys ready? When James said he'd be meeting you here to evangelize at the Halloween dance, I didn't think you'd be up for it. I'm impressed."

Not noticing the stunned silence that greeted his words, he continued, "I'll be back at ten-thirty to pick you up," he said. "Keep the faith!" He drove away with a wave.

For a moment all of them stood there, gaping at the departing van. Then, after it had disappeared into the darkness, a gabble of panicked voices broke out.

"What just happened?"

"Did he say EVANGELIZE?"

"This was James' *main event?*"

It was clear that everyone was as surprised as Allie, but her first instinct was to put as much distance between her and the Catholic weirdness as she could. "Well — see you guys!" she said, waving and hurrying toward the dance.

George gaped for a moment as the white angel vanished through the massive bank of doors. "Hey . . . wait!" he finally said, but Allie was long gone.

Not knowing what else to do, he looked around. Sparrow Hills kids in costumes — normal Halloween costumes — stood in clumps, smoking, talking, and looking curiously at the group of "saints." The JP2 kids instinctively huddled together.

"Whose idea was this?" Liz said in a panicked voice.

"James' idea," George said tightly.

"Can't we just walk back to our school through the woods?" Brian asked.

"Hey, you kids!" A strange adult in an African mask was walking toward them, making pushing motions with his hands. "No loitering outside!" he said crisply. "If you're going to the dance, get inside!"

There were groans and arguments from the other groups, but teacher-chaperones were herding everyone through the doors, and before the JP2 kids could get away, they were inside.

The lobby was filled with crowds of students, dressed in an amazing variety of costumes. At first glance, George saw a bunch of vampires, some movie characters. Some kids were dressed up as rap stars, one guy dressed up as Austin Powers, and even a few kids dressed up as Zorro. There was even a guy dressed up as a toothbrush.

But the John Paul 2 kids got more than a few stares and smirks as they moved through the crowd.

"Nice costume," someone called out at Liz. "What are you supposed to be, the knocked-up grandma?"

"Hey, Peter Pan!" someone said to a reddening Brian. "Nice sword! But someone ripped your cape!"

"Hey, your Holiness! Come here and bless me!" a girl dressed as a go-go dancer said.

J.P. moved forward, an eager look on his face; but Celia grabbed him by the collar. "You are *not* blessing that girl," she said between gritted teeth.

"I don't think they're going to let us in. See? They're checking I.D.s at the door." Liz whispered.

George figured she was right, but when they reached the table in front of the entrance to the gym, the gorilla asking for identification roared at him, "Peterson! Burke! What a surprise!"

"Coach?" George said hesitantly.

"Yeah, that's me," the gorilla said in Mr. Lamar's voice, and tapped itself on the head. "Are these other kids from your school?"

"Um, yeah," George said. "Actually, it's pretty much the *whole* school."

Mr. Lamar laughed and stamped the back of their hands with a pumpkin stamp. "No problem. Enjoy the dance. Happy Halloween!"

He waved them through the double doors, and they were engulfed by the darkness within.

SIXTEEN

SAINTS
VS. SPOOKS

ALLIE STOPPED RUNNING ONCE SHE GOT through the main doors. She felt a twinge of guilt. *I shouldn't have done that.* But the thought of handing out Catholic tracts at the coolest dance of the school year was enough to make anyone panic.

She decided not to think about it anymore. She craned her neck to look for Tyler, Nikki, and the rest of her friends among the bizarre and spooky costumes in the lobby. An involuntary shudder passed through her when she saw students dressed in trench coats and hoods as *Praxor's Game* characters. *Calm down! Where's Tyler?*

"Babe!" a familiar voice called out. "Over here!"

Allie breathed a sigh of relief as she spotted Tyler standing in a corner of the lobby, wearing a pinstriped suit, shades, and slicked-back hair. Madison was with him, looking bored and sophisticated as usual. She was wearing a black cocktail dress, fishnets, spike heels, and a glittery witch's hat.

"What, are you supposed to be an angel or something?" Tyler said as Allie walked over.

"Brilliant, Holmes," Allie said. "And you're the God-father."

"Something like that," Tyler said, flashing his usual toothy smile. "I thought you'd be stuck hanging with the Catholic kids."

"I ditched them," Allie said. "Hey, Madison. Great costume."

Madison nodded slightly. "Yeah, I guess," she said in a languid voice. "I like your angel wings. Kind of fitting, you know?"

"I don't know about that," Tyler said with a smirk. "Just kidding!" he said hastily when Allie glared at him.

She didn't get Tyler sometimes. "What are you guys doing out here?"

"*I* was going out to catch a smoke," Madison said distantly. "Speaking of which . . ." She walked away.

"Come on," Tyler said, grabbing Allie's arm. "Wait till you see the haunted house. It is *awesome*."

Allie let herself be led away, trying not to dwell on the fact that her boyfriend had been hanging out with one of the hottest girls in Sparrow Hills. *Stop imagining things*, she told herself.

The Halloween dance was the most popular event at Sparrow Hills; so popular, in fact, that they had to use more than one gym. The main cafeteria had dancing and food, so Tyler and Allie went there first. The "Monster Mash" was blaring as they stepped through the doors.

"Want to dance?" Tyler yelled in Allie's ear.

"Not yet!" Allie yelled back. She was still annoyed with Tyler. "Show me the haunted house first!"

Tyler grinned. "You got it, babe!" He led her across the crowded dance floor, through hordes of furiously dancing kids, to the other side of the gym. The doors there normally led to a hallway; but now the threshold was decorated to look like a monstrous open mouth. TUNNEL OF TERROR, a large sign read over the door, with a subtitle: ABANDON ALL HOPE, YE WHO ENTER HERE. A row of pointy teeth brushed their heads as they passed through.

Oh brother, Allie thought. *Abandon all hope? That's so cheesy. The teeth are pretty cool though . . .*

Inside, the hallway walls were covered in the predictable haunted house style, with black fabric on the walls and the lights covered with blue cellophane. Spooky organ music was playing.

"Is this it?" Allie whispered to Tyler as they walked down the hallway. "It's not too bad . . ."

"AAAAAAAUUUUGGGHHHH!" Two dark figures rushed toward her. She screamed and dug her nails into Tyler's arm.

"Ow!" he said, and burst out laughing. Then Allie realized the figures were Flynt and Brock in flowing black robes. Flynt was grinning through white face paint. Brock wore a skull mask that hid his smile.

"Got you, Weaver!" Flynt crowed, and they melted back into the shadows.

Allie took a shaky breath.

"You scared, babe?" Tyler said. "You almost cut me with your nails!"

Allie tried to laugh it off. "That was pretty cool."

Tyler didn't know how much the dark figures of Flynt and Brock had looked, for a moment, like the trench-coated figure in a hallway just like this one. Scared? She'd been *terrified.*

It's just a haunted house. You're just freaking out for no reason. That's *the truth.*

But wasn't there someone, probably here right now, who really *was* out to get her? Wasn't *that* the truth? Allie didn't *like* the truth: it was too scary.

"Babe, you're like, cutting off my circulation," Tyler muttered.

"Sorry," Allie whispered, loosening her grip. At that moment, she didn't care if Tyler called her babe, and was a bully, and had been hanging out with Madison. He was big, and strong, and solid. *He* could protect her. That nerdy little Truth Guy . . . she wasn't so sure.

The dance turned out to be inside one of Sparrow Hills' gyms; and as George pulled open one of the double doors, he was immediately blasted by a wave of talking and loud music. The place was packed. There were crowds everywhere . . . loud music . . . smoke machines . . . kids in costumes dancing frenetically.

"Isn't this kind of . . . creepy?" Celia asked behind him.

"What did you expect? It's Halloween," George said.

It was a *little* creepy, though. People wore weird costumes — some of them pretty gruesome — and, with the dim lights, the smoke, and the clashing music, the effect was unsettling.

J.P. didn't seem to mind; he headed for the food, then the dance floor, chatting with everyone he met. Celia and Brian stayed close to George. Liz slouched behind them, embarrassed.

"Where's Allie?" Celia yelled in his ear.

"I don't know," he yelled back.

"I think we should find her," Celia yelled.

"What? Why?" George yelled. "She ditched us!"

But Celia grabbed him by the arm and pulled him back out of the gym. In the hallway again, she said, "We should find Allie, George."

"Why? She's probably hanging out with her friends. She obviously doesn't want to be seen with us." *Or with me*, he thought bitterly.

Celia didn't reply for a moment: she seemed to be deep in thought. "Look, I really can't explain it. I just think we should find her."

George sighed in exasperation. "Fine." It wasn't like things could get any worse.

The Tunnel of Terror took Tyler and Allie to the wrestling gym, or THE LOVE SHACK, according to the glittery sign over the doors. Inside, the gym had been turned into a dance floor. The lights of half the gym were turned off and the music, while still loud, was more of the slow-dance kind. The other side of the gym, still had the lights on, and there were some kids playing basketball and goofing off — mostly freshmen, she guessed, or the kind of kids who didn't like dances.

"*Now* we get to dance," Tyler said.

"Sure," Allie said. It wasn't the most romantic setting, but it would do.

Tyler pulled her onto the dance floor. He put his arms around her and they swayed slowly to the music. Allie felt the sudden urge to do something crazy — kiss him, or put her head on his chest and cry, or something. She was still scared, and she still didn't know why.

For a while she didn't say or think anything — she just let Tyler lead her as they swayed clumsily back and forth on the dance floor. She ignored the fact that he was a horrible dancer, or that his hands were hot and sweaty on her back — she just let the soft, sweet music wash over her.

Most of all, she ignored the Truth Guy, who suddenly seemed to appear and start asking questions: *Does Tyler love you? Does he care about you? Can he really protect you? Does he even want to?*

Go away, Truth Guy, she said back. *I don't care. I just want to dance with my boyfriend.*

George walked up to J.P., who was chatting with a couple of cute girls. "Come on," he said, grabbing his arm, "We need to find Allie."

"George!" J.P. said, fixing him with a manic smile. "I was just talking to Melissa and Tiffany here. Mel, Tiff, this is my buddy George. He's the best wrestler in the state — went to the championships last year."

Melissa smiled flirtatiously at George. "*Really?*" she said. "Are you on the wrestling team? Nice costumes, by the way. You two make a good match."

"Yeah, sure, whatever," George said impatiently. "J.P., we really need to find Allie."

"Allie Weaver?" said Tiffany. "She went that way," she pointed to the opposite side of the gym. "With that big jock — what's his name, Tyler."

"Thanks," George said, and started to drag J.P. away.

"Aren't you guys from that Catholic school?" Tiffany said. "What are you doing here, anyway?"

"We're *evangelizing!*" J.P. said, throwing his arms out in a papal gesture. "Isn't it obvious?"

Tiffany didn't laugh. "Really?" she said. "That's kind of neat. I really do like your costumes too, by the way."

"Yeah, they're original," Melissa chimed in. "I liked the pope," she added. "I was really sad when he died."

George was astonished. "Oh, well," he stammered, and found himself digging in his pocket. "Maybe I have something about him . . ."

"Here," J.P. said, and walked up with an uncharacteristically serious expression. He handed Melissa a pamphlet with the title *John Paul the Great: A Pope for the Ages.* "There's some really cool stuff in there about him."

"Cool!" Melissa said. "Thanks, uh . . . what was your name again?"

J.P. colored a little. "I *told* you," he said. "J.P."

"No, I mean your *real* name."

"That *is* my real name!"

"Okay, come on," George said, dragging J.P. away.

"Can I get your number?" J.P. yelled.

"Come *on!*" George said, trying not to grin.

After a few more songs, Allie wasn't feeling quite so romantic any more, but Tyler wouldn't let her go. He held her close and whispered, "Allie . . ."

"Mmmm, yeah?" Allie responded, shifting uncomfortably. Her back was starting to get itchy.

"I've really missed you . . ."

"Thank you," Allie said, and then thought that wasn't enough. "I missed you too."

"Hey Allie . . . You look really hot tonight."

Allie didn't know what to say. She felt hot, but only because Tyler's sweaty hands were pressed against her back. It was getting kind of gross. The only thing she could do was nestle closer to him and wish desperately that he would just shut up and dance with her.

"When I saw you tonight," Tyler said. "The first thing I thought was how sexy you looked."

Was that supposed to be a compliment?

"I just saw you there, and I was like . . . wow! She is *soooo* hot. What a babe. Wow." His hands shifted again on her back, and Allie suddenly became aware that he was trembling with excitement.

This whole thing seemed . . . familiar, somehow. Why was that?

Suddenly she remembered how George had looked, just a few hours ago, when he had seen her in her costume — how his jaw had dropped, and what he had said: *Wow. You look beautiful.*

Then the Truth Guy was at her elbow again. But this time he wasn't asking awkward questions. *You're beautiful, Allie,* was all he said, over and over again. *George was right. You're beautiful.*

Suddenly she felt sad. George had said she was beautiful. And she had ditched George to be with this guy, who said that she was "hot" and "sexy." George's jaw had dropped when he had seen her; Tyler had practically licked his lips . . .

Allie pushed Tyler away as gently as she could manage. "I — I think I have something in my eye." She put her hand over one eye, being careful not to smudge her mascara. "Be right back."

Tyler gave her a funny look. Was he annoyed? Angry? "Sure, babe," he said grudgingly. "I'll be here."

She started to walk away but ran into someone with a jolt. She cursed under her breath and muttered, "Sorry."

"Allie?"

It was George.

Allie looked very, very flustered as she backed away from him. "George! Uh . . . hey. What are *you* doing here?"

George found himself at a loss for words. *I came looking for you,* he wanted to say. *Because Celia said I should find you . . . and because* I *wanted to find you.* But he couldn't say that. It would sound stupid.

"Peterson!" Tyler Getz strode forward. He wasn't smiling now. He looked furious. "What are *you* doing here?"

George felt a flash of irritation. He did *not* want to deal with Tyler right now. "What, do I need your permission?"

"You don't go to school here," Tyler snarled. "How did you get in?"

"Coach let me in, if you need to know."

"Yeah, Coach Holy Roller just loves you religious types, doesn't he?" Tyler smiled sourly. "That's probably the only reason he let you and the shrimp join the squad."

Couples around them stopped dancing and began to look in their direction.

Tyler turned to Brian with a nasty grin. "Hey, Burke," he said, nodding mockingly to Brian, J.P., and Liz. "Cool costumes. You guys *really* fit in. Especially Peterson. A Catholic priest. Guess we better keep the kids away."

Shock and indignation spiked through George's chest. "What?"

"I *said,*" Tyler said, relishing the words, "we better keep the underage boys away from you, Peterson. We know how Catholic priests are . . ."

215

The anger hit George like a bowling ball, punching into his stomach and nearly taking away his breath with its force. "Take that back," he said hoarsely.

"Take what back?"

"What you said about Catholic priests."

"What if I don't want to?"

"Then I'll make you."

"Make me how?"

George stared into Tyler's eyes. "Let's go."

Tyler chortled. "You asking for a smackdown, Peterson? Right here?"

"I'm not asking you for nothing," George growled. "I'm *telling* you that I'm gonna take you down. Right here. That is, if you're up for it. Come on. I know you've wanted to have a go at me — well, here's your big chance."

Tyler's eyes glinted. "Sure," he said in a low voice, almost a whisper. "Oh, sure, Georgie boy, I am *so* up for it. Okay, listen up!" he shouted to the whole gym. "Kill the music, Billy!"

The music suddenly stopped; apparently the DJ was a buddy of Tyler's. All the dancers on the floor stopped, too, looking towards them with curious expressions.

"Sorry to interrupt," Tyler said, flashing a smile. "But I have a little announcement to make. Me and George Peterson here are going to have a special exhibition match, right here, right now. Feel free to gather around and watch! Tell your friends! Spread the word! I guarantee it'll be quite a show." He turned back to George, his smile more shark-like than ever. "Whaddya say, Peterson? We can pull out a mat over there," he jerked his thumb towards the other end of the gym, "and we'll do it."

"Sounds good to me," George didn't drop his gaze.

Tyler chuckled again. "Man, I'm going to *love* this, Peterson," he said. "Thank you *so* much. Let's go."

They both made their way to the other end of the gym, and pulled out one of their practice mats from under the bleachers. "I got my gear in the locker room," Tyler said. "Be right back, Peterson." He strode away.

George suddenly became aware that there were more and more people coming into the gym; apparently the word was spreading quickly.

"George!" Celia said, running up to him. "What are you *doing*? Are you crazy? You can't start a fight here!"

"He's not starting a fight," Brian said. "They're just going to have a match. It's okay."

"Oh yeah?" Celia said angrily. "I don't see how it's okay . . ."

"He's defending the honor of Catholic priests," Brian said solemnly.

"Seal," George said. "I have to do this."

Celia opened her mouth to reply, but he cut her off. "Look, remember how you said that we *had* to find Allie, but you didn't know why? Well, I just *have* to do this, okay?"

Celia looked bewildered for a second . . . and then, throwing up her hands, she backed away.

Thank God, George thought. With his heart still pounding, he began to unbutton the cassock. Luckily he was wearing clothes that would work for wrestling underneath: shorts, a T-shirt, and sneakers. There were a couple of hoots and whistles from the rapidly growing crowd as he pulled the cassock over his head and handed it to Celia.

"Make sure this thing stays safe and doesn't get dirty or anything."

"Hey, George!"

George looked up at a kid in a werewolf costume. It was Mahoney, the freckle-faced rookie, and he looked both excited and kind of nervous. "You're gonna wrestle Tyler, right?"

"Yeah," George said.

"Cool," Mahoney said. "Kick his butt for me, okay?"

"Uh . . . sure," George said. "Will do."

There was one more thing to do. Disregarding any thoughts of how he might look to anyone, he went down on one knee, bowed his head, and closed his eyes.

"Lord . . ." he muttered, and then realized that he didn't know what to say; he wasn't even sure if God would approve of what he was doing. "Lord," he began again. "Please let me do well. I guess I'm sticking my neck out again, but this time I'm not going to complain. I was dressed up like a priest tonight . . . and I guess that means that I have to do well to make priests look good. Please defend me as I go into battle. Uh . . . may your will be done. Amen."

"Are you done?"

He looked up, and there was Tyler, glowering at him, dressed in his Sparrow Hills singlet, wrestling shoes and headpiece.

George got up; and Tyler tossed him another headpiece.

"Thanks," George said, taken aback.

"I don't want to accidentally rip your ears off," Tyler said casually. "It'll look bad on my record."

"That's really big of you," George shot back, and strapped the headpiece on. "So, are we gonna get somebody to ref this?"

"Why?" Tyler sneered. "You want someone to rescue you when things get rough?"

"No," George said. "I just want it to be fully documented when I smack you down. Anybody want to ref?" he called to the crowd. "Anybody?"

For a long moment, there was no reply. He saw several Sparrow Hills wrestlers in the crowd, but from the looks on their faces they seemed to be on Tyler's side. Flynt and Brock were standing together with arms folded and smirks on their faces. Next to them was Allie, shifting back and forth with an anxious look on her face. *I wonder if she's worried about Tyler, or me . . . Better not think about it right now.*

"Come on," he said. "We need a ref!"

Finally, somebody stepped forward: Henderson, one of the veterans, a big guy who filled the 212-pound class on the Sparrow Hills squad. "I'll ref for you guys," he said in his deep, husky voice.

"Okay," George said, breathing a sigh of relief. He didn't know Henderson very well; he was a quiet guy. But he had never joined in either the hazings or the teasings of Brian. *That's as good as I'm gonna get*, he thought. *I just hope he's fair.*

"You guys want to do this the usual way?" Henderson asked. "Three periods? Two minutes each?"

"Sure," George said.

"I don't think it'll take that long," Tyler sneered.

Henderson checked his watch. "Okay," he rumbled. "Take your positions."

As he and Tyler faced each other, the noises became louder in the crowd. George heard catcalls from the crowd: "Get him, Tyler!" "Let's go, Getz!" Someone started a chant, "Ty-ler, Ty-ler . . ." and the crowd took it up with enthusiasm.

"Go George!" Celia yelled, apparently back on his side again. J.P., Liz, and Brian stood next to her, easy to pick out in their saint costumes.

For a moment George glanced up at the crowd; there were Sparrow Hills kids gathered all around, and more in the bleachers. In that moment, all the grim, bizarre costumes seemed sinister. It was almost as if he was surrounded by witches, monsters, and demons. A crazy thought shot through his head: *Maybe this is what the martyrs felt like, in the Coliseum.*

"*GO!*" Henderson roared.

SEVENTEEN

CHOOSING SIDES

THIS IS CRAZY, ALLIE THOUGHT AS TYLER AND

George lunged at each other. *I can't believe this is happening.*

"Who's keeping score?" someone asked.

"Take him down, Tyler!" Flynt yelled.

"Hey, is anybody keeping score?" asked another wrestler whose name she didn't know.

"Nah, Matt, it'll be over before that," Brock said.

"I don't know," Matt said. "Peterson's pretty good . . ."

George and Tyler were locked together, straining and shifting. They looked evenly matched.

"*TAKEDOWN!*" Flynt yelled. "What did I tell you? Yeah, Tyler!"

Tyler had knocked George off his feet and was using his powerful shoulders to force George's torso down.

"Pin him! Pin him!" yelled the crowd. It looked as if the match would be over in seconds. Already Henderson was lying down, watching for the instant George's shoulders touched the mat.

"Go, Tyler!" Flynt yelled. "Allie, you see what's going on? He's gonna pin him!"

People all around chanted, "Ty-ler! Ty-ler!" and Allie found herself joining in. "Ty-ler! Ty-ler!" she yelled.

But I don't want either *of them to win,* she thought. *I want it to be a tie. Please, God, let it be a tie . . .*

The crowd roared. George had done something — she hadn't seen what — to get free, and now *he* was on top.

"Escape!" Flynt snarled. The effect was grisly in his white face paint. "That kid is slippery!"

"No way, man! That's a reversal!" Matt objected.

"It's an escape!" Flynt retorted. "Two to one!"

"He's got control!" Matt shouted back. "Two to two!"

Allie had no idea what they were talking about, but she saw Tyler struggle, and with a massive heave, he ripped free of George's grasp. Now both wrestlers fell back, panting heavily.

"Getz escape!" Flynt crowed. "Three to one!"

"Three to two!" Mahoney retorted. "Good thing *you're* not reffing, Flynt!"

A moment later, both wrestlers were grappling again; and this time, it was George who got the takedown; he wrapped his hands around Tyler's waist, got Tyler's head between his legs, and heaved him to the ground.

"Come on, Tyler!" Brock screamed; but try as he might, Tyler couldn't seem to escape from George's grasp.

But George couldn't pin Tyler either. Both boys grappled until Henderson yelled, "STOP!"

"Peterson's up by one," Brock grunted. "That's how Henderson's gonna score it, anyway."

Sure enough, Henderson yelled out, "Peterson's up four to three! Ready?"

The two combatants trudged out to face each other again. Tyler still looked trim in his Sparrow Hills singlet, but George looked a little the worse for wear with his now-rumpled T-shirt and sweat pants.

"*GO!*"

Immediately Tyler charged at George, wrapped his arms around him, and threw him to the mat. Allie gasped, and the crowd roared, and several wrestlers cried out, "Takedown! Another takedown!"

"Come on, George!" someone on the other side of the crowd yelled — it sounded like Celia.

Tyler forced one of George's shoulders down to the mat, but George had managed to get one arm free, and was propping himself up with it; it looked excruciatingly painful. But Tyler kept bearing down, and again it looked like a pin was coming.

With a roar, George pushed Tyler off of him, and then grabbed both of Tyler's legs. For a long time both wrestlers panted and heaved in a deadlock.

"That ties it up," she heard Flynt yell.

The stalemate went on for a long time, neither combatant able to gain the advantage. Finally, Henderson yelled "*STOP!*" and they separated.

It could go either way at this point, Allie thought. *But which way do I want it to go?*

George put his hands on his knees and panted heavily. He wished he had some water; that last bout had been tough. He wished he had his singlet, too; Tyler kept grabbing his shirt when they were locked up.

How am I gonna win this thing? He had known Tyler was good, and he wouldn't have bet on himself in a match between them. They hadn't ever wrestled each other before: Coach Lamar had never matched them . . . George realized he was just going on instinct out there: he didn't have a plan.

"Come, on, think!" he whispered to himself. Tyler's got more upper body strength — but he's slow. I can keep getting points on escapes, but that's not going to do me much good if he keeps taking me down. Two points per takedown, only one point for an escape.

"You ready?" Henderson asked him.

"Yeah," George grunted, and walked out to face Tyler once again. Tyler wasn't looking so cocky anymore; but he still had a confident look on his face. *He knows he can win on points*, George thought. *I've got to pin him to win this thing.*

"George! George!" He heard Brian's voice from behind him, and without thinking, he looked around.

"Hey, Peterson! Let's go!" Tyler shouted.

"You're a biker, George!" Brian yelled. "A *biker!*"

So what? What is he talking about?

"Peterson!" Henderson yelled. "Are you ready or not?"

George turned back to Tyler and nodded. *I'm a biker. So what?*

"GO!"

Tyler didn't rush him this time; maybe he was getting tired. They both trudged forward warily and got into a lock. When Tyler tried to heave him off his feet again, George kept his feet firmly planted. Then Tyler grabbed George's left thigh, and yanked . . . but George was ready for that too; besides, he had a lot of leg power from . . .

Biking. That was it. Tyler had stronger arms and shoulders — but George had stronger *legs*. From biking. He just had to get in the right position . . .

But they were still locked up, and he wasn't going to throw Tyler. So the only solution was . . .

George relaxed his tensed shoulders, and immediately he fell, borne down by Tyler's strength. He hit the mat, and knew that he was now down on points. Now he *had* to pin Tyler to win.

Using every ounce of speed and cunning he had, George wrapped both legs around Tyler's waist, locked his ankles behind Tyler's back, and then pushed and twisted at the same time.

Tyler wasn't expecting that. George was able to flip him over with ease, and suddenly he was on top, his face only a few inches away from Tyler's.

"Come on, George!" a familiar voice yelled.

He looped both arms underneath Tyler's armpits, immobilizing them, pressed his chest against Tyler's chest and *pushed*. He felt Tyler's panic as he realized he was trapped. George continued to push relentlessly, getting onto his knees to give himself more leverage. Slowly, Tyler's chest went down . . . down . . . until his shoulders hit the mat.

"Come *on*, George!" The voice yelled again, growing more shrill and excited. It couldn't be Allie, could it?

Tyler gave a massive, desperate heave with his shoulders, forcing them up for an instant. But George forced him down again, and he felt both shoulders hit the mat . . . one second . . . two seconds . . . it had to be more than two seconds by now, right?

Henderson's palm slapped the mat. "*PIN!*"

That's it, George thought dazedly. *I did it.*

He let Tyler go, rolled off him, and lay on the mat, taking deep breath after deep breath, as the roar of the crowd washed over him.

Brock looked stunned. Flynt was shaking with silent fury. But Allie didn't care; she was screaming her heart out now as Henderson lifted George's arm into the air. "*Yes!*" she whooped. "All *right!*"

The whole crowd was cheering for George now; even some wrestlers were joining in, especially the younger ones. She glimpsed J.P. jumping up and down like a maniac, his pope hat falling off; Celia was hopping with joy.

Suddenly Allie noticed that Flynt and Brock were staring at her in astonishment. *What am I doing?* she thought. *Uh . . . this might look bad . . .*

"What's going on here?"

Silence fell as Coach Lamar strode into the gym. He was still wearing the gorilla suit, but he had taken off the mask, and there was a surprised, angry look on his face.

"Getz! Peterson! What's going on here?"

Tyler and George froze. Neither of them said a word.

"We had a match, Coach," said Henderson. "Tyler and George wrestled. I officiated."

"Really?" Coach Lamar said. "Who won?"

"George pinned in the third period. But Tyler was up on points."

"It was awesome!" Mahoney said. "The best match I've ever seen!"

"Okay, quiet, everyone!" Coach Lamar said. He was still frowning but looked less angry. "Getz, Peterson. Are you both okay?"

"Yeah," they both mumbled.

"Good. Because if either of you had gotten hurt, you'd *both* be off the squad. You too, Henderson. I don't want to see my best players down with injuries because of an unsupervised match. Now get out of here. I don't want to see your faces in this school again until Monday. Got it?"

They nodded mutely and looked relieved to not have any worse punishment.

The crowd started to disperse, and Allie watched as the JP2 students greeted George enthusiastically, hugging him and slapping him on the back.

I should congratulate him, she thought. *I really should. That was a great match.*

"Babe." Tyler grabbed her arm. He had a grim, dark look on his face. "Let's get out of here."

Weary but exhilarated, the JP2 kids waited outside Sparrow Hills for Mr. Costain to pick them up. George was sore and tired, but that was nothing compared with the warm, light feeling he was still basking in. He knew exactly what the feeling was: *victory.*

The others seemed to feel it too: J.P. was still bouncing around like a rubber ball, telling anyone who'd listen what a cool match it had been; Brian had a broad smile on his face; and Celia was full of praise for George's exploits.

Liz sounded the only sour note, standing apart, a glum look on her face. "I can't believe he saw me!" she said.

"Who?" Celia asked, puzzled.

"My boyfriend," Liz said. "Rich Rogers!"

"You have a *boyfriend?*" Celia said.

"I don't know if I still do," Liz whimpered. "He saw me in this get-up and said it was stupid. He *laughed* at me!"

"You know, I think I like this guy!" J.P. dodged nimbly out of the way of Liz's purse as she hurled it at him.

"It's not funny!" she said. "We just started dating! My

parents don't know. He was already freaked out by my school, and now he must think *I'm* a freak too!"

George shook his head. He was having a good night, and he wasn't going to let Liz ruin it. He remembered hearing Allie cheer for him even though she was supposed to be on Tyler's side.

"There's Dad!" Celia said suddenly. Sure enough, the Costain minivan had just pulled into the Sparrow Hills parking lot. An odd silence fell, as everyone remembered how they had gotten to Sparrow Hills in the first place.

"So, how did it go?" Mr. Costain said, as they silently piled into the back seats. "Where's James?"

No one answered. "Come on," Mr. Costain said. "Did you evangelize anybody?"

That was such a crock!" Tyler said for the twentieth time to the crowd of sympathetic people in Madison's living room. Girls shook their heads, and Flynt and Brock grunted in agreement as the theme from *Nightmare on Elm Street* played on the stereo.

Allie, sitting next to him on the couch, checked her watch discreetly, tired and vaguely depressed.

"No kidding, dude," said Brock. "It was just a lucky break. Freak accident."

"It *was* a freak accident!" Tyler said. "A dumb trick. I should have won," he turned to Allie. "Babe, you saw the whole thing. What do you think?"

She shrugged. "You both seemed really good."

"Yeah, yeah," Tyler scowled. "And then Coach comes up and yells at us. What's *his* problem, anyway?"

"Well, at least you didn't get in trouble," Allie said soothingly. Tyler needed to calm down; she was starting to get a headache.

Tyler looked darkly at the carpet. "It was a crock," he muttered. "Just a fluke."

"You're taking this a little hard," Madison observed from a nearby chair, passing Tyler a pumpkin dish of candy corn. "It wasn't a real match or anything."

"Don't worry about it," Flynt said. "It was just a stupid fluke. It won't happen again."

"Yeah," Tyler muttered. "Yeah."

This is getting pathetic, Allie thought. "Be right back," she said pushing aside the curtain of black and orange beads that covered the doorway.

"Hey, babe!" Tyler yelled after her. "Get me a beer!"

Allie stood in the dining room, staring into the mirror over the bar. She had taken off the angel wings, her mascara was starting to run, and her hair was getting frizzy. *I look terrible.*

You're beautiful, the Truth Guy said softly.

Whatever. She rubbed her eyes. *What am I doing here?*

I gave away a tract," J.P. said.

"Yeah, to a cute girl you were hitting on!" George said.

"That's better than nothing," Mr. Costain said as they pulled out of the Sparrow Hills parking lot. "Evangelizing is really hard work. But you never know what kind of seeds you'll sow."

Thoughtful silence greeted his words. George sighed and cooled his forehead against the window. *I wonder if I sowed any seeds tonight. Probably not. But I guess it's possible.*

EIGHTEEN

JAMES' REVENGE

HAS JAMES COME IN YET?" GEORGE SAT

next to Celia in homeroom. It was the Monday after Halloween. Everyone was a little bleary.

"No," Celia said, stifling a yawn. "I hope nothing happened to him Friday night."

"Nothing happened to him," said Liz. "He set us up, Celia! Don't you get it?"

"Think of how bad you'll feel if something bad really *did* happen," Celia pointed out.

"That's right," Brian said. "You never know . . ."

"You people are all mental!" Liz said. "I *hope* that something bad happened to him! He tricked us into *evangelizing* at the public school!"

"Yes indeed. And how did it go?" James was standing in the doorway with a darker version of his usual grim smile. "I couldn't help noticing you *talking* about me. That seems to happen a lot, doesn't it?"

"What does that mean?" George said brusquely.

James only kept smiling, I-see-a-hypocrite style. "Nothing." With that, he walked to his usual place in the back of the room, ignoring the glares in his direction.

"How's everyone this morning?" Mr. Costain said, entering the classroom. "None the worse for wear, I hope?"

There were only mumbles in reply, but Mr. Costain didn't seem to notice. "We'll start the Rosary now. Let's pray that the school passes inspection tomorrow so that we can put this permit business behind us. George, why don't you lead us?"

Why should today be any different? And today, George

wasn't feeling the least bit prayerful — just really, really ticked off with James.

During prayers, he planned his confrontation with James. He was itching to demand an explanation and barely noticed what he was saying.

"Hail Mary, full of grace, the Lord is with thee . . ." he said for the hundredth time. An uncomfortable thought struck him. *You're not really full of grace yourself, right now, are you? James might be right. Maybe you* are *a hypocrite.*

The sting of the realization kept him quiet until lunchtime, when Allie pulled him aside. "Are you going to talk to James, or what?"

"I sure am," George said, rousing himself. "Right now."

"Good," Allie said. "I was beginning to think that no one would. Hey," she added, almost as an afterthought, "good job Friday night."

"Thanks," George said, hoping his features didn't betray the pleasure he was feeling. "How's Tyler?"

"Fine," Allie said. "A little mad, but he'll get over it."

They were the last people to come to the cafeteria. Everyone was sitting together at one table, except James, who was sitting at another table by himself, as usual.

Suddenly feeling up to the task, George tossed his lunch on a table and walked right toward him. The others saw what was happening and scrambled out of their chairs for a closer look.

George stopped in front of James, crossed his arms, and glared at him.

"Do you want something?" James said.

"Yeah," said George. "I want to know what you did Friday night."

"I read a chapter of Aquinas and went to bed," James said, smirking. "Why?"

"Did you tell Mr. Costain that we wanted to evangelize at Sparrow Hills?"

"Yes," James said. His smile vanished, and he fixed George with an icy stare. "I did."

"Why?"

"Well, I was thinking about it," James said. "And I decided that you people probably didn't want to do something that was *my idea*." He stressed the last two words viciously. "And I didn't want to show up, since hanging out with me was such a *waste of time*. Isn't that break right?"

George felt the words ring uncomfortably in his head. "So, what? You conned us into going out evangelizing. But why?"

James leaned forward. "To make a point. Do you get it, now, Peterson? Or are you still a little slow, even for a dumb jock?"

"Yeah, maybe I am," George said coldly. "I don't get why you would do something so mean."

"Oh, you don't? Was it any meaner than pretending you liked somebody's idea when you really thought it was a *waste of time?* That's what you said, wasn't it?"

Celia gasped. She suddenly looked horrified. "Oh, James! You . . . you heard us talking, didn't you?"

"Yes, I overheard your patronizing conversation," James snarled. "Listen carefully: I don't want to be part of your little society. I don't want to be your buddy. I don't want your condescension. And I don't want to be patronized." He glowered at them all. "I just want to be *left . . . alone.*"

237

There was silence. George could tell Celia was about to cry, but all she did was say softly, "If that's what you want, James, we'll do that."

But Allie wasn't so easily put off. "Hey, jerk!" she said, elbowing past the others. "It's not our fault that you're such a loser! Now you're blaming Celia for just being nice to you? What, are you an idiot or something?"

"Fancy a dumb blond like *you* calling *me* an idiot," James sneered.

"Oooh, good comeback!" Allie snapped, tossing her hair. "Just because you're smart, you think you're better than us? You know what you are? You're a *Pharisee*, that's what you are! You say you're a Catholic, but you're just a hypocrite!"

James turned pale, and for a moment George thought he was going to strike her. But he sat back instead, the smug smile began to play on his face.

"So Miss Lapsed Catholic is lecturing me on Christianity," James said. "You think I'm a hypocrite? What about you? Playing at being a Catholic when you're with the Catholics. This is all just a game to you, Miss Weaver, isn't it? The only reason you're acting like a Catholic now is because it's — " he spat out the word, " — convenient. But what are *you* really risking?" He paused, his eyes narrowing. "Nothing."

Allie opened her mouth, closed it again, then turned and ran out of the cafeteria.

James laughed and laughed, but no one else joined in. Then he seemed to realize the rest of them were staring at him.

"Go away," he said evenly. "I don't want to talk to you anymore."

Having silenced everyone in the school, he grabbed his tattered brown lunch bag and stomped off in the other direction.

"Wow," said Liz after a moment. "This place is turning into a soap opera."

Celia walked numbly back to her seat. George wanted to go after Allie, but decided he'd better take care of Celia first.

"Hey," he said. "You okay?"

Tears were trickling down Celia's face. "I'm so ashamed," she whispered. "I really wanted to help him. I thought I *was* helping him. I didn't mean to be condescending . . ."

"You weren't, Seal" George argued, squatting next to her. "He's just being a jerk."

Celia shook her head. "I shouldn't have been saying things behind his back," she said. "It was just wrong. I —"

"Oh, shut up," said Liz, butting in. "You can't fix the whole world, Celia."

"Yeah," said George. "Stop trying to save the human race — it's already been done."

Celia had to laugh. She wiped her eyes. "Let me see if I can go find Allie and talk to her."

"And I'll go find James, and throw rocks at him," Liz said. ". . . KIDDING, Celia!"

No one had much of an appetite after the scene with James. Celia went to the bathroom to wash her face. Liz and J.P. drifted off, talking. Only Brian was able to finish his lunch. George watched him eat it.

"Why isn't Mrs. Flynn ringing the bell for next period?" George glanced at his watch. "It's quarter after."

"She's not here," Brian said. "J.P. said she was giving a talk at some women's retreat."

George sighed and got up. "We'd better go to class," he said, wishing that the school could carry its own weight without his help. He crumpled his bag into a ball and aimed for the trashcan.

CRASH!

One of the windows had shattered. A shower of glass fell to the floor and a small, dark object skidded to a halt at their feet.

It was a brick.

George and Brian looked at each other — and then, both getting the same idea, sprinted for the entrance.

But there was no sign of the culprit outside. The only things moving were the mostly bare branches of trees waving in the wind. The evergreen bushes around the school looked undisturbed.

By the time they got back inside, Mrs. Simonelli, J.P., Mr. Costain, Celia, and Liz had gathered in the gym and were surveying the damage.

"Did you see who did it?" Liz asked. "We heard the crash — "

George shook his head.

"Not again!" Mrs. Simonelli was pale, and her voice shook with rage. "Who keeps doing this?"

"I don't know," Mr. Costain said evenly, but George

could see he was unusually upset. "They seem determined to put us out of business."

The students all gaped at him. He sighed and said, "You might as well all know that when we signed the lease, we became responsible for the maintenance of the building. If we can't keep it in repair, we could lose the lease." He took off his glasses and looked around at the students. "I know that you been having some fun with your pranks, and I haven't said anything until now, but you should all know that any damage that's done to the school as a result of a prank . . . endangers the existence of this school." He looked from one student's face to another's. "So if any of you have been responsible for this or know who is responsible . . ."

"Pranks!" Mrs. Simonelli said bitterly. "Crickets, cows, and now bricks! These students are running wild! Dan, I've tried not to say anything about the way you've been running things around here, but you are entirely too lenient with these students, letting them leave the building, go down to the store, do who-knows-what between classes!"

"Tammy," Mr. Costain said quietly.

George raised his hand. "Excuse me, sir. This isn't the first time a window's been broken?"

Mr. Costain looked at him grimly. "It's the sixth time."

"Yeah!" said J.P. unexpectedly. "That's what my mom said, and I told her that the polter . . ."

Mrs. Simonelli cut him off. "I don't think you students realize how much work and sweat and labor goes into running a school! I don't think you're really grateful for all the hard work your parents have put into this! Do you know how many hours I've put into preparing lessons and teaching — as a volunteer? I wouldn't be surprised if it's a student breaking these windows . . . a student who doesn't want to be here, and who wants to see our school closed." She glowered around the group. But she seemed oblivious to the fact that her own daughter had gone white.

"Excuse me," Brian said tentatively. "Can we look at this logically? Where was each of us when the brick was thrown?"

"I was in my room, with my daughter Elizabeth," Mrs. Simonelli said.

"Therefore," Brian said, "we know that Liz, at least, didn't throw that brick through the window."

Mrs. Simonelli nodded, and Liz looked at Brian gratefully.

"And George and I were in here together when the brick was thrown," Brian said.

"And I was in the office on the phone," Mr. Costain said, apparently content to have Brian continue his inquiries.

"Was anyone outside?" Mrs. Simonelli demanded.

Celia raised a shaky hand. "I was," she said, "Looking for Allie. But I didn't find her, and I didn't see anyone else around the school." She swallowed. "I guess that's not a very good alibi."

"Oh, come on!" Liz spoke up. "*No one* thinks you threw the brick. Unless you've gone completely psycho in the last thirty minutes."

Mr. Costain smiled wryly. "I think I can vouch for my daughter's sanity. Where were you, Mr. Flynn?"

"Uh — " J.P. jumped. "Um. I was, uh, sitting in a classroom, studying."

"J.P.," Celia said reproachfully. "Were you?"

"Yes!" J.P. said, then squirmed. "Okay, so I was studying on my laptop."

"And what were you studying?" Mr. Costain probed.

J.P. hung his head. "*Praxor's Game*," he muttered. But George, looking hard at J.P., wasn't so sure that he was telling the truth.

"Ah," said Mr. Costain. "Some material for confession, Mr. Flynn." He looked around. "Where's Mr. Kosalinski?"

"Here," James stumped into the room, looking warily at the group. "What happened?"

"Where have you been since you left the cafeteria?" George demanded.

James snorted. "In the men's room," he said loftily. "Recovering my good temper."

"Did anyone see you there?" George asked. but Mr. Costain intervened.

"I did," he said. "I can vouch for Mr. Kosalinski."

George glanced at Brian, who looked troubled. In the silence, they heard someone quietly opening a door. There were light footsteps in the hallway, and then a figure came into view.

It was Allie. She started when she saw everyone looking at her.

"You!" exclaimed Mrs. Simonelli, pointing her finger in wrath. "You broke the window!"

Allie's mouth dropped open. George could see her looking past them to the shattered glass.

"Tammy — "

Mrs. Simonelli turned on Mr. Costain. "See what happens when you let just *anyone* into the school? She doesn't want to be here, she's never wanted to be here, she's been missing for the past half-hour, and now she's sneaking back into school! What more proof do you want?"

"Tammy, that's enough!" Mr. Costain thundered. "One more word and I will *fire* you!"

Mrs. Simonelli's eyes widened, and she stopped.

Mr. Costain turned around. "Allie," he said. "Let me explain."

But Allie was already gone.

Allie plunged through the woods. They didn't want her in the school. She didn't belong here. They thought she was faking it, playing at being Catholic —

Well, aren't you?

The quiet thought struck her hard.

In fury she turned around. "Go *away!*" she yelled at the Truth Guy. "Leave me alone! I just wish you would — quit it!"

"Allie?"

She halted, startled. But the voice was human, and familiar. She turned to see George trudging through the fallen leaves toward her.

"You okay?" he asked.

"I guess," she mumbled.

He looked around. "Who were you yelling at?"

She knew her face was bright red. "No one. Just blowing off steam."

"I can see why," he said. He nodded toward Chimney Rock behind her. "I thought I'd find you here. Going to SpeedE.Mart?"

"Maybe. No." She halted in confusion. "George, I don't belong at your school."

"Don't listen to Mrs. Simonelli," he said gruffly. "I've known her since I was six. She's always going wacko about something. She says stuff she needs to get off her chest, and then feels guilty and apologetic about it for years afterward." He shook his head. "She drives my mom nuts. Just ignore her."

"But," Allie drew a deep breath, "James said I was pretending to be Catholic. When it was convenient. Do *you* think that's what I'm doing?"

George looked at his shoes, then straight in her eyes. "Sometimes, yes."

Allie was shocked; she hadn't expected him to be so straightforward. "What?"

"Wrestling tryouts," he said. "The Halloween dance. You know what I'm talking about? Those times you were ashamed to be seen with us."

Her face grew hot again. She was mad at herself: she'd asked him for a straight answer, and he'd given her one.

"Okay," she said grudgingly. "Anything else?"

George looked away. Then he looked back at her. "What about Tyler?"

"What about him?" All her defenses rose. Tyler was her boyfriend, her link with her friends and old life back at Sparrow Hills. She wasn't going to give up Tyler to be Catholic, or whatever it was they wanted.

"Allie," George said suddenly, speaking quickly. "I know you don't want to hear this, but Tyler is *not* a good guy. Not for you, not for anyone. I've seen him in the locker room at wrestling practice. He looks at pictures. Of girls."

"What do you mean, he looks at pictures?"

"Porn," George said, his face red. "It's a sin. I mean, Catholics believe it's a sin."

"Tyler isn't Catholic."

"But it's still wrong. He's cheating on you. You know what I mean? With those other girls in the magazines. You don't deserve a guy like that, and he doesn't deserve you." He looked her in the eye again, and then looked down at his shoes.

Allie suddenly became aware that someone else was coming through the woods. They turned and saw Mr. Costain.

"Hello!" he said, looking out of place trudging through the leaves in his suit and tie. "May I join you?"

"Sure," George said, glancing at Allie.

"Actually, I'd like to speak to Miss Weaver for a moment," Mr. Costain said. "If you'll excuse us, George."

Hands in his pockets, he stood beside Allie.

"Mr. Costain," she blurted out. "I didn't throw that brick."

He looked at her solemnly. "I believe you, Miss Weaver."

Gratitude surged through her. But Mr. Costain continued.

"But even if you had thrown that brick, I would still want you at our school."

"Why?" Allie asked, and added, "Don't tell me 'because it's good for me,' right?"

"No," Mr. Costain said, "Because it's good for *us.*"

He looked at her a moment longer, then winked. "I'll have to ask you to be patient with our Mrs. Simonelli. Please forgive her."

"That's okay," Allie murmured. "George said she gets a little wacky sometimes."

George flushed, and Mr. Costain coughed. "Well, all of us have our moments, Catholics in particular. Shall we go back inside?"

NINETEEN

THE BIG DECISION

AT HOME AFTER SCHOOL, ALLIE TURNED UP

the music loud on her MP3 player, fell on her bed, and stared at her bedroom wall. *This is so not fair, Truth Guy. Now you've got George doing your dirty work.*

But she wasn't convinced. It seemed unfair to accuse Tyler when he wasn't around to defend himself. Besides, she *liked* dating Tyler. He was big and strong, handsome and popular. He wasn't perfect — big surprise. He acted like an idiot with his little boys' club — another big surprise. But he didn't do it in front of her, and she felt safe when she was with him.

He calls you hot, the Truth Guy insisted. *He calls you babe. He never calls you beautiful.*

Allie's cell phone rang. She pulled it out and sighed when she saw who it was. "Great timing," she muttered, putting the cell phone to her ear.

"Hey, babe! What's up?"

"Nothing much," Allie said. "What's up with you?"

"I was just thinking: next Friday's gonna be our five-month anniversary."

"Oh, yeah! You remembered!" she said. *So there, George. So there, Truth Guy.*

"Yeah. I was thinking — maybe we can go out to dinner or something. Whaddya think?"

"Sounds good," Allie said. "That's real sweet of you."

"Hey, what can I say? Gotta take care of my babe, make sure she's feeling all right."

Determined to prove George wrong — or at the very least, to *really* get to know Tyler, Allie decided right then to have a *serious* conversation with him. "Hey, Tyler, I've been thinking . . ."

"Yeah?"

"Um, where do you think our relationship is going?"

Tyler seemed bewildered. "I don't know. We're just having fun, I guess."

"Do you have any plans for the future?"

"Plans? What are you talking about? Why do you have to get heavy all of the sudden? I just want to have a good time with you, that's all."

She tried to explain herself, but had to give up.

"What's all this about?" Tyler said finally. "What's bothering you?"

Allie swallowed, and tried bringing up something that had been a forbidden subject up to now: religion.

"I don't know, just wondering . . . What do you think about all this Jesus stuff?"

Tyler hesitated a minute. "Well . . . I never really thought about it, to be honest . . ."

"Not even a little bit?" Allie said, disappointed.

"Well, all I know is that every religious person I've ever met has turned out to be a stinkin' hypocrite."

Allie thought about Celia, George, and Mr. Costain. "I don't know if you've met enough religious people. They're not all that bad."

"Maybe." She heard him yawn. "But look at what those priests did to those little kids! And those televangelists, always asking for money . . . Look, I really don't want to talk about this, okay?"

"Why?"

"Because I don't want to offend you." He yawned again. "Sorry, babe. I'm worn out. Got to rest up for Sectionals next Saturday."

"Oh," Allie said grumpily.

Who do you think broke the window?" Brian asked George a few days later. They were walking up through the woods to wrestling practice. The season was coming to an end, which meant extra practices and more tension as the Sparrow Hills squad got ready to compete in bigger competitions.

"I don't know," George said, kicking a stone out of the way. He'd been trying to keep his nagging doubts about J.P. to himself.

"Everyone seems to think J.P. did it," Brian said. "He doesn't have a really good alibi. And he's always coming up with these outrageous stunts."

George thought about the stink bomb. "You might be right," he said slowly. He liked J.P. — he'd known him since grade school — but the youngest Flynn had always been unpredictable. "But he said he was playing one of those video games his mom had banned."

"But the game wasn't on his laptop when Mr. Costain confiscated it," Brian said. "I heard Mrs. Flynn talking to Mr. Costain about it."

"I wish J.P. wouldn't lie about stuff," George said. "How can anyone trust him?" He sighed and changed the subject. "Hey, I won't be able to go over those moves with you before practice. Coach wants to meet with the varsity squad for the half-hour before we start."

"You're officially an upperclassman now?" Brian said.

"I guess so," George said, cracking a smile. "Maybe Coach heard some good things about the match with Tyler . . . He wants to prep us for the Sectionals."

"How do the Sectionals work again?"

"They're the first round of the playoffs," George said, wondering how a smart guy like Brian could be so ignorant of basic sports stuff. "You win Sectionals, you go to the Division Championships. You win the Divisions, you go to States."

"And if you win States?"

"You get a nice big trophy and your name in the paper," George said, kicking a rock off the path. "Why? You getting ambitious?"

Brian laughed easily. "No. I'm still looking forward to wrestling someone for real."

George frowned. He had been anxious about how Brian would do in the Sectionals because none of the teams they'd competed with had had anyone in Brian's weight class and all his wins had been by default. That would change in the Sectionals, and Brian would be going up against the elite of his class. "I wish you had more experience," he said.

"I'll be fine," Brian said.

"But, Brian . . ."

"No, seriously, don't worry, I'll be fine," Brian said. After a pause, he added, "I'm stronger than I look, you know."

"Well . . ." George hesitated. "All the same, maybe you and me can practice a bit more together. How about on

Saturday, we show up a bit early, before the rest of the squad, and we'll go over some moves?"

Brian laughed. "What, you want to practice the day that the Sectionals are held? At the last minute? What good will it do?"

"It does a lot of good to practice right before," George insisted. "Be there at 9 a.m. I'll ask the coach to open the gym early for us."

"Okay, okay," Brian said, shrugging. "If it'll make you feel better."

veritatissplendor: hey george!
    gpwrestler27: whatsup
veritatissplendor: i just had a great idea!!
veritatissplendor: lets all go to the sectionals
veritatissplendor: to watch you and brian wrestle!
veritatissplendor: like a class trip!
veritatissplendor: now i have my license
veritatissplendor: i can drive us all.
    gpwrestler27: thatd be awesome seal
    gpwrestler27: btw i dont need a ride
    gpwrestler27: have to practice early w brian
    gpwrestler27: momll drive me
veritatissplendor: no prob bob.
veritatissplendor: is your mom coming?
    gpwrestler27: no she has to work
veritatissplendor: too bad
veritatissplendor: ill see if i can get the others JP2ers too
                     come too
veritatissplendor: i just IMed Liz about it
    gpwrestler27: dont bother james
    gpwrestler27: liz wont go

gpwrestler27: she only likes basketball
[italianstallioness has joined the conversation]
  italianstallioness: hey selia this iz liz
  italianstallioness: if u can drive me i will go sure
  veritatissplendor: liz that is awesome! :)
gpwrestler27: wunders never sease
  italianstallioness: keep ur smart comments to yrself
  italianstallioness: georgie boy ;->

Hey," Allie said as she got into Tyler's car that evening. She had decided to dress up for the occasion, with jewelry and a black stretch velvet top. Carefully she slid into the seat next to him, trying to not to crease the freshly-ironed blue skirt that matched her eyes.

"Hey," Tyler said. "Wow, you're looking nice."

Well, at least he didn't say hot, Allie thought hopefully.

"How are we going to get in?" she asked as Tyler pulled into the parking lot of La Chinchilla, one of the nicer restaurants downtown. "Isn't there a bar?"

"I know someone who works here," Tyler said.

Cool. Allie thought. *He really planned this.*

The hostess looked up as they came in and immediately said, "Hey, Tyler!"

"Hey, Megan," Tyler said, flashing her a smile. "Can we get a table?"

"Sure!" Megan said warmly, adding quietly, "Just don't order any beers."

Tyler laughed. "No problem, honey," he said.

"Good evening, sir, your ID?" Megan said in a louder voice. "Please follow me . . ." She led them to a booth tucked away in a private section of the restaurant.

"Honey?" Allie asked Tyler as they sat down. "What does that mean?"

"Nothing, babe," Tyler said.

"How do you know her?" Allie persisted.

"Geez, *somebody's* suspicious!" Tyler said. "She's Brock's older sister."

"Oh," Allie said, and felt bad for being so mistrustful, especially when he had gone out of his way to get her into a real restaurant.

After a few minutes of uncomfortable silence, their waitress came over, a tall blonde. "Hi, I'm Carrie," she said, sliding some water glasses on their table. "What'll you be having tonight?"

"Hey there," Tyler said easily, taking a long look at Carrie in her tight shorts and low-cut white blouse. "I'll have the steak-and-cheese quesadilla and a Coke. How about you, babe?"

"Um . . ." Allie was too busy watching Tyler, who was *still* looking at the waitress, "I guess . . . I'll have the caesar salad. And an iced tea."

"Okay!" Carrie pranced off. Tyler watched her go, before turning back to Allie. "Let's talk," he said.

"What about?" Allie growled.

"How's the freak school going?"

"That was only funny the first fifty times you said it."

Tyler's eyebrows shot up. "Okay, okay," he said. "How's the *Catholic* school going?"

"Fine," she said shortly. She wasn't interested in talking about the goings-on at John Paul 2 to Tyler, who would either mock them or be bored by them.

"Well, things are going pretty crappy at Sparrow Hills,"

Tyler grumbled. "Ever since the Halloween dance, everybody thinks they're a comedian or something. I've totally lost respect."

"What do you mean?" Allie said.

"I mean," Tyler said, taking a gulp of water, "that none of the rookies got any respect for me, and I'm getting smart comments from all the people that . . . well, I'm getting a lot of smart comments."

"Oh," Allie said, feeling grimly satisfied. "I see."

"And then Coach had to invite Peterson to our veterans meetings!" Tyler said. "Like, as if being a veteran doesn't mean anything anymore!"

"Really?" Allie said. "Well, I mean, he has wrestled before . . ."

"You don't understand! It's a respect thing! I worked hard to get where I am, and now he just comes and gets everything *handed* to him, just because Coach is sweet on him! I don't understand it!"

"Well, the important thing is the team, right?" Allie said, yawning. "I mean, maybe you're just making a big deal about nothing. No offense."

Tyler looked as though he'd been mortally insulted. "You don't understand," he grumbled, taking a sip of water. "The Sectionals are tomorrow, and I'm the team captain, and nobody's respecting me . . ."

Carrie came back with their drinks and Tyler's expression changed. "Thanks," he said, flashing her one of his patented smiles. "Thanks a lot."

She smiled back, and laughed a little. "No problem."

Tyler once again indulged himself with a long look as she walked away.

He's just being stupid, Allie told herself. *I'm his girlfriend.*

Then Tyler reached over and took her hand. "So Allie, I was thinking . . ."

This sent her into instant confusion. For some reason, she and Tyler hadn't held hands much — he was more of an arm-around-the-shoulder kind of guy — and she had always been bothered by that. Normally, if he had grabbed her hand like he was doing now, in public, she would have thought it was sweet and romantic. But, for some reason, she didn't.

"What were you thinking?" she asked, trying to sound playful.

". . . Maybe after dinner, we could spend some time alone. To celebrate."

"Really?" Allie said, trying to convince herself that this was cute and harmless. "Doing what?"

He shrugged, "Nothing much."

"I hope so," Allie said lightly. "We shouldn't mess around, you know. I'm a *Catholic* school girl."

"I don't know, I've heard some interesting stories about you Catholic school girls . . ." Tyler said.

Allie suddenly felt queasy. "That's not funny," she said, pulling her hand away.

"Aw, come on, Allie," he said, taking her hand again and stroking it. "Lighten up. You're always so uptight."

He leaned over, and kissed her.

It happened so quickly that Allie had no time to react . . . and then it lasted a little longer. It lasted too long. She pushed herself away.

"What?" Tyler said softly; but there was an edge to the softness.

"Nothing," she whispered back. "Sorry."

He was a good kisser. A *very* good kisser. She needed time to think.

"Give me a few minutes," she said. "Uh . . . I have to go to the ladies' room."

"Okay," Tyler said, smiling.

"Be right back." She got out of the booth with as much dignity as she could muster.

Once in the bathroom, she locked herself in one of the stalls and sat down to think. Two opposite and extraordinarily powerful emotions clashed inside her.

One was like a sweet, enveloping mist. It told her go back to their table and let Tyler kiss her again. *You're lucky to have a guy like him. He* does *like you. Didn't he just prove it? Relax. Enjoy yourself a little.*

The other was like an alarm bell. *He's playing you! He is so playing you, and you're letting him!*

So what? You can play him *too. It's not a big deal. Come on, it's not like you've never been kissed before. . .*

Celia wouldn't like it! It's not right!

So what? You're not like Celia. You never will be.

Allie sighed. She felt shaky and she didn't *like* it. She wanted to be in control. She didn't want to listen to either voice right now; at least not yet. She wanted to date Tyler, and be kissed by him . . . but she wanted Tyler to be like George, to be shy and tell her she was beautiful. She wanted to be Tyler's girlfriend; but she didn't want to be Tyler's it trophy girlfriend. She wanted to be cool, admired, and bad like Madison, but she wanted to be pure, sweet, and good like Celia . . .

Truth Guy . . . ? she thought fleetingly.

It took her a while, but she finally decided to go back and give Tyler another chance. *He's only a teenage boy with raging hormones,* she thought. But she had to set some ground rules. Tyler had to stop flirting with other girls. That was minimum, wasn't it? And maybe she could find a way to bring up the porn thing. Maybe he'd listen to her if he really cared. He would definitely *not* get to kiss her or do anything else with her until they had an understanding.

She took a deep breath, unlocked the door, and walked out of the bathroom.

As she walked up to their booth, the first thing she saw was Tyler talking to Carrie, who was giggling and writing something on a piece of paper. The second thing she saw was Carrie giving the slip of paper to Tyler, who slipped it into his pocket with a grin.

Instantly, she was struck by several different emotions, all at the same time. Astonishment: *He just got her number!* Anguish: *But he just kissed me!* Rage: *How could he do this?*

But then all of these emotions were swept away by something else: something so bright that it was blinding, so sweet that it was painful, and so real that it was irresistible: the truth. *It's over. I'm gonna dump him. I've* already *dumped him.* She suddenly felt sharp, focused, and *totally* in control. It was a good feeling.

She walked up to the booth, which was now set with the food that Carrie had delivered.

"Hey," Tyler said as she sat down. "It took you long enough. I was starting to wonder what happened — "

"Tyler," Allie said, smiling sweetly. "We're done."

The look on Tyler's face was perfect. "What?"

"We're done," Allie repeated calmly. "Get out of here, please. You are officially dumped."

And that was that. There was a lot of noise, of course, before Tyler was convinced that she was serious. And then there was some more noise as he tried to figure out why. He kept asking if it was George. But she didn't tell him. She figured he already knew. She just kept on asking him to leave. And eventually, since the manager was hovering near their table, Tyler left. "Don't expect me to give you a ride home!" he said as he stomped out.

She waved at him cheerfully. "See ya!"

She was alone. People were staring at her, but she hardly noticed. She was too astonished with herself. *I can't believe I just did that.* She hadn't even come close to losing her temper. Tyler had done all the yelling.

Allie looked at their food, and realized that she was hungry. Her mom had given her some money, so she could pay the bill. But she had no idea how she was going to get home.

Celia's got a license.

Thanks, Truth Guy, Allie thought happily. *I think I might like you.*

"Celia? It's Allie. I have a favor to ask you . . ."

Allie turned to the food, and dug in. It was the best meal she had ever had.

Thanks a lot!" Allie said as she got into the front seat of the Costain minivan about twenty minutes later, "You're a lifesaver!"

"No problem," Celia said, looking at her curiously.

"Uh . . . you can make it up to me by telling me what's going on?"

"Tyler brought me here on a date," Allie said, checking her mascara in the passenger-side window. "But he started hitting on the waitress, so I dumped him."

Celia stepped on the brake a little too hard and Allie almost bashed her head on the dashboard as the minivan jerked to a stop.

"Oh! Sorry!" Celia said hastily as she pulled out of the parking lot. "So . . . You broke up with Tyler?"

"Yep," Allie said. "Broke up."

"Oh . . . I'm sorry?" Celia said tentatively.

"Don't be," Allie said, smiling. "He had it coming."

"So . . . you're alright?"

"I'm fine. I just needed a ride home." Allie took a deep breath. She felt unbelievably light and happy; the happiest she had felt in a long time. She felt like dancing, or dressing up, or going shopping.

"Hey, Celia!" she said. "Let's go shopping tomorrow! Me and you!"

"Really?" Celia said. "Oh, I'd love to, but . . ."

"What?" Allie said. "Come *on*, Celia, me and you never have fun together."

"No, it's just that . . . ." Celia sighed. "George and Brian are going to the Sectionals tomorrow, and I promised George I'd come . . ."

"Oh, the Sectionals," Allie said. "Can I come?"

"Isn't Tyler going to be there?"

"Yeah, so what?" Allie said, and then laughed out loud. "I don't care."

And she didn't.

TWENTY

THE HAZING

ARE YOU SURE SOMEONE'S HERE?" GEORGE'S MOM said as they pulled up to Sparrow Hills' main entrance.

"Sure I'm sure," George said, opening the door and stepping out. "Coach said someone would open the gym for me." It was a cold, fresh morning, and he felt rested and ready for the day. It was funny, but big meets relaxed him more often than not.

He shouldered his bag, jogged over to the main entrance, and sure enough, the center front door was unlocked. "It's good!" he shouted, waving at his mom.

"All right! See you later!" she called back, and started to drive away. "Good luck!" Then she was gone.

As he made his way through the silent, darkened hallways, George found his thoughts turning back to Allie. *I wonder how her date with Tyler went. Probably great. Okay, maybe I'm just being jealous.*

Suddenly he heard voices echoing down the hallway. Who's that? I didn't think there was anyone else here this early . . .

He turned the corner and ran right into Flynt and Brock.

"Hey, Peterson!" Flynt said. "About time you got here!"

"Hey, Flynt," George said warily. "What do you mean?"

"Dude, didn't you get the message?" Flynt said. "Coach wanted the varsity squad to come at nine to help load mats and stuff into the bus."

"Really?" George said. "I was just coming in early to practice."

"Don't you think you're ready?" Brock said.

George shrugged. "Never hurts to be prepared." He had no intention of telling Flynt and Brock about meeting Brian early to practice.

"Whatever," Flynt said. "Anyway, for once I'm glad to see you, Peterson. Only four guys showed. Come on."

They went down the hallway, talking and laughing. George followed, annoyed. *Why didn't Coach tell me about this? I thought we'd have the whole gym to ourselves.*

Wondering where Brian was, he checked his watch. Flynt and Brock led the way over to the closet in the back of the gym where the mats were stored. It was the size of a small garage and held stacks of wrestling mats, volleyball poles, hockey goals, and even gymnastic equipment. "We got to get all the mats out of here," Brock pushed open the doors. "Come on."

Still preoccupied, George stepped into the closet and looked up.

There stood Tyler, looking right at him. His face was a bit pale, but he grinned. "Hey, Peterson," he said. "How's it going?"

Out of the corner of his eye, George saw Flynt lunge for him. He spun around, to meet him; but Brock leapt on his back, and then Tyler pinned his arms to his sides. For a moment George grappled, trying to stay upright. Then he fell beneath the three of them. Pain shot through his shoulder as it made contact with the hard wooden floor. He was pinned down.

Tyler laughed. He grabbed a handful of George's hair and jerked his head up, hard. "Does that hurt?" he growled viciously.

"What . . . are . . . you doing?" George said between gritted teeth.

"I'm just having fun," Tyler said. "Just like you've been having fun with my girlfriend."

"I have *not* been having fun . . ." George started to say; but Tyler stuffed a dirty sock into his open mouth, and Flynt smeared a piece of duct tape over it. He tried to reach up and rip it off; but he was too well pinned.

"We gotta get some rope or something," Flynt said. "There's not enough duct tape to tie him up."

"Check over there," Tyler said to Brock, and George seized the moment to struggle, twisting in their grasp, until they lost hold of him, for a moment. He was on all fours in a second and scrambling to his feet, heading for the door . . .

Flynt snarled. "Whoa!" he heard Brock yell. "Hold him!" Tyler barked.

A moment later, George was pinned again, dazed and trying to get his breath back. Flynt was on his stomach and Brock was sitting on his head while Tyler rummaged in the closet.

Brock had his face mashed to the floor and George could no longer see what was happening. All he could do was lie there thinking of all the things he wanted to say to them, and wish that Coach Lamar would walk into the gym. Maybe Coach Lamar was in his office right now, going over stuff for the Sectionals. *If only I could make some noise!*

He saw Tyler's feet again, and then something dropped to the floor: rope, white nylon cords from the volleyball net. "Here," Tyler said. "Flynt, you tie him up. Brock, help me hold him down."

Brock's chest pressed down on George's shoulders, immobilizing them. Then Tyler dug his knees into George's calves painfully, pinning them to the floor. George struggled again, but this time there wasn't any loosening of the grip. Flynt yanked his hands back and crossed them together. "Hold his hands!"

Brock and Tyler held his struggling wrists as loop after loop of cords was wrapped around his wrists, swiftly and mercilessly. Then his wrists were yanked down cruelly, and Flynt said, "Okay, give me his ankles. No, cross them. Yeah, like that." He sounded so calm and unruffled that it was almost frightening.

George's ankles were pulled up off the ground; he tried to kick, but Tyler had too good of a grip. Then the cord went round and round his ankles, and then it too was pulled tight. George's legs were bent backwards now, off the floor; he tried to pull them down, but only succeeded in stretching his arms painfully.

"Yeah, that's it," Flynt said, satisfied. "Got him hogtied."

"What do we do now?" Brock said.

"Shove him behind the mats where no one'll see him," Tyler said.

Flynt and Brock heaved George over a stack of mats and dropped him onto a wrestling mat in the back corner of the huge closet.

George struggled, rolling back and forth on the mat as he tried to yank an arm or leg out of the knots.

"He can still move," Brock said in a worried voice. "He might make enough noise to give us away."

"Hold on a sec," Flynt said. "You got any more rope?"

A few moments later, Flynt wrapped a loop of cord around his neck and then tied it back to his legs. It wasn't tight yet, but George knew that if he tried to pull free again, the cord would strangle him.

"Saw this in a movie," Flynt said. "Pretty cool, eh?"

"Great, fine, whatever. As long as he stays quiet," Tyler said. He squatted down next to George. "You know what we're going to do with you, Peterson?" he said, putting his face level with George's.

George didn't even try to reply. He concentrated on meeting Tyler's gaze, trying to ignore the anger, hate, and shame surging through him.

"Nothing," Tyler breathed. "We're just gonna leave you here. Let you sweat a bit while we give Burke what's coming to him. After we're done with Burke, maybe I'll let you out; maybe I won't. I haven't really decided yet."

George's words were smothered by the gag, which turned them into a barely audible growl. Tyler only laughed grimly. "Coach told me you and Burke were coming in early to use the gym, and I was just thinking last night . . ." he put a heavy hand on the back of George's neck, and pushed. For a moment the cord around George's neck tightened, and he couldn't breathe. Panic welled up in him . . . and then Tyler let him go. "I was just thinking that if Peterson is always interfering with my business, maybe I'd just interfere a bit with him. So you want to make Burke a man? Well, I'll un-man him. Not that it'll take too much work." He stood up. "See you around, Peterson. Enjoy the show."

He vanished behind the mats, and George heard the

271

door creak closed behind him. Then he was alone in the darkness.

George struggled in vain for a few minutes, but it was no good. Then the door opened. He twisted his head around, trying to see; but the pile of mats that was hiding him blocked his view.

He heard Brian's voice. "Uh . . . what are we doing?"

George's heart froze. He struggled again, and tried to yell through the gag. Brock coughed loudly to hide the sound.

"I told you, dude," Flynt said casually. "We're setting up some mats for a demonstration. Come on."

"Oh, okay," he heard Brian's voice say. "Have you seen George around?"

"George? No," Brock said. "Were you supposed to meet him here or something?"

"Hey!" Brian's voice suddenly was full of alarm. "What are you doing — hey! Stop!" George heard a scuffling sound, some grunting, and all the while Brian's voice yelling, "Hey! *Hey!* Let me go! Unhand me! I'll — "

"Shut up, Burke," Flynt said, and there was silence.

"We got something for you. Stay right here."

Flynt appeared above the pile of mats. He grinned at George and snatched up a plastic bag that had been lying there. He pulled some items out of the bag: a bra, a blonde wig, and a pair of high-heeled shoes, then scrambled back over the mat. "Take his shirt off, Brock. We got some new clothes for the homeschooler."

With his heart pounding and his face growing hot, George had to listen as they stripped Brian's shirt off and forced him into the bra. Then they ripped off his shoes and jammed the high heels on him. Apparently the shoes were too small; Brian cried out in pain as they did so. Finally, they plopped the wig on his head.

"And now the final touch," Flynt said, and pulled something else out of the bag; something small that George didn't recognize immediately.

"No!" Brian gasped. "No, stop it!"

George leaned up as far as the cord would let him and caught a glimpse of Flynt grabbing Brian's head with one hand, and, then, as Brock broke out laughing, he put lipstick on Brian's face.

"It's our new mascot!" Flynt said, and laughed gleefully. George was forced to let himself fall back on the ground, choking for breath.

"What now?" Brock said.

"Most of the squad's probably coming in right now," Flynt said. "Go get them. Tell them you got something to show them!"

Brock ran off, and Flynt stayed there, keeping Brian pinned to the ground. George heard deep shaky breaths coming out of Brian.

"Aw, you scared?" Flynt said after a while. "Sowwy, Bwian, but Peterson ain't here to help you this time. You wondering where he is?"

Brian made no reply.

"I saw him a little while ago. He came in before you did," Flynt said. "He said you'd be coming in. Poor guy, he was so tired. Kept complaining about how he had to sit with you all the time, holding your hand. I felt sorry for him. I wonder where he went."

"Where is he?" Brian said, and his voice was angry. "Did you beat him up too?"

"I *told* you, Burke," Flynt said in a mock-patient voice. "He must have taken off. He said he was so sick of you always hanging around, pretending to be a wrestler."

George's heart seemed to twist in his chest. *God, please don't let Brian listen to him . . . please.*

There were footsteps and voices as the other wrestlers came into the gym. He heard Flynt jerk Brian to his feet and shove open the door. "Hey, check out the home-schooler!" he yelled. "He just found his real self!"

Laughter greeted his words, and catcalls followed.

"Woo! Woo! Nice!"

"Looking good!"

Flynt must have let Brian go, because George heard feet pounding on the ground, the high heels making an odd clocking sound as Brian half-limped, half ran from the gym. There was more laughter.

George turned his face to the wall. He didn't even want to think anymore. Someone — probably Brock, he guessed — closed the closet door, and he was plunged into darkness.

But he could still hear what was going on. "Nice one, Flynt!" he heard Tyler say. "A sight for sore eyes!"

Suddenly he heard another voice: Coach Lamar's. "Hey! What the *hell* is going on here?!?"

There was dead silence. "I don't want to believe that I just saw that," Coach Lamar said. "Tyler, you want to tell me what's going on?"

"Uh, yeah, sure, Coach," Tyler said, and something about his voice told George that he was trying hard to appear stern and serious, and not laugh. "Okay, idiots! Who dressed Burke like that?"

"We didn't do it!" several voices responded.

"Okay, who *let* him dress like that?"

Laughter broke out again. "Okay, that's enough," Lamar yelled. "That's *enough*, do you hear?" After a long pause where you could hear a pin drop, Mr. Lamar spoke again. His voice was thick with fury. "I'm ashamed of you. Every one of you. Here we are, on the day of the Sectionals, and are you acting like a *team?* Are you acting like *men?* I don't think so!"

"And if I ever find out who did this," Mr. Lamar continued. "I will personally make sure that they never wrestle again. You got that?"

There was a surly mumbling response from the team. "I said, you got that?" Mr. Lamar said.

"Yes, sir!" came the response, louder now.

"Good," Mr. Lamar growled. "Get your gear and get your butts on the bus. *Now!*"

George's heart sank as he heard the sounds of the team moving out of the gym. He realized that there was no way Tyler, Flynt, and Brock were going to let him go now; at least, not until Mr. Lamar had calmed down. And that meant that he was going to *miss* the Sectionals!

George was so full of anger it took all his self-control to restrain himself from struggling too much; he knew what would happen if he did. *Okay, think. How am I going to get out of this?* He tried to move his feet experimentally. No good — he couldn't move them back at all without tightening the strangling cord. But he could move them forward a bit. Would that loosen the cord that was tied to his wrists? No, it wouldn't. It was tied too tight. He was so frustrated that he kicked down his feet in rage, and the strangling cord tightened again, choking him.

With a supreme effort of will, he forced himself to stop struggling. *Okay, Okay. Calm down. You can do this . . .*

Then he heard footsteps: one pair of footsteps. Someone was coming back. George tensed, trying to keep down the irrational hope that someone had seen him and was coming to free him.

The door creaked open, and something was tossed into the closet.

"Here's your gear," came Tyler's voice. "You heard Coach, Peterson. He's on a rampage."

He walked over and untied the cord around George's neck. "That Flynt is an idiot," he muttered. "I can't have you dying on me, Peterson." He straightened. "I gotta run. The Sectionals and all. Too bad I'm going to have to wrestle your guys for you. Carrying the team to victory by myself, as usual. Hey, catch!"

With a laugh, he tossed something at George's face. "Maybe you'll find someone in there to keep you company." It was a *Playboy* magazine.

Tyler waved mockingly and shut the door. George listened to his footsteps as he jogged out of the gym.

Then George rolled over, kicking the *Playboy* out of his vision. He swallowed against the gag, and listened. *So this is what you get for sticking your neck out and being Catholic.*

Nothing.

Failure.

TWENTY-ONE

SECTIONALS

WOW, CELIA SAID, LOOKING UP AS THE THREE girls got out of her car. "This is a big school. You must feel right at home, Allie."

"No way," Allie said. "This is a city school. I'm from the suburbs."

"Me, too," Celia said. "Cities always make me nervous."

"Oh, you guys are so lame," said Liz, slamming the car door. "This is exciting."

They stood on a wide, crowded sidewalk, near the entrance to Parrington Central High School, the largest school in the area. This was where George and Brian were going to be wrestling. *And Tyler,* Allie thought with a twinge of nervousness. Some of her newfound courage was seeping away. She didn't feel good about seeing Tyler right now.

"Shouldn't we go in?" Celia said brightly.

"It's almost noon right now," Allie said, checking the clock on her cell. "They started half an hour ago."

"I hope we haven't missed any of George and Brian's matches," Celia said.

Liz shrugged off her coat, "Whatever. I'm just here to meet Rich." She pulled some blush out of her purse and began applying it, checking herself with a mirror as they walked.

Allie looked skeptically at Liz's short skirt and low-cut blouse, an outfit that Mrs. Simonelli definitely would *not* have approved of. "Why are you dressed like that, anyway? This is a wrestling match, remember?"

"I gotta look good," Liz said. "Or else I'll end up with no boyfriend, like you two."

They walked into the school, paid the five-dollar admission fee, and went into the cavernous main auditorium. It was three times as big as the Sparrow Hills main gym, with a huge scoreboard and bleachers that looked as if they could seat thousands.

"This is a *high school?*" Celia said, gaping.

"I guess so," Allie said, who was more concerned with locating the Sparrow Hills team. She searched the bleachers, for the familiar black and red of Sparrow Hills. There seemed to be dozens of schools represented here.

"Well, I'd love to hang out with you two single losers, but I gotta go find Rich. See ya later," Liz said as she disappeared into the crowd.

"Freshmen," Allie said, rolling her eyes.

"We better hurry up," Celia said, making her way up the bleachers through crowds of wrestlers, students, and parents.

"Look! There's Sparrow Hills!" Allie said, pointing to a group with familiar red-and-black jerseys. On the floor below, were a bunch of wrestlers. Mr. Lamar was yelling at one of the matches in progress, and he didn't look too happy.

When they got to the bleachers in front of the Sparrow Hills team, they found Liz there, looking very cool and pleased with herself. She sat next to a guy with a mass of long curly hair. Allie assumed he was the famous Rich Rogers.

"Hey, Liz!" Celia said, and made her way over to them.

Liz gave them a look that seemed to say that she was too cool to talk to them. That didn't stop Celia from sitting down right next to them. Allie followed suit.

"Hi!" Celia said. "You must be Rich. I'm — "

"Rich, these are two girls that go to my school," Liz said in a bored voice. "Celia Costain and Allie Weaver."

"Uh, hi," Rich grunted, then looked at her again. "Hey, did you say your name was Allie Weaver? I think we met at the Guerins' house last year."

"Oh, yeah." Allie had crashed Rachel Guerin's graduation party with Madison and Ginger. Now that she thought about it, she had a dim recollection of this guy being there too. He was a sophomore like Allie, but he'd never been in any of her classes.

"Maybe you can take *me* to some parties now," Liz said, cuddling his arm and gazing at him admiringly.

Rich laughed and patted her hand. "Sure, sure, babe."

Celia and Allie exchanged looks. *This is SO sad*, Allie thought.

"So," Celia said. "How's Sparrow Hills doing?"

"Not too good," Rich said. "They've lost every match so far. It's weird; I heard they were pretty good this year. Didn't they pick up a new guy . . . Peterson?"

"Yeah!" Celia and Allie both said. "He's from our school," Celia said. "Has he wrestled yet?"

"That's the strange thing," Rich said. "He didn't show. I heard the guys on the team talking about it."

"Huh?" Celia said. "That's weird . . ."

Something's wrong, Allie thought. She looked down at the row of Sparrow Hills wrestlers sitting on their assigned bench. She could only see the backs of their heads. She frowned, and went from wrestler to wrestler. Sure enough, there was no George. And where was Brian?

"Brian!" Celia yelled. "Hey, Brian! Up here!"

Brian was walking up the aisle at the base of the bleachers, away from the main floor. He was wearing the red-and-black Sparrow Hills singlet, and there was a grim, determined look on his face.

"Brian!" Allie yelled, and at last Brian looked up and his face brightened.

"Celia! Allie!" he said. "I'm — "

But just then the crowd around them roared. One of the Sparrow Hills wrestlers was pinned.

"Oh, give me a break!" Rich shouted. "You're terrible!"

They met Brian at the base of the bleachers. "I'm glad you're here," Brian said, glancing back at the rows of bleachers. "It's been awful."

"Because the team is losing?" Celia said.

"It's not just that. Never mind," Brian said, going red.

"Where's George?" Allie said.

"I don't know," Brian said in consternation. "We were supposed to meet this morning to practice, but he didn't show up. I thought maybe he was coming later, but he hasn't showed."

"That's crazy." Celia said. "George wouldn't have missed this for the world. Something must have happened to him!"

"That's what I think, too," Brian said. "Look, I can't stay long. I was just going to find a pay phone. I'm getting really worried."

Allie felt a surge of anger. *I bet Tyler has something to do with this.* "I'll be right back," Allie snapped, and headed for the main floor.

She made her way to the Sparrow Hills wrestlers. Mr. Lamar looked up in surprise at her approach, and said. "Hey Allie! What are you doing here?"

"I'm looking for Tyler," Allie said. "Where is he?"

Mr. Lamar frowned. "Right over there," he said, pointing to the ring. "And from the looks of it, he'll be back soon. I don't know what's wrong with the team today: first Flynt's out with a shoulder injury, now Tyler's off — "

Tyler was in the middle of a match that was going badly for him. His opponent had him down. Suddenly the ref slapped the mat with an open palm and blew his whistle.

"Well, there you go," Mr. Lamar said in a disgusted voice. "Go ahead and talk to him, if you want to."

"Thanks," Allie said.

Tyler was walking dejectedly back to the bench. When he saw her, he scowled. "What do *you* want?" he said.

"I'm looking for George," Allie said. "Have you seen him?"

"No," he spat, and walked away.

"Are you sure?" Allie persisted, following him. "No one knows where he is."

"You seemed really interested in George all of a sudden," Tyler said, glaring at her. "That's real interesting. Not very surprising, but interesting."

"I just wanted to know where he is, since he *does* seem to be missing," she said in what she hoped was a reasonable tone.

"Well, I don't know," Tyler said. "So leave me alone." He stalked back to the benches.

He's lying, Allie thought. She felt another wave of anger. *I can't believe I dated him. Now what?*

When she got back to Celia and Brian, Celia was talking on her cell phone to someone. "Where did you drop him off? Okay. Thanks." She snapped the phone shut as Allie walked up. "What did you find out?"

"Tyler said he hadn't seen him, but I think he's lying."

"Okay," Celia said. "George's mom said she dropped him off at Sparrow Hills this morning, and she saw him go into the school."

"But he wasn't there," Brian said. "I never saw him; I didn't even see his gear."

"Maybe we should go back to the school anyway, just to make sure," Allie said.

"Maybe we should call 911," Celia said. "I wish Dad wasn't out of town this weekend . . ."

"Let's go to Sparrow Hills," Allie insisted. "Right now. Maybe he's still there."

"Okay, okay," Celia sighed. "I'll tell Liz we're taking off. Maybe her boyfriend can drive her home. Brian, you should tell Mr. Lamar that you think something happened to George. Maybe he can find out what happened."

"Okay," Brian said. "I'll do that. I can't be any more unpopular anyway."

"Oh, and Brian," Allie said. "Good luck today."

Brian looked startled and then smiled briefly. "Thanks," he said. "I'll need it."

George worked relentlessly to get the sock out of his mouth. He couldn't loosen the ropes around his wrists and ankles, but at least he could move his head against the ground. So he had scraped away at the duct tape, over and over again, until finally it began to peel away. Now it was almost off.

Finally! With a cry he spit the sock out of his mouth. It fell to the floor in front of him, looking wet and very chewed up. The duct tape dangled in strips from one side of his mouth: he must look really stupid.

For a few minutes he lay there, enjoying the freedom of being able to move his jaws. Then he thought about his next move. It wouldn't do any good to yell for help; the school was empty and no one knew he was here. Wouldn't it be great if no one ever found out? If he could free himself, then no one would ever need to know how Tyler had humiliated him and kept him from wrestling in the Sectionals.

Not that I'm going to let Tyler forget this. I'm going to get him back. I don't care how.

But if only he could avoid looking ridiculous in front of everyone in Sparrow Hills . . . He thought of the newspaper articles about his performance last year, and winced to think of making the paper this year only as the object of Tyler's stupid hazing.

No way am I going to let the school janitor find me like this. Or the cops . . .

He had to get his hands or feet free. He tried with all his might to break the cords. But it was no good: the nylon was much stronger than he was. His exertions allowed him to straighten his legs some more, but they didn't get him free.

"Okay, okay," he muttered, trying not to give up. Maybe he could loosen something else. Groping with his fingers, he discovered that the cord from his feet to his hands was a simple loop tied with a single hard, tight knot. Maybe, just maybe, he could untie that knot.

He bent his wrists back as far as they could go and reached for the knot with his index and middle fingers. He could almost reach it. Over and over again his fingers brushed it. "Come *on!*" he grunted, and yanked with his feet, trying to bring the knot down just a tiny bit more.

It wouldn't budge. His muscles twitched and throbbed from being tied in this unnatural position. It wasn't fair. Suddenly he was angry with God.

YOU got me into this.

You tricked me into this. Oh, sure, it was fine when I first started praying: You helped me win matches and get to States. But what gives? Now, the more I pray, the more trouble I get in. I try to do the right thing, and look what happens to me!

He was so angry, he was blinking back tears. He wasn't sure if it was pain or stress or just the disappointment of feeling betrayed by God.

What do You want from me?

You know, I'm not so sure I want to keep bringing You with me if this is what You do to me . . .

Can't You just let me be a regular guy? Just one of those normal Catholics, like Liz or the guys at St. Lucy's?

Why do I have to be a SPECIAL Catholic, a John Paul 2 High kid? I'm just so sick and tired of being . . . called.

Weary, sore, and humiliated, he put his head down and prayed.

Whatever.

Whatever You want.

. . . I guess that's what's going to happen anyhow.

You don't drive fast enough!" Allie said for the hundredth time, as they drove up the road to Sparrow Hills.

"It won't help George if we're *dead*," Celia pointed out patiently, and came to a stop at the stop sign.

"There are no cars here!" Allie said. "Come *on!*"

"That's no excuse," Celia carefully looked both ways before stepping on the gas. They sped up the road, and turned into the parking lot. There were a few cars in the lot, but the building seemed dark and empty.

Once they came to a stop, Allie jumped out of the car, ran over to the main doors and yanked on them.

"They're locked!" she said in despair to Celia, who had just run up.

"What about the side door?" Celia said, and the two of them hurried around the building to the metal doors that opened onto the basketball court.

"Locked," Celia tugged at them. "There's got to be another way in. Let's just go around the school building and check all the doors."

There didn't seem to be anything else to do. The two girls hurried across the grass, rounding one big massive brick corner after another, looking for more doors. But every time they found one, it was locked. Eventually they found themselves approaching the main entrance of the school again.

"This is ridiculous," Allie said. "I swear I'm going to break this door down if it's not open." She was feeling so reckless and desperate now that she grabbed the handle and pulled, knowing full well that it would be locked. It opened.

"Oh!" Allie was so surprised she just stood with her mouth open for a moment. "Oh, thank God!" She pulled the door fully open and started through.

"Allie! Wait! Look!" There was something in Celia's voice that made Allie stop.

"What?" she said, turning around impatiently.

Celia was looking at the deadbolt. She turned the lock and a piece fell to the floor with a clatter. "This lock's been broken," she said.

"Oh." Allie shrugged. "Lucky for us, I guess."

"Don't you get it?" Celia said. "This door was locked a few minutes ago. Someone must have just broken it. That means someone else is *already* inside."

George lay in the darkness, resigning himself to the inevitable. The team would come back eventually, and Tyler and the others would untie him once they had a chance to do so without anyone noticing. They were probably counting on him being too embarrassed to say anything. The worst thing was, they were right. He just wanted to go home and forget this day had ever happened.

RATTLE. RATTLE RATTLE RATTLE.

It was the first sound George had heard in hours. For a moment he was too shocked to recognize it. *Sounds like someone's trying to open the gym doors.*

Suddenly he was caught in a turmoil of conflicting emotions. His aching muscles screamed for relief and urged him to yell for help, but he wanted to find out who it was first. It was stupid, probably his pride, but he was cautious . . . He listened.

But the rattling sound had stopped, and George felt a sudden panic well up in him. He changed his mind.

"Uh-Hey!" he called out. "Who's there?"

Only silence answered him. "No," he whispered. "Come on. HEY!" he yelled. "IS ANYONE THERE?"

Still nothing. He swore.

"Hel-LOOOOOO?"

George's spine prickled. A voice had spoken — a weird, raspy, singsong voice. Under other circumstances George might have found it funny.

"Hey!" he yelled back. "Can you help me?"

"You need HELP?"

"Yeah! Sort of!"

"Aw . . . you need some help?" The voice sounded sympathetic.

"Yeah!" George yelled, throwing caution to the wind. "I'm locked in the closet!"

"And all alone?"

"Yeah!" George said, wondering what this guy's deal was.

"And nobody knows you're here?"

"YEAH!" George shouted. "Some guys on the wrestling team tied me up and left me here! I've been in here for hours! Can you help me?"

There was no reply.

George waited impatiently. Maybe the guy had gone off to get help, but George hadn't heard any footsteps.

"Heh heh heh." There was a low, nasty laugh, as if someone had just played a cruel joke and was shamelessly amused by it.

Then there was silence again. George listened, feeling uneasy. Was this some kind of stupid prank?

"Hello?" he finally said. "Are you still there? Are you going to get help, or what?"

"Heh heh heh, heh heh heh." The snickering laugh continued. It sounded like the guy was really amused. *Really* amused, so amused that he couldn't help laughing, and

he couldn't stop laughing. It sounded like he found the whole situation hilarious.

George tensed, his stomach churning. Suddenly he felt it might be better to have a closet and locked doors between himself and someone like that.

And that might not be enough.

Allie and Celia stayed close together as they ventured down the darkened hallways of the school. Sparrow Hills didn't have a lot of windows in the hallways, so it was hard to see.

"How can we get to the gym from here?" Celia asked.

"This way, I think," Allie murmured. It was easy to get lost in Sparrow Hills. The hallways were dim and full of shadows. It was creeping her out. Their footsteps seemed very loud, echoing down the halls.

Is someone else really here? Allie thought. *What burglar would rob a school?* She thought of kids with too much time on their hands, vandalizing the school over the weekend for kicks, kids who were so bored that they would do anything for fun, even fire a gun with blanks at a girl . . .

"We shouldn't even be here." Allie muttered. "What are we *doing?*"

Celia didn't answer for a moment. "Well," she said finally, "We're trying to find George. Maybe we have to rescue him. You know what this reminds me of?"

"No," Allie said, irritated.

"*St. George and the Dragon.* Have you ever read that book? This princess Una has to find St. George so he can fight the dragon — "

"What?"

"It's like *we're* on a quest to — "

"Rescue St. George?" Allie snapped. "That's backward!"

"Not really. Sometimes the knights of King Arthur were rescued from dungeons by fair maidens. Girls had to do the rescuing sometimes. It's like something out of G. K. Chesterton," Celia added dreamily.

Allie grimaced. Celia was starting to talk like her dad. "Don't start quoting that C. S. Eliot guy — " she said.

"Do you hear that?" Celia said.

"What?" Allie said, and listened.

"*Heh heh heh heh . . .*"

The sound echoed down the hallways, faint and far. Allie had heard that laughter before.

"What is that?" Celia whispered. "It sounds like someone's in the school . . ."

"Celia," Allie said, urgently. "We have to call the cops. *Right now.*"

TWENTY-TWO

THE SPLENDOR
OF TRUTH

CALL THE COPS? WHY?" CELIA SAID.

"The guy who shot at me is here!" Allie said.

"The guy who shot at you?" Celia said, baffled. "You got shot at?"

"At Sparrow Hills!" Allie whispered furiously. "That was me! That's why my mom sent me to John Paul 2 High! The kid who shot at me laughed at me and that's *his* laugh!"

Celia's mouth dropped open. "Oh! Are you sure?"

"Sure I'm sure!" Allie whispered.

The laughter stopped, and there was silence again.

"Who are you?" George yelled. "What do you want?"

There was no answer . . . but George, listening intently in the dark, could hear other sounds: the soft *clink clink* of metal, as if someone was getting a tool out of a toolbox. "What do you want?" he shouted again.

There was a piercing sound, incredibly loud after the silence: *SKREEEECH*.

It happened again, and again, taking on a rhythm: *SKREECH SKREECH SKREECH SKREECH . . .*

Who are you?" A faint voice echoed down the hall.

Allie grabbed Celia's arm. "Who was that?"

"*What do you want?*"

"That's George's voice!" Celia said. "We've got to find him!"

"Wait, Celia!" Allie said urgently. "there's a *crazy* guy here too!"

295

"Okay, okay," Celia said, and reached into her purse. "I'll call . . ."

A screeching metallic sound echoed down the hallway.

"What is that?" Allie whispered.

"I don't know."

It was an ugly, piercing sound, like some kind of animal screaming: *SKREECH SKREECH SKREECH* . . .

"It sounds like a dragon," Celia breathed.

"Oh, shut up, Celia!" Allie whispered. She was creeped out enough as it was. "Get your cell phone out!"

Celia dug through her purse. "It's not here!" she said. "I must have left it in the car! Do you have yours?"

"No," Allie said angrily. "It's in my purse, and I left that in the car like an idiot."

"What do we do now?"

Allie didn't reply. All was silent, except for that horrible sound: *SKREECH SKREECH SKREECH* . . .

Allie bit her lip. Everything in her wanted to run, to get out of here. She started backing down the hall. "We're leaving."

"But Allie — " Celia grabbed her hand. "George!"

Better George than me, Allie thought. But she stopped.

Celia urged, "The truth is, if we leave George now — "

Truth. The word jarred in Allie's consciousness. "Not now, Truth Guy," she muttered.

"What?"

"Nothing," Allie said. "It's just that I keep imagining . . . this guy following me." She gave a shaky laugh. "Like your dad's poem, that nerdy Truth Guy following me and not leaving me alone."

"Have you tried following *him*?"

"What?"

"Well, do you think . . . maybe . . . it's Jesus?"

"The Truth Guy is Jesus?"

"Well, Jesus did call himself the Truth," Celia whispered. "And He said the truth would set you free. So try following Him. See where He goes. Isn't it worth a shot?"

At any other time, Allie wouldn't have paid much attention. But now, in the dark, she took a deep breath. Feeling foolish, Allie closed her eyes and thought, *Okay Truth, I'll follow you.*

There was a moment of stillness. It continued. Allie blinked, looking around. The horrible screeching sound had stopped.

"Heh heh heh, heh heh heh!"

Laughter echoed down the hall, much louder than before. She shuddered. It was the laugh she had heard many times in nightmares, and now it was *here*, and real. The air around her tingled with danger.

But the screaming panic inside her had died down.

"Come on," she said. "Let's get closer."

They edged down the hallway again. Celia pointed and whispered, "We must be real close to him. Look up."

Allie peered into the darkness. There was a turn ahead, where another corridor joined with theirs.

"He must be around that corner and down the hall," Celia whispered. "Maybe we can see him, if we . . ."

"I'm coming to get you!"

Allie almost jumped up and ran away. The malice in the eerie, raspy voice was unmistakable.

"Maybe we should go back!" Celia whispered.

"Just wait right there!"

"Wait a sec," Allie whispered back, fighting to control herself. The voice didn't seem to be talking to them. And she knew, somehow, that running away would be disastrous.

"Okay, Truth, what should we do?" she muttered.

Chase him away.

Allie cocked her head, mystified. Where had *that* come from? *Chase* the shooter?

SKREECH SKREECH SKREECH. The sound started up again.

"Allie," Celia whispered suddenly. "I . . . I just had this crazy idea."

"Me too," Allie said.

"I think we should just chase this guy away." Celia whispered. "I know it's crazy, but . . ."

"I was thinking the same thing!" Allie whispered back. "We should run down the hall, yelling and screaming."

"And maybe he'll just run away," Celia finished. It sounded crazy. But Allie felt recklessly confident. Like she had felt when she dumped Tyler.

"We should make *lots* of noise," she said. *If only we had some pots and pans.*

"Omigosh!" Celia's eyes widened. "Hold on a sec." She opened her purse and pulled something out.

"When I was looking for my phone, I found this."

Celia handed Allie a small tin can with a plastic horn on the top.

"Is that an air horn?" Allie whispered, bewildered.

"Yes!" Celia whispered excitedly. "George took it from J.P. at the All Saints' Day Party!"

"Okay, okay, give me that!" Allie said, grabbing the horn from Celia. "Let's go."

"What should we yell?" Celia whispered.

Allie waved a hand impatiently. "It doesn't matter."

"Let's yell, *Veritatis Splendor!*" Celia whispered.

"Veri . . . what?" Allie whispered back.

"The Splendor of Truth," Celia whispered, and grinned. "My IM name."

"Oh . . ." Allie thought about it, and grinned back, "Okay."

The *SKREETCH SKREETCH SKREETCH* continued as they drew closer . . .

. . . and then stopped. There was a loud clattering sound, and then they heard the voice one more time: *"Here I come! Ready or not!"*

There was the ugly screaming sound of metal scraping metal. Allie cringed.

Chase him, Allie! Chase him now!

She took a deep breath and closed her eyes. *Here goes nothing. Come with me, okay?*

She jammed a thumb down on the air horn button.

HOOOOOOOOOOOOOOOOONK!

The deafening blare of the horn filled the air. Allie and Celia leapt from their hiding place screaming "*Veritatis Splendor!*" at the top of their lungs, the air horn sounding like a trumpet, challenging their enemy to battle.

They could see very little in the dark, but Allie distinctly made out a dark, burly figure kneeling by the doors that led to the wrestling gym. Then she saw it get up and . . . run away.

When they got to the doors, no one was there. A broken hacksaw blade lay on the floor; the door to the gym was halfway open, its bolts sawn in half.

George braced himself against the wall, knowing that there was almost nothing he could do to defend himself. But if that nut was going to come after him, George wasn't going to go down without a fight. He waited, knowing that whenever that guy finished breaking down the gym doors, or whatever he was doing out there, there was going to be trouble.

Then, the strangest thing happened: he heard a blaring sound like a trumpet, and voices — *girls'* voices — shouting, and then running footsteps.

What the — ?

The footsteps skidded to a halt.

"George?" A voice called out.

"I'm in here!" he yelled hoarsely, warmth and relief spreading through him as he recognized the voice.

The door to his prison swung open. Celia Costain climbed over the pile of mats and dropped beside him, her black curly hair framing her relieved face. He'd never been so glad to see his oldest friend.

And then the last person he wanted to see him right now appeared: Allie Weaver.

Celia was kneeling next to him. "Where are your hands tied?" she asked.

"Behind," he grunted, not looking at Allie, and rolled over on his back.

Celia gasped. "Omigosh! That must hurt!"

"Just let me loose." George said, trying to avoid looking at Allie.

"These knots are tight: no wonder you couldn't get out," Celia said. "I wish I had a knife . . ."

"I'll get the hacksaw," Allie said, her voice sounding odd. She vanished while Celia dug a water bottle out of her purse.

"Thanks," George breathed after she had given him a long drink. "The guy — sawing through the bolts? Did you see who it was?"

Celia shook her head as Allie returned. "No, we didn't — here, Allie, give it to me. There's a short length here I can cut . . ."

George lay still as Celia patiently sawed at the cord while Allie waited, looking around nervously.

There was a snap and suddenly he could pull his arms away from his legs, and with a groan of relief, he sat up, his muscles unkinking. Then Celia cut the ropes that held his wrists together while Allie worked on the ropes that bound his ankles. In a few minutes, he was free, and sat back on the ground feeling sore and shaky.

"Are you okay?" Allie asked hesitantly.

"I think so," George said, avoiding her eyes. He took another drink of water and tried not to let her see how his hands were shaking. "Did you guys drive over here? How long did it take you?"

"About an hour."

"Really? What time is it?"

"Almost four. Want us to drive you to the meet?"

"Almost four." George considered but shook his head wearily. "By the time we get there, the Sectionals will be almost over. It's probably wrapping up now."

"Let me help you up," Celia said.

"So who the heck was that guy?" he said, getting to his feet a bit shakily.

"I was going to ask you the same thing," Celia said. "Allie thinks . . ." She looked to Allie expectantly.

Allie looked a little hesitant. "Let's go outside," she said. "It's too dark in here."

So that sound was him sawing the lock open with a hacksaw," Celia finished filling George in on the details.

"And that was you and Allie, with an *air horn*?" George said. They were sitting on the grass outside Sparrow Hills, close to the door with the broken lock, watching the autumn sky darken into evening. There was no sign of the stalker. He must have made a quick escape.

"And this guy . . ." George said. "Allie, you think he was the one who shot at you?"

Allie closed her cell phone. She had just called the cops, and they were on their way, "I was sure it was him when I heard that laugh," she said, shaking her head. "But I could be wrong. It was kind of like a bad dream, you know?"

"Yeah," George said thoughtfully. "But you might have really recognized him . . ." He rubbed his wrists slowly. "I wonder what he was doing here today?"

Allie shrugged. "Staking out the school again," she said shakily. "He has some kind of a plan, George, I know it."

She hadn't meant to sound so panicked, but her voice cracked, and Celia squeezed her shoulders.

"It's okay," she said. "Remember, Allie? The Truth Guy? He's with you."

"Yeah," Allie said, flushing with slight annoyance at how Christ had gotten under her radar. She saw the rope burns on George's wrists, and remembered how guilty she had felt, seeing George humiliated and beaten. If she had broken up with Tyler earlier . . . if she hadn't dated Tyler.

"Tyler did that to you, didn't he?" she said softly.

He nodded, his face set.

"I broke up with him last night."

A light seemed to turn on inside him. For the first time, he looked her in the face. "You did?" he asked, as if he didn't really believe her.

She nodded, "I guess he didn't take it so well."

"Guess not!"

George flushed again, and she had to grin — *he looks so cute when he's embarrassed*— then suddenly George was looking in her eyes with his hazel eyes, and she felt her own face turning red. She tried to keep locking eyes with him, but couldn't keep it up. Shyly, she looked down at her shoes and caught a glimpse of him grinning at *her*.

He started to stretch, a little stiffly. "So, how did you guys find me?"

"You weren't at the match," Celia said. "Brian thought that something might have happened to you. So I called your mom, and she said she'd dropped you off here."

George did a double take. "Brian was at the meet?"

"Yeah," Allie said.

"I thought he'd quit the team," George said, then added, almost to himself. "I guess he was stronger than I thought."

"When we saw him, he hadn't wrestled yet," Celia said. "He didn't look so great. This would be his first time wrestling in a match, right?"

"Yeah," George said. "Yeah, it would be."

There was silence, then George said, "You know, if it's not too weird — why don't we pray for Brian right now?"

"Sure," Celia said, and Allie nodded.

George closed his eyes and crossed himself. The girls did the same. Then George bowed his head, cleared his throat, and said, "Our Father, who art in heaven . . ." He was beginning the Divine Mercy Chaplet, just as if they were in school.

But this time, instead of zoning out, Allie listened to the words as though she were hearing them for the first time. Part of her thought, *you know, George really* means *it when he prays. Maybe that's why Mr. Costain always has him lead prayer, because those words actually mean something to George. He's really talking to God, right now. It's part of who he is. That's why he's so different from Tyler.*

She felt a surge of warmth. *And it's why I like him*, she realized. *I really, really like this guy.*

The bus filled with Sparrow Hills wrestlers pulled into the parking lot. George waited apprehensively next to Allie and Celia, as it drew near. They could hear laughter from the wrestlers inside.

"Home-school-ER! Home-school-ER!"

"I can't believe it!" Celia blurted out angrily. "They're *still* making fun of him."

"Peterson!" Mr. Lamar bellowed from the bus, jumping down as it came to a stop.

"Mr. Lamar!" said George, running to meet him. "Listen, I know you're not gonna believe this, but . . ."

The rest of the wrestlers piled out of the bus. A few looked grumpy, and most looked tired. But a bunch of underclassmen were exuberant. They had been making all the noise. There was no sign of Tyler, Flynt, or Brock.

Then Brian came down the steps, wearing an embarrassed smile. "There you are, George! Hey, Allie. Hey, Celia," he said. "You'll never believe what happened . . ."

"There's Burke!" one of the wrestlers said. "Let's hear it for him!"

Soon nearly all the wrestlers were clapping and chanting again, "*Home-school-ER! Home-school-ER!*"

"Burke is going to the Regionals," Coach Lamar said. "Along with Tom Mahoney, and Marshall Vickson — both freshmen *you* trained, Peterson."

George's heart jumped in his chest. "Brian! You actually got to wrestle?"

Brian grinned. "Twice! And I won both times." His expression turned to concern. "But what happened to you?"

When George had finished, the coach said grimly, "I thought something was up. Burke told me that something had happened to you. Well, I can tell you right now that Getz is off the team. And so are Flynt and Brock; that's why Mahoney and Vick got to wrestle tonight: they took Flynt and Brock's places. Those three will be lucky if they don't get expelled. I don't know where they took off to." He shook his head angrily. "Getz was stupid to keep you out of the match, Peterson. He had to wrestle in your place, twice; he barely won the first time and got pinned the second time. I'm sorry you weren't there."

"Yeah," George said, trying to find the positive side. "I guess there's always next year." Next year, he could wrestle without Tyler and his goons being on the team.

"But you brought us some winners, anyway," Coach said, slapping Brian on the back. "You brought Burke along to tryouts, and I'm sure glad you did. The whole squad owes you for that."

George hadn't thought of that, but now that Coach had said it, a feeling of warmth came over him. "Thanks," he muttered, embarrassed. God worked it all out.

"And I have to say I like having homeschoolers on the team," Coach Lamar said, grinning at Brian. "They're a good influence on the other guys. You too, George," he added as an afterthought. "You're not homeschooled, but you're a Catholic school kid, aren't you?"

"Yeah," George said, and actually felt proud. "Yeah. I'm a John Paul 2 High kid."

Well," Coach Lamar said, looking concerned and baffled. "That's just strange. What do you think, Hal?"

Officer Jordan was kneeling and examining the sawed-through deadbolt lock on the front door. He stood and shook his head. "We got breaking and entering and damage of school property; that is, if we ever catch the guy.

How do you know this guy, anyway?" he said, turning to Allie.

Allie gulped. "No, you don't understand," she said. "I *don't* know him. I just recognized his laugh . . ."

"Oh yeah, sorry," Officer Jordan said. "You said it sounded sort of like the guy who shot at you, right?"

"Right," Allie said. "But I . . . I could be wrong, I don't know." Her heart sank.

"What do you think?" Coach Lamar said.

"Well," Officer Jordan said. "It's not like I don't take this sort of thing seriously, Arthur; I do. And I'm ready to believe this intruder had ill intent . . . but the bottom line is, we don't have a lot to go on. I'll dust the doors and hacksaw blade for prints, and I'll see if I can get a forensics team down here, but . . ."

"But don't count on it?"

"Yeah. I mean, all you got is a hacksawed door or two, really. That's all."

Allie turned away, feeling hopeless. "I can't believe there's not going to be more . . ." she muttered to George and Celia. Liz was there too, having been dropped off by Rich at the school so she could meet Celia for a ride home. "They've got to find the guy and stop him."

"Well, at least you got to hear his voice," Celia said. "And we got to see him."

"Yeah, but it doesn't mean much," Allie snapped. "And I didn't really get a good glimpse. Did you?"

"No," Celia sighed. "I didn't."

Allie's cell phone rang. She opened it wearily and put it to her ear. "Hello?"

"Who is this?" a frantic voice said. "Is this Allie? Allie Weaver?"

"Yeah, this is Allie," Allie said, alarmed. "Who's this?"

"Allie, this is J.P.!" the voice said. "J.P. Flynn! Listen, uh . . . who else is there? I mean, from our school?"

"George is here." Allie glanced around, "And Celia, and Brian. And Liz. Why? What's going on?"

"Just get down here right now!" J.P. said frantically. "And bring everyone you can!"

Do you see J.P. anywhere?" Celia whispered.

Allie nearly fell after tripping on a hidden tree root. "How should I know where he is?" she whispered back crossly. "I don't even know what we're doing here! It's just going to be some more bull . . ."

Suddenly someone grabbed her hand and steadied her. "Watch yourself," George said quietly.

His hand was warm, and strong. She found herself looking in his eyes again. "Um," she said. "Thanks."

He didn't say anything, just grinned at her then looked ahead and kept walking. But he didn't let go of her hand.

"Where exactly are we supposed to meet — ?" Brian whispered ahead of them.

"Quiet!" Suddenly, J.P.'s voice came from the underbrush. "Is that you guys?"

"Yeah, it is," George said. "The gang's all here."

"Minus James, who just wants to be *left alone*," Liz inserted.

"Shhhh!" J.P. appeared in a dirty white T-shirt and jeans with a crazed look on his pale, freckled face.

308

"Thank God you guys got here in time!" he said. "I've been staking the place out all day, and he's been here for ten minutes . . ."

"Who?" Brian said. "Not the poltergeist?"

"One and the same, my friend," J.P. said, and pointed.

Allie rolled her eyes, but consented to look.

The John Paul 2 High building was only fifty feet away, and right as she looked, she saw some movement in the parking lot next to the woods.

"He was using a spray can," J.P. whispered. "There'll be graffiti on the school on Monday . . ."

"Oh!" Celia said breathlessly. "I see him!"

Allie peered through the woods, her heart beating fast; and sure enough, she could make out a thin figure walking alongside the school. He was holding a can in one hand; and suddenly he raised it to the wall and started spraying.

"Oh my gosh!" Celia gasped. "I can't believe it! How could he *do* that? What are we going to do?"

"Never fear, Celia," J.P. said, fishing a cell phone out of his pocket. "This is the best part. Here comes the exorcism!"

He pushed a few buttons on the cell phone . . . and instantly pandemonium broke loose. The lights of the school turned on, and there was the sound of alarm bells going off; sirens, air horns, and even the familiar school bell.

The figure started, and he bolted away from the school into the woods.

"Yeah! That's right, you'd *better* run!" J.P. crowed as the rest of them jumped up in amazement.

"Come on!" George said, and took off running after the man. Allie kept pace with him, everyone else following.

But even before they reached the woods, they heard the sound of a car starting.

"He's getting away!" George gasped, and dropped Allie's hand to sprint towards the road. But — too late! — a pair of red taillights sped away.

"Oh, man!" George said, panting as he watched the car drive off. "Did anyone get the license plate number?"

"It was too far away," Brian said.

"AWWWWWWW YEAH!" J.P. was standing in front of the school doors pointing at them and laughing his head off. "Who's your daddy? That's right! Who's your daddy? I was RIGHT, there WAS a polterGEIST! I was RIGHT, there WAS a polterGEIST!" He started doing an incredibly stupid dance, right there in front of the school as they all watched him with open mouths.

"But now he got away," George said in some frustration. "If you had just told us what you were going to do, we could have cornered him or . . ." he stopped, and then threw up his hands and grinned. "Okay, way to go, J.P. The poltergeist was real."

"He was RIGHT . . . there was a polterGEIST," Brian repeated, and smacked himself. "I can't believe I just said that."

"Pretty cool trap, huh?" J.P. said, running up to them.

"J.P.," Celia said. "I'm *so* sorry. I really did think it was you."

"Yeah, I did too," Liz said. "Sorry."

"How did you get those alarms to go off?" Brian asked, with an impressed look at the school, where the lights were still on and bells were still wailing.

"Oh, most of it's running through my laptop," J.P. said. "Recordings, you know. But the lights were on timers that I ran through my computer, and . . ."

"You did this all *yourself*?"

"Yeah, well, when I finally realized that I was up against a *professional*, I started working really hard at catching him. I had to work on it before school and during study halls . . . The least I could do was scare him away if he came sneaking back."

"So," George said after a long pause. "I guess we all misjudged you."

"Don't worry about it," J.P. said, spreading his arms in a generous gesture. "The important thing is that the *truth* has finally triumphed, right? Like my namesake said, Verify the Spender!"

Silence, punctuated by giggles from Celia and Allie greeted his words. Brian sighed and shook his head. Liz rolled her eyes. "What?" George said.

"I think he means *Veritatis Splendor*," Allie said. "You know, the Splendor of Truth."

"You know what that means?" Brian said.

"Well, I paid attention *sometimes* in Theology," Allie said playfully. "But . . . I think it means more to me now," she said to herself. The Truth Guy, who had been following her around, *had* saved her, somehow or another . . . and the truth had helped her save George . . . and now, she remembered, it was *her* turn to do the following.

"Veritatis Splendor," she whispered again, and for the first time she thought it sounded beautiful. "Veritatis Splendor! Wow!"

"Uh, Allie?" George was giving her a strange look. "Are you okay?"

She smiled at him. "Never better."

COMING SOON
BOOK 2:

THERE WAS A RUSTLE FROM THE DARKENING FOREST

to his right. It was ever so slight, but George's ears caught it. He pretended not to notice, his mind racing to form a plan of action. They were at least a minute's run from the school, probably more through the woods in the snow and the dark. He could outrun whoever it was, but Allie . . .

"Everything's fine," he said out loud, then whispered to Allie, "When I move, run!"

He took a step, made as if to take her hand.

"GO!" he shouted, and whipped around in a low crouch, ready for anything. Allie took off toward the school without hesitation.

He wanted to buy Allie more time before he made his escape, but the sound of her tearing through the woods was gone, and there was no sound of pursuit. Maybe there really wasn't anybody there.

Or maybe it wasn't Allie they were after.

Slowly, silently, he approached an old, hollowed-out tree near the frozen stream a few yards from Chimney Rock.

Suddenly the surrounding forest was alive with sound and movement. He'd caught something by surprise; whatever it was jerked back from the tree, causing clumps of snow to drop from the overhead branches. Snow landed on George's head startling and blinding him for a moment. He put his hands up out of reflex to ward off any blows and quickly shook the snow off.

He heard a cracking sound, and a scraping, and saw a person wearing a black trench coat stumble across the ice to the opposite bank — James?

No. Whoever it was took off into the woods, glancing back as they ran.

George caught a glimpse of a face, perhaps looking back to see if anyone was following. It was a face distorted with surprise and anger, staring wildly, only turned toward him for a moment.

But that moment was long enough for him to recognize the menacing glare of Tyler Getz . . .

JOHN PAUL 2 HIGH
has a website and forum at
www.johnpaul2high.com

Imagio CATHOLIC FICTION
FROM SOPHIA INSTITUTE PRESS®

Imagio Catholic Fiction seeks to counter the despair, cynicism, and amorality of today's youth fiction with stories for young readers that feed faith and build virtue.

Our books are not disguised sermons but compelling stories told in a contemporary voice: entertaining young readers while at the same time presenting to them a moral universe in which God is real and active, and in which religion, family, and friendship are goods to be reverenced.

Sophia Institute Press®

Sophia Institute® is a nonprofit institution that seeks to restore man's knowledge of eternal truth, including man's knowledge of his own nature, his relation to other persons, and his relation to God. Sophia Institute Press® serves this end in numerous ways: it publishes translations of foreign works to make them accessible for the first time to English-speaking readers; it brings out-of-print books back into print; and it publishes important new books that fulfill the ideals of Sophia Institute®. These books afford readers a rich source of the enduring wisdom of mankind.

Sophia Institute Press® makes these high-quality books available to the general public by using advanced technology and by soliciting donations to subsidize its general publishing costs. Your generosity can help Sophia Institute Press® to provide the public with editions of works containing the enduring wisdom of the ages. Please send your tax-deductible contribution to the address below. We also welcome your questions, comments, and suggestions.

For your free catalog, call:
Toll-free: 1-800-888-9344
or write:
Sophia Institute Press®
Box 5284, Manchester, NH 03108
or visit our website:
www.sophiainstitute.com

Printed in the United States
202989BV00001B/94-264/P